PRAISE FOR *BACKHAND*

"An expansive set of intriguing characters and . . . sharp dialogue."

—*Kirkus Reviews*

"A treat. Anna is the most realistic of the new breed of private investigators, and the most level-headed as well."

—*Romantic Times*

"She is the sort of private eye who produces a cup of tea rather than a bottle of Bourbon out of the desk drawer, and she makes mistakes and leaves loose ends undone. Just like life. [Anna Lee] has been away too long."

—*The Sunday Telegraph Review*

"Darned good."
—*Daily News,* New York

PRAISE FOR LIZA CODY

"Move over, Sam Spade, Hercule Poirot, and Jane Marple. Meet Anna Lee . . . the best of the newly ordained female detectives on the scene."

—*San Diego Tribune*

Also by Liza Cody

DUPE
BAD COMPANY
HEADCASE
UNDER CONTRACT
STALKER
RIFT

BACKHAND

#6

Liza Cody

BANTAM BOOKS

NEW YORK   TORONTO   LONDON   SYDNEY   AUCKLAND

This edition contains the complete text
of the original hardcover edition.
NOT ONE WORD HAS BEEN OMITTED.

BACKHAND
A Bantam Crime Line Book / published in association with
Doubleday

PUBLISHING HISTORY
Doubleday edition published February 1992
Bantam edition / January 1993

CRIME LINE and the portrayal of a boxed "cl" are trademarks of
Bantam Books, a division of Bantam Doubleday Dell
Publishing Group, Inc.

ISBN 0-553-29627-2

Published simultaneously in the United States and Canada

Bantam Books are published by Bantam Books, a division of Bantam
Doubleday Dell Publishing Group, Inc. Its trademark, consisting of the
words "Bantam Books" and the portrayal of a rooster, is Registered
in U.S. Patent and Trademark Office and in other countries. Marca
Registrada. Bantam Books, 666 Fifth Avenue, New York, New York
10103.

PRINTED IN THE UNITED STATES OF AMERICA

OPM   0 9 8 7 6 5 4 3 2 1

BACKHAND

Chapter 1

A HIGH-PITCHED WAIL split the silence. It pulsed through the room and made the dog howl. Anna turned the key and there was a sudden hush. The dog scampered to the door and whined to be let out.

Johnny said, 'This siren has at least three quarters of a mile range. As I've just demonstrated, if the electric supply is cut off it will operate on battery power.'

'Most impressive,' the big man said.

'The electronic sound has completely superseded the old bell,' Johnny went on. 'But we brought one along in case.'

'That won't be necessary.' The big man glanced at the stack of hardware in the middle of his carpet.

It was a large room, painted cream, with the mouldings picked out in white. Apart from the carpet and a few canvas chairs it was unfurnished. A woman with hair the colour of old gold sat attentively against the wall listening to Johnny's pitch. But Johnny addressed himself exclusively to the big man. Given a choice, Johnny always concentrated on the men.

'The system you select depends to a great extent on your own unique security requirements,' he was saying now. 'There is an enormous choice on the market, but Brierly Security has the expertise to ensure a wise decision. Shall I begin with the infra-red?'

'How about tremblers?' the big man asked. 'Guy I know in Miami swears by them.'

Anna looked at the dog. It was still upset but no one had thought to let it out.

'Honey,' the woman said suddenly, 'why don't you and Mr Crocker talk tremblers. I'll acquaint Miss Lee with the layout.' She rose and stretched.

'We'll thrash out the technical details, Lara.' The big man smiled indulgently.

The woman's expression was sweet but a flash in the powder-blue eyes warned Anna that indulgence was not required. She got up and followed her out. The dog raced across the empty hall, its claws slipping on the polished boards.

'Technical details,' the woman said neutrally. 'What do you think?'

'Well, Mrs Shomacher . . .' Anna began.

'Mr Shomacher's my brother,' the woman cut in. 'I'm Lara Crowther. I know how the British are about Mr and Mrs, but if you don't mind, I'll be just plain Lara.'

'Anna,' Anna replied, thinking that Lara Crowther would have to neglect herself considerably if she wanted to be just plain anything. She was probably in her mid fifties but nothing had been left to nature and it was only the ropy folds of skin under her chin that gave her away. Her golden tan did not speak of a summer spent in England.

'Why don't you take a look around on your own,' Lara said. 'I'll make us some coffee. Technical details. I know my brother. He's gismo crazy and if I read your colleague right . . .'

'He likes the hardware too,' Anna said, smiling. 'But he does know what he's doing.'

'Oh, I'm sure,' Lara said hastily. 'But you're on commission, right? So the more you sell, the more you make, right? Oh, don't get me wrong, I'm not saying you'd gyp Donald. I had your firm checked out before I rang.' Pale blue eyelids fluttered harmlessly over the baby-blue eyes. Anna grinned.

'I don't mind spending money on security,' Lara went on. 'But I don't want to be up to the eyes in state of the art technology. Do you get me?'

'Alternative security,' Anna said.

'Right.' Lara turned towards the kitchen.

'Do you plan to keep the dog in the house?' Anna asked.

'I didn't mean quite *that* alternative,' Lara said. 'I don't mind some gismos.'

'It's not that. It's just that animals loose in a house can trigger

2

some alarms, and before I start I need to know what normal conditions would be.'

'See what I mean?' Lara showed a mouthful of gleaming white teeth. 'I'll bet Donald never thought of the dog.'

The big yellow Labrador was certainly no guard-dog. It followed Anna from room to room, and every time she stopped to make a note or take a measurement it presented her with a gift: a paperback in the bathroom, a sponge in a bedroom, a slipper in another bedroom. She was forced to accept these objects, otherwise the poor dog would prance in tighter and tighter circles looking more and more anxious. When she took one, however, he would lay back his ears, wag his tail and take on an expression of intense relief.

She arrived in the kitchen with her notebook in her mouth and her arms full of bric-a-brac.

'Put them on the table,' Lara said. 'I'll get rid of them when he isn't looking. I should have warned you. That dog's got his retriever instincts all balled up.'

If proof were needed of Mr Shomacher's interest in technology the kitchen was it. An operating theatre on the flight deck of a supersonic aircraft was how Anna described it later. It was not the sort of room to become the warm hub of family life. Lara Crowther had made coffee in a tall, stainless steel coffee pot and poured it into straight-sided white cups and sat down.

'Well?' she asked.

'Well,' Anna said. 'You're lucky in that the design of this house allows you to be as simple or as fancy as you like. You have three entrances: front, back and from the garage. They all connect with a single space – your entrance hall. So by covering that you can take care of a number of factors in one go. There aren't any major problems with upstairs because there are no abutting roofs or overhanging trees. There's the garage roof, of course, but no windows on that side.'

She stopped. There was no point going further until she had some idea of how the house would be used and what there was to protect.

'Yes?' Lara said, encouragingly.

'It's a question of what you want from security.'

'Sounds like a philosophical question.' Lara sipped her coffee and smiled. 'I know there's no such thing as total security. I've got an apartment in New York.'

'So you know that anyone determined enough can break in anywhere.'

'Right.'

'So, do you just want to discourage the casual opportunist?' Anna asked, 'or do you want to go a bit further?'

'A bit further,' Lara said firmly. 'Donald will want to go all the way. But only as a project, if you see what I mean. He isn't paranoid, he just wants what he thinks is the best . . . the latest.'

Anna regarded Lara over the rim of her cup. The next question, put crudely, would be, which of you signs the cheques? Anna, as a representative of Brierly Security was not supposed to ask crude questions. Someone, Martin Brierly or Beryl Doyle, would already have made enquiries. They might even have received payment for the advisory service the firm offered: advice Anna did not want to give to the wrong person. She decided on an oblique approach.

'How long have you been over here, Lara?' she asked and smiled in a sociable way.

'Oh, I'm here on and off all the time,' Lara said. 'That's why I'm helping out now. I'm a buyer for a chain of fashion stores. They keep me travelling. Donald has only been here a few months. He's been staying in a company apartment in Kensington. Now it looks as if he'll be here for a couple of years at least, so his wife and family want to join him.'

'So he bought a family house,' Anna said. It was a big neo-Georgian house: five bedrooms, three bathrooms. 'Small children?' she asked.

'Growing and grown,' Lara said. 'Does that make a difference?'

'It can do,' Anna told her. 'There are a lot of considerations. For one thing, the harder you make it for thieves to get in the harder it is to get out yourself. So if there was a fire . . .'

'Right,' Lara interrupted, grimacing. 'Small kids might make a difference. Like dogs.'

'Yes.'

'Well, I'm sure glad I talked to you,' Lara said. 'There's more to this than just the hardware.'

'Won't Mrs Shomacher want to be consulted?' Anna asked.

'No,' Lara said quickly. 'She'll want to decorate, buy furniture and all that, but she'll want the basic structural decisions to be made already. That's where I come in.' Lara paused. 'She isn't very . . .' She paused again. 'Anyway, I have to make sure that when Donald plumps for a security system it'll be something she can handle on her own.'

'He listens to you?' Anna thought about Donald Shomacher's enthusiasm for the most complicated pamphlets Johnny had shown him.

'Oh, yes.' Lara blinked guilelessly, and Anna believed her.

'Well then . . .' Anna got up. 'I'll have a look outside. I've already drawn a floor plan. But good security starts outside.'

Lara walked with her to the front door just as Donald Shomacher and Johnny came out of the drawing room.

'You going outside?' Mr Shomacher asked. 'Honey, there's the neatest device you ever saw with miniaturized heat-sensitive TV cameras and a console you can put in the hall. I figure if we mount one in front and one out back we can get maybe a hundred and eighty degree sweep . . .

'That's nice,' Lara interrupted. 'But why don't we let these people get on with their survey before it rains again?'

Chapter 2

ANNA TOOK HER shoes off in the car. Both she and Johnny were wearing sober business suits. Johnny loosened his tie and ran a hand through his crinkly hair. He was driving a nearly new Volvo Estate which gave them plenty of room for all the demonstration equipment.

'Hooray for Hollywood,' he said at length. 'Did you cop the size of that Jacuzzi in the master bedroom?'

They were leaving Barnes behind and crossing the river back towards Kensington.

'What're you going to do?' Anna asked. 'Wire it up with miniature TV cameras and a monitor over the master bed?'

Johnny grinned. 'The bloke's gadget-mad,' he said. 'Could've been a lovely little job if that bleeding sister of his hadn't stepped in and wrecked it. He didn't say the wife was a spam-head.'

'You should've asked.'

'Don't have to, do I?' Johnny said. 'Not with you there to do it for me.'

'Could've saved us a couple of hours.' Anna was irritated. It was not the first time Johnny had ignored the human element in his passion for electronics. A short while ago it had expressed itself in cheap watches, calculators and telephones. Now that Brierly Security, along with most of the security industry, had gone up-market he was in his element. He loved the toys. He loved his new car with its phone, its electric windows, the quadraphonic stereo he had installed himself. He knew everything about bugs, anti-bugging devices, and the whole technology of surveillance. It was only a pity, Anna thought sourly, he didn't have the opportunity to use it. He should have worked for one of the classy City firms. But although Johnny admired class he was not himself classy enough to fit in. Underneath it all he was still the ex-Signals

Corps wide boy at heart, a little too ready to cut corners or do a deal. And Brierly Security, for all its expansion, was still a small firm nibbling away at the private end of the market.

Kensington High Street might have become flashier and trashier over the years, but Martin Brierly had not changed, nor had his personal assistant and office manager Beryl Doyle. An atmosphere of small-minded, tightfisted respectability still hung over the office.

Nowadays Anna had a room to herself, furnished with a desk, typewriter and swivel chair. But it was a narrow sliver of a room and the walls were glass from the waist up. It had a glass door too, so Beryl could still see if Anna had taken her shoes off under the desk or left her tea mug on the floor. Beryl, of course, had her own office: a sentry box which stood guard over the supply room, the copier and the switchboard. Brierly Security now employed a receptionist who was also switchboard operator, but Beryl had a nose for private calls: an agent only called home in the gravest emergencies. No one liked to have Beryl monitoring the outside lines which she did if she suspected anyone of taking liberties with the company phone bill.

Anna laid her notebook open on the desk. She took paper from the drawer marked 'stationery' and some graph paper from the drawer marked 'plans'. It was time to write up the preliminary report on the Shomacher account. She could have done it with her eyes shut. To her right, behind the glass, she could see Johnny on the phone to the supplier. To her left was Tim's empty cubicle, and beyond that Phil's. Bernie, on the other side of the corridor was writing up a court report. Sean was next to him, and Anna could see him pretending to work. Soon, when he thought it appropriate, he would get up and tap on Bernie's door, asking for advice or reassurance. Sean was a new addition to the team. He wanted to get on, and he had chosen Bernie to be his mentor. A wise choice, Anna thought.

But Bernie preferred to pick his own protégés: as he told Anna, over a quiet drink one rainy evening, he was getting too old to train a puppy – especially one whose interest in the job was solely commercial. 'He wants to make a career for himself,' Bernie complained. 'I don't think he's interested in anything but that. Promotion was too slow in the police, that's the only reason he's here. More money. Bugger him. I never could abide a climber.'

Anna yawned. The preliminary report would have to be on Mr Brierly's desk next morning. There was a new client to see at eleven, and a follow-up job in the afternoon. The new client was a Turkish shopkeeper who wanted a potential manager vetted, and the old one was another security job. All Anna had to do was check that the equipment was of the type she had recommended and that it worked.

She leafed through her desk diary. Every day, for a month ahead, a scribbled note told her where she should be and who she should be talking to. She yawned again. There were no gaps left open for surprises.

Chapter 3

IN HOLLAND PARK the few remaining leaves were brown and brittle. Anna walked north to Holland Park Avenue wondering how many pick-up cricket games or soccer matches she had seen in the time she had been coming home this way. How many children grizzling because they had to go home for supper, how many pairs of lovers on benches, how many elderly ladies giving the squirrels their tea? They all ran together, like one very long walk. I should change my route, she thought, go the long way round. Anything for a change. But there were far worse ways to come and go than through one of London's parks, especially when it was dry and shafts of evening sun filtered through the trees.

At one time Anna had used the route for a run. But that wasn't possible any more. She could hardly think of a recent occasion when she had not been forced to turn up for work in respectable clothes and shoes. She couldn't arrive sweating and with her hair in a tangle. Clients expected tailored suits and shiny briefcases, and Beryl saw to it that clients got what they expected.

A couple of years ago a memo, initialled by Martin Brierly himself, had been circulated in the office. It detailed a Proper Dress Code and caused a lot of crude humour about cross dressing. But the code was adhered to, and overnight Brierly Security changed from quietly informal to rigidly smart. 'Might as well still be in bloody uniform,' Bernie grumbled, fingering his chafed neck. 'This is going to look right inconspicuous on obbo in Kilburn.'

That was in the early days. It had been a long time, Anna thought, since there had been anything as different as an observation in Kilburn. Walking through the park that evening in September she realised that her job had been reduced to that of a saleswoman. She represented, not so much a private detective agency, as the manufacturers of security equipment. She could be selling double-glazing or cosmetics for all the excitement she got out of the job now, or for all the judgement she put into it.

'A rep, a manky, boring rep,' she muttered to herself as she watched her shiny tan shoes emerge and disappear from under the hem of her linen skirt. 'That's what I am.'

She kicked a stone and sent an overweight pigeon scuttling into the bushes. The pigeon was too well fed and too accustomed to the idiocies of humans to take off and fly.

Anna looked at it glumly. 'You and me, kid,' she said, and walked on.

Chapter 4

A BOUT TWO YEARS ago the small hardware shop, one of the
few left where you could buy a handful of loose washers,
closed and had been replaced by an interior decorator's show-
room. The old corner shop which gave paperbags full of broken
biscuits to pensioners was now West London Video Services, and
Selwyn's favourite pub had become a wine bar.

'It's creeping gentrification,' Selwyn complained. He hadn't
noticed the loss of the hardware or corner shops, but the wine bar
hit him where it hurt. He prowled the area counting cars with
new registration numbers and noting the fresh paint and carriage
lamps.

'We're becoming respectable,' he said fearfully. 'The Waterford
crystal's catching up with us.'

'Look at the house prices,' his wife Bea said. 'If we didn't
already live here we couldn't afford it.'

Selwyn and Bea had the flat beneath Anna's. Their house
was owned by Mr Chatterjee who until recently had needed a
prolonged campaign of bullying even to replace broken tiles on
the roof.

'He wants to repaint the front,' Bea said puzzled, 'we didn't
ask him to, did we?' She was delighted until Anna pointed out
that it probably meant Chatterjee was intending to sell the house.

The couple's response to the threat was typical. They quarrelled.
Bea totted up the family's resources and decided that they could
probably afford a mortgage if they moved out to somewhere
small in Ealing or Acton. It was time they stepped onto the bottom
rung of the property ladder. Selwyn however had different ideas.
'Acton be buggered,' he snorted. 'What I want is a place in
Brittany, or Normandy, or Tuscany. What about a little white
house next to a taverna on some unknown Greek island?'

'What's the difference between a French mortgage and an English one?' Bea asked.

'I don't know,' said Anna. 'What's the difference between a French mortgage and an English one?'

'I'm not joking,' Bea said. 'I couldn't pay a French one because I can't speak French and I couldn't get a job over there and support that impractical sod I'm married to.'

'Support me!' Selwyn roared. 'What are you talking about, woman? What you support are lace curtains and shepherd's pies and duvet covers from Habitat. All I need is time, and space, and light.'

'We'll see about that,' said Bea, and the next day she took a train to Swansea leaving Selwyn with time, space and light but no shepherd's pie or clean sheets.

'She's left me,' Selwyn said, amazed and not a little impressed. 'There's fidelity! There's love, honour and obedience!'

'Bea never promised to obey you,' Anna pointed out as she shoved him back into his own flat. 'She's far too intelligent.'

It was the first battle, and Bea won it. Without her, Selwyn had no brick wall to beat his head against, he was a warrior without a war, and besides he got hungry. He wrote, he telephoned, and finally he went to Swansea to bring her back.

'There will have to be some changes round here,' Bea said, tipping cold tea bags into the rubbish bin. 'My mother says I've given him enough rope. Poetry is all very well but it doesn't pay the gas bill.'

Selwyn's friends watched with horrified disbelief as Selwyn committed the final act of capitulation. He got a job.

'Two incomes!' Bea cried, as letters from estate agents poured through her letterbox. Selwyn, teaching English and drama to a group of dyslexic teenagers, barely had the energy to protest. More often than not he came home to find Bea armed with particulars of yet another suburban prospect and had to spend his weekend touring the furthest reaches of the Central Line. It looked as if his typewriter had been silenced for ever, and it was many months since Anna had been greeted by the sight of Selwyn, pint mug in hand, beckoning her into his paper strewn front room. His shabby old cardigan had made way for a tweedy jacket and nowadays his trouser button stayed put.

Selwyn's trouser button was significant. Just as Selwyn lost the first round of the war with Bea, so his belly lost its battle with his waist band. Previously it had burst triumphantly through all attempts to contain it. Now, what with the job which gave him little opportunity for snacking between meals and the anxiety of living by the school bell, he lost weight. The Selwyn Anna knew and occasionally loved was fading away.

This evening however the sound of her key in the latch brought Selwyn to the door. A crimson wine stain, just where the hated tie should be, decorated the front of his shirt and his eyes gleamed with bonhomie.

'Look what I've got,' he shouted. 'Come in, come in, and see.'

'I am in,' Anna said, shutting the front door behind her. Bea appeared at Selwyn's shoulder.

'Be quiet or you'll wake him,' she said. 'Quex is back.'

'You weren't expecting him, were you?' Selwyn asked, tiptoeing thunderously back into his flat. Anna was not expecting Quex. He was supposed to be in a Middle Eastern oil field, not sprawled unconscious on Bea's new sofa. Anna looked at him with a mixture of affection and irritation. He lay on his back with his head on a cushion, his curly black beard pointing to the ceiling and his left leg bent. His right leg was stretched across the arm of the sofa and obstructed the door to the kitchen. That was one of Anna's problems with Quex: he was so big that there was really nowhere to put him where he did not obstruct something.

'When did he arrive?' she whispered.

'Heaven knows,' Bea said. 'He was here when I got back. He must've picked the lock or something.'

'I wish he'd wake up,' Selwyn added, in the tone of a child who wanted to play.

'Why didn't he go up to yours?' Bea asked. 'Haven't you given him a key yet?'

'Why didn't he go to his own place?' Anna said evasively. 'And I keep telling you, Bea, your locks are child's play.'

'They're supposed to be,' Selwyn retorted. 'How else would I get in when I lose my key?'

'*Haven't* you given him a key yet, Anna?' Bea persisted.

'Yes,' Selwyn put in, 'when are you going to make an honest man of him? If I have to become middle-class and respectable I don't see why he should escape.'

'Seriously, Anna,' Bea began, with centuries of chapel-going ancestors to back her up. 'Isn't it about time . . ?'

'Where are you off to now?' Selwyn asked.

'Shopping,' Anna called back from the hall. 'He'll be hungry when he wakes up and I've only got a couple of chicken legs in the freezer.'

'Get a take-away,' Selwyn said. 'It'll be like before the bloody estate agents.'

Chapter 5

'Y OU ARE GIVING a party perhaps?' Mr Lal enquired politely.

'It's just for four,' Anna said, as always slightly embarrassed by the amount Quex could put away.

'Ah, your big friend has returned.' Mr Lal grinned as he poured the Indian lager Anna had asked for. 'I have not seen him for many months.'

'Nor me.'

'He is keeping well?'

Anna laughed. 'He hasn't gone off yet in spite of the heat,' she said.

'You are making a joke,' Mr Lal announced disapprovingly. 'All the same, I will miss you when you move away.'

'I'm not moving,' Anna said. 'It's Mr and Mrs Price who are house hunting.'

'But surely . . .' Mr Lal, suddenly awkward, started to wipe the bar. He said, 'Your order will be completed in only a few minutes more.'

'What have you heard, Mr Lal?' Anna asked, worried because Mr Lal was an elder at his local temple and in general knew what was going on.

'Oh, it is nothing, I'm sure.' He made another pass with his cloth over the already spotless bar. 'Rumours,' he said and inspected a row of sparkling glasses. 'You know how people do talk.' He rearranged the brass bowls full of spicy titbits. 'Well, actually,' he said and turned his attention to the pile of menus. Anna sipped her lager and waited.

'Well actually,' Mr Lal said, leaning both elbows on the bar. 'I'm surprised you have not already been informed. Mr Chatterjee sold your house ten days ago.'

'What!' Anna cried. 'We weren't told anything. The house isn't even on the market.'

'Private treaty,' Mr Lal said, looking sympathetic while enjoying himself immensely. 'I'm so sorry to tell you this bad news. It is quite wrong that you have not been informed. But in any case probably what I am saying is simply evil gossip so you must not worry.'

'Not worry!' Anna exclaimed. 'Mr Chatterjee sells our house without even a by your leave . . .'

'Maybe he has not sold,' Mr Lal said comfortably. 'He talks, you know, sometimes as if he has done the thing he only means to do.'

'Who bought it?'

'West London Properties,' Mr Lal said promptly. 'But I am sure it is not true. I am sure we will be seeing you and Mr and Mrs Price for a long time yet.'

But Anna, walking home burdened with several heavy bags, was certain that it was true.

Chapter 6

'HE CAN'T DO that!' Selwyn said furiously. 'This is my home. This has been my home for eleven years.' His fork swept in an all-embracing arc around the room and lost its load of lamb pasanda on the way.

'Don't wave your food around,' Bea said. She stooped and mopped up the mess with a paper towel. 'We'll just have to move a bit quicker, that's all.'

'Move,' Selwyn yelled. 'Over my dead body! I'll barricade myself in rather than be pushed out by a poudrette of property developers.'

'Poudrette?' asked Anna.

'A sort of manure,' Quex said. 'It's a mixture of night soil and . . .'

'Please!' Bea interrupted. 'Not when we're eating.' She patted her lips. Selwyn glared at her.

'This is too much,' he roared. 'I become a bloody teacher to suit you. I wear a tie. I trot around looking at bathroom fixtures and louvred doors in Chigwell every weekend. I have not written a blessed word in a year. And now you attack my vocabulary. The worm will turn. There will be more than strong words from now on.'

'I never thought of "poudrette" as a particularly strong word,' Quex mused.

'I think it was "night soil" Bea was objecting to,' Anna added, enjoying what was now the rare sight of Selwyn in full cry.

'You stay out of it,' Bea snapped. 'What's so wrong with having a house of your own? I just want somewhere that's mine – where I won't have to apologize to my friends and family – where I won't have to share a hall.'

'Your turn now, Leo,' Selwyn said. 'All these years and now

she tells you she's had to apologize for sharing a hall with you.'

'That's not what I said. Anna understands.'

'She would!' Selwyn cried. 'She spends all her working life, these days, selling paranoia to people with property. Security, my arse! It's the haves making damn sure the have-nots stay without.'

Even Quex had stopped eating. The mountain of pilau rice in front of him was becoming cold.

'It's not security she sells,' Selwyn went on at the top of his voice, 'it's fear. Fear of some poor bastard crossing your threshold unannounced.'

'Have you ever been burgled?' Anna asked angrily. 'Because if you ever had you wouldn't be talking such codswallop.'

'I haven't been burgled because I don't own anything anyone else wants.'

'That's the trouble,' Bea said, suddenly close to tears. 'We don't have anything I want either.'

'Speaking of homes,' Anna put in before the conversation became a quarrel. 'What's wrong with yours, Quex?'

'I rented it out for six months, remember? The six months isn't up so I'm temporarily homeless.'

'Yes, but why? You're supposed to be working.'

Quex carved a deep crater into his mound of rice and spooned some raita into it before he spoke. 'The old man died,' he said eventually. 'I had to go back to Ireland.'

Anna stared at him and noticed in a rush all the things she should have noticed an hour ago if it hadn't been for the commotion caused by Mr Lal's bombshell. He was not as sunburnt as he should have been, his hair and beard were neatly trimmed and his clothes were clean.

'Why didn't you say?' Selwyn asked angrily.

'I just did.'

'You could've stopped us talking all that twaddle.'

'When could I ever stop you talking twaddle, Selwyn?' Quex was the only one eating. 'I'm a simple chap,' he went on with his mouth full, 'if I'd wanted your sympathy or whatever I'd've asked for it.'

'Yes, but your dad,' Bea said. 'I am sorry.'

'Thank you.'

He seemed subdued, Anna thought, but whatever he was feeling did not put him off his food. She found herself quite unable to say anything because she didn't know what the death of his father meant to him. He looked up and caught her eye.

'Not to worry, Titch,' he said with a half smile.

'You going back to work?' she asked.

'No.'

This meant there was a big change coming. All Anna knew was that Quex's family were country people with some land in Ireland and that Quex was the one who had got away. She did not know why his father's death meant he would give up his job and she avoided the question.

'You'll want to stay awhile?' she asked instead.

'If you don't mind,' he said formally.

'All right.'

'For Christ's sake!' Selwyn exploded, 'what are you two playing at? I mean, it's like he's booking a hotel room. Where else would he stay?'

'Belt up, Selwyn,' Anna said, 'you don't understand.'

'You're too right I don't,' Selwyn said. 'How long are you two going to pussyfoot around? I mean, why doesn't he have a key? Why didn't he have a key ages ago? You've been seeing each other long enough.'

'Such tact!' Quex said, grinning amiably. 'Like the lady said, Selwyn, belt up.'

'And anyway, who knows how long it'll be before we're all out on our ears.' Anna started to eat again but without much appetite.

Chapter 7

LATER, WHEN THEY were upstairs and alone, Quex said, 'Well, I suppose it's nice to see Selwyn with a bit of spirit again.'

'Except he's popping off in all directions at once.' Anna was still smarting from Selwyn's interference and not inclined to treat the born-again maverick charitably. She was clearing a space for Quex's clothes in her cupboard and hoping against reason that he had given up singing while he showered first thing in the morning. Perhaps it was the size of her flat but already she was beginning to feel squeezed out.

More likely it was the size of Quex. Anna often wondered whether, had he been a normal size, she would be able to take more of his company. She was very fond of him, she admired him, she even liked him a lot, but after a few days close to him she always felt as if he had used up all the air.

Normally she only saw him on the three or four times a year when he was home on leave. Even then, he had his own place in Fulham so they never lived on top of each other. By moving in, even for a short time, he was breaking an unspoken rule.

'You should have seen Selwyn at university,' Quex mused. 'Talk about spirit . . . well, spirits, beer, wine – you name it. We were writing a review, with three other chaps, and he was so pissed he started talking in spoonerisms. You know, I heel in my fart, that sort of thing. We got him to write it all down and it was a brilliant piece.'

Anna looked at him as he sat on the edge of the bed. He seemed to be looking backwards and inwards in a way that was quite uncharacteristic. He never talked about university. Sometimes she thought it was an example of his tact, for, where Selwyn often took great delight in showing up her relative lack of education, Quex never did.

'We lived in this big old house,' he went on, 'sleeping bags on the floor, no electricity, people coming in all day and all night. Fantastic! It was my first spell away from home.'

Anna smiled. People born a little closer to the breadline than Quex or Selwyn didn't have the same romantic view of living rough.

'My father would've been furious if he'd seen it,' he continued, and Anna stopped smiling. If Quex was re-evaluating his relationship with his father in all this talk of houses and homes, the issue was a serious one. He glanced up and caught her looking at him.

'Getting ready to be all sensitive and sympathetic?' he asked. 'That's not like you.'

'Ungrateful sod,' Anna retorted, turning away. 'It's not like you to get slushy and nostalgic either.'

'Was I?'

'Not half.'

Quex started to unlace his size fourteen shoes. 'Just what I came to get away from – the sanctification of a perfectly ordinary old man. I thought, who's the least sentimental woman I know?'

'Me?'

'So I came here.'

'Well, you're wrong,' Anna said grumpily. 'If I was the tough nut you yearned for I'd chuck you and your extra, extra large cotton shirts out in the gutter.'

'Unsentimental, not sadistic.'

'So don't droop around on the edge of the bed or you'll ruin the springs. If you want to do something useful, go and put the kettle on.'

'That's my girl,' Quex said, and padded out of the bedroom in his enormous nylon socks. Anna sighed and kicked his shoes under the bed. The phone rang. Quex poked his head round the kitchen door. 'I gave your number to some people,' he said apologetically.

Anna lifted the receiver. 'North London Home for Distressed Chemical Engineers,' she said brightly.

'Anna Lee?'

'Er, yes?' She pulled a threatening face at Quex who disappeared smartly.

'Lara Crowther. We met this morning.'

'Of course,' Anna said in her best agent-to-client voice. 'What can I do for you?'

'I shouldn't be ringing you so late or at home,' Lara said without regret, 'but you looked like the kind of person I could ask. Where do you play tennis around here?'

'Tennis?'

'Yeah. You do play, don't you?'

'Well, sometimes.' Anna frowned at the receiver.

'So where do you play?'

'Er, Battersea Park.'

'That a club?'

'No.'

'Oh, public courts.' Lara paused. 'Well, never mind. It'll do. When?'

'What?' Anna started to laugh. 'Are you asking me out to play?'

'Sure,' Lara said, surprised. 'Don't you want to?'

'Why not?' Anna said. 'But it'll have to be at the weekend.'

'Okay. Saturday morning?'

'Make it Sunday,' Anna said, suddenly smelling burnt toast from the kitchen.

'Sunday then. Nine-thirty,' Lara said and hung up. Anna blinked and hung up too.

'Who was that?' Quex called from the kitchen.

'Lara Crowther. A client. She wants to play tennis on Sunday.'

He came in with two mugs of tea and a plateful of charcoal-grilled toast. 'Tennis is part of the service these days?' he asked.

'No. Service is part of the tennis.' Anna estimated that he had spread nearly half a pack of butter on the toast and that there would be no marmalade left for breakfast.

Chapter 8

'WHAT I WISH,' said Mr Kemal, 'is that you see into the references this man brought.'

Anna looked at the papers he handed her. There were three in all and they were dated four years ago. She said, 'William Herridge has been in your employ for four years now?'

'Yes,' Mr Kemal agreed. 'But at that time he was only a salesman. I ask for references but I do not have time to contact these people. Now I wish to promote this man. My business is expanding, there are three shops for him to manage and I will not always be in this country.'

'Very well.' Anna placed the references in her briefcase. As she did so she noticed that Mr Kemal was wearing carpet slippers. She envied him. Her own shoes pinched.

'I wish also to know if this man is in debt.' He drank from the cup of weak coffee his secretary had brought in when Anna arrived.

'Most people buy on credit,' Anna suggested.

'This I know very well.' Mr Kemal smiled tolerantly. 'But can they keep up the payments? I wish to know what is his credit rating.' Anna made a note on the client form.

'Also I wish to know if this man is someone I can really trust.'

'You mean prison record if any?' She made another note.

'Of course that.' He took another sip of coffee. 'But also I have heard that there is a list that employers may consult to make sure.'

'To make sure of what?' Anna had a shrewd idea of what he meant but as it was the most disagreeable side to this kind of job she wanted Mr Kemal to spell it out.

'To make sure this man is not a troublemaker.' Mr Kemal spread his hands. It was obvious. 'I wish to know if he belongs perhaps to a trade union or one of those left-wing organisations.'

'Such as?'

'Oh, those who make trouble, who make nuisance against the government and military.'

'I see.' She hid her distaste and made another mark on the client form.

'Greenpeace!' Mr Kemal said suddenly, delighted to have found an example. 'They have boats. They make trouble for Her Majesty's Royal Navy. I wish to know if this man perhaps belongs to Greenpeace.'

Dutifully, Anna wrote 'Greenpeace'. What a world, she thought.

Chapter 9

'THAT'S WILLIAM, NO middle initial, Herridge,' Beryl said, clattering on the keyboard with reinforced pink fingernails. 'You're absolutely sure it's Herridge with a D? Only I never know with your spelling and I don't want to waste another Directory fee on your carelessness.'

'Herridge with a D,' Anna said through tense lips.

'National Insurance number,' Beryl droned. 'Is this a seven or a one?'

'One,' said Anna. It was perfectly clear.

'Date of birth. I do wish you wouldn't perch on the edge of my desk.'

'It's my legs,' Anna said. 'You make such a to-do over a simple PAD search my legs get tired.'

'Political Affiliations Directory is not a charitable institution,' Beryl said primly. 'Every name we put through costs money.'

'Pernicious Antisocial Disaster, if you ask me,' Anna muttered.

'What did you say?' asked Beryl, who had heard clearly. 'An employer has a perfect right to check out the suitability of an employee.'

'Ever put your own name through?' Anna asked sweetly. 'I mean wouldn't it be awful if someone had joined a suspect political organisation under your name?'

Beryl glared. 'Well, I'd know who to blame then, wouldn't I?'

'Yes, but that would be the end of you. Once you get on the Directory you never get off it.'

'I've voted Conservative all my life,' Beryl said furiously.

'Well, swipe me!' Anna said. 'I'd never've guessed.' She made her exit whistling the Red Flag.

At the end of the corridor, past all the agents' glass cubicles, was a door marked 'ONLY'. It was the old rec-room refurbished.

To begin with the sign had read 'EMPLOYEES ONLY' but an anonymous wit had changed 'EMPLOYEES' to 'PLAYERS'. Later, Beryl changed 'PLAYERS' to 'STAFF'. 'STAFF' was then replaced by 'STIFFS', and now through lack of inspiration on both sides, 'ONLY' was the sole survivor.

'What're you grinning about?' Johnny asked as Anna came in. He was playing a lunchtime hand of poker with Phil.

'Just nattering with Beryl.' She filled the kettle for tea.

'Got the last word?' Tim said. 'Left her speechless, did you?'

'Brilliant,' Anna said. 'Sheer genius. Tea anyone?'

She made tea for Bernie and Tim, and then squeezed half a cup out for Sean who came in late and always wanted what Bernie was having.

Tim sat close to Anna and said, 'Since you're in such a good mood, how about a favour?'

'What?' Anna asked suspiciously. Of late, Tim had been dressing more and more like a politician. He was beginning to talk like one too.

'You've got a job this afternoon, right?'

'Right.'

'North London?'

'Tottenham.'

'Then you've got to come back here and finish off what you started this morning. Am I right?'

'So far.'

Tim smiled winningly. 'It's just that I've got one in Islington but I'd like to get home early so if you did mine and I did yours we'd both be closer to home. Save time, right?'

Bernie leaned across Sean and said, 'Syl's put two apples in my lunch. Want one, Anna?'

'Thanks.' Anna took the apple and glanced at Bernie. One of his eyelids drooped fractionally over a sleepy eye. Otherwise, his expression remained impassive. She said, 'Sounds like a good idea.'

'Great,' Tim said with obvious relief.

'I haven't said I'll do it yet,' Anna said. 'What is it?'

'Just someone who wants an alarm system.'

'Anything special?'

'Not really.'

'Not really?'

'Well, just a room with a few paintings in it.'

'Oh.' Anna was beginning to catch on. 'Well, Tim,' she said innocently, 'you know paintings aren't my thing. I don't know my art from a hole in the ground.'

'You don't have to,' Tim said, beginning to look anxious. 'It's just an ordinary security job.'

'Islington, you say?'

'Well . . .'

'Not Camden Town?'

'Well . . .'

'Not Belitha Road, Camden Town?'

'Oh shit a brick,' Tim said.

'Not the Hon. John Daubney, Belitha Road, Camden Town?' Anna went on inexorably.

'Give me a bleeding break!' Tim groaned. 'Why do I always cop the Hon. John? He gets these flutters about that crappy collection of his, calls in security. I go over, hold his trembling hand for three hours, and then the silly sod dillies and dallies and never even buys a sausage.'

'Well, don't try and palm your neurotics off on me.' Anna took a bite out of Bernie's apple. 'I've got enough of my own. Islington, my foot!'

They all had their nuisances, but the Hon. John Daubney was famous at Brierly Security. He was what they referred to as 'social work'. There were several over the years who called up for advice when what they really wanted was someone to chat to for an afternoon. Next time they felt lonely they might call in a heating expert. The Hon. John was different in that he was a persistent security freak. Sometimes he called the police, but mostly he called Brierly Security and, as he was prepared to pay a consultation fee for the privilege, Beryl always took his requests seriously. He was a beautifully mannered old gentleman who laid on China tea and cucumber sandwiches for his victims, but there was no escaping the fact that he was achingly dull. No one at Brierly Security was at all surprised that he had to pay people to listen to him. The trouble was that *they* were not paid enough.

'You're a hard woman, Anna Lee,' Tim grumbled.

If she was hard, she reflected later in the afternoon, it was probably because she was bored rigid. Pick up the phone, dial a number, 'Can I speak to Mr Watkins, please?'

'Mr Watkins isn't available just now. Can I help?'

'Mr Watkins wrote a reference for a Mr William Herridge four years ago. I'd like to speak to him about it.'

'Is that Herridge with or without a D?'

'With. When will Mr Watkins be available?'

'Herridge with a D. If you leave your name and number Mr Watkins will get in touch at his earliest convenience.'

And pigs might fly. Draw a deep breath, dial the next number, 'Can I speak to Mr Richard Pickles, please?'

'Mr Pickles is no longer employed by Miller Casuals.'

'Do you know where I can get in touch with him?'

'Putting you through to Personnel now.'

Click. Hum. Dead silence. Start again.

Chapter 10

'YOU SIT. I'LL COOK,' Quex said. Anna *was* sitting. She had her feet up on his lap and he was massaging her pinched toes. His enormous hands enveloped her feet like the mouth of a whale.

'Be reasonable,' she said, 'If you cook I'll have to wash up. And washing up after you isn't restful.' It was like clearing up after a landslide. Anna was comfortable. If she had been alone she would probably have made a sandwich and watched television.

Selwyn banged on the door and came in bristling. 'Panic stations!' he shouted. 'Bea got hold of West London Properties. We have to be out in eight weeks.'

Quex grabbed Anna's feet to stop her jumping up. He said, 'Calm down, old chap. They can't chuck you out till you've found somewhere else. There are laws, you know.'

'A pox on their laws!' Selwyn shouted. 'This is war. Leo – all that stuff you've been peddling – locks, alarms – I want the lot – booby traps, boiling oil, water cannon. I'm barricading myself in.'

'Don't listen to him,' Bea said, appearing behind Selwyn. 'I'm making an offer for that little place in Potters Bar.'

'If you move to Potters Bar,' Selwyn thundered, 'you go on your own. I will not be budged for speculators.'

'We'll see about that,' Bea said, turning away. 'But you'd better come down now: I'm putting your chop under the grill.'

When she had gone, Selwyn sat in the armchair opposite Anna and Quex. 'It's no good, you know,' he said quite evenly. 'I won't go to Potters Bar – not now, not ever. A man has to make a stand somewhere and I'm making mine here.'

'It's not the speculators,' Quex said quietly. 'It's middle-age you're making a stand against.'

'What makes you such a pillock?' Selwyn asked.

'Raw talent,' Quex told him.

'Well, in spite of that I'm glad you're here. West London Properties may think twice when they know it's me and Man Mountain they're up against.'

'Oh, Jesus!' Anna said, pulling her feet free and standing up. 'Now we have the Butch and Sundance of Shepherds Bush. I don't want to move any more than you do. But if we must we must.'

'Spoken like a true pragmatist,' Selwyn said disdainfully. 'You go to Potters Bar with Bea and see how you like it.'

'Not me. I've got my own ideas.'

'Well, so have I,' Selwyn retorted. And then as her words sank in he said, 'It's funny, isn't it? I never really thought we'd split up — the three of us.'

'Four,' said Quex.

Anna looked at him and retreated into the kitchen. It was a shambles. Quex had made lunch for himself and not washed up. She thought about booby traps. Were they set for or by boobies, she wondered, and if she stuffed Quex's head in a blender would it count as a crime of passion?

As she set the kitchen to rights she heard the murmur of men's voices. She took her resentment out on three pounds of King Edward potatoes. The little kitchen steamed gently and she opened a window. The sash was sticking — a job someone else would have to do. She decided to mash the potatoes. That was always an aggressive act.

Chapter 11

AT EIGHT-THIRTY on Sunday morning Anna was lacing her tennis shoes and wondering if her ancient Dunlop racket would bust a gut the first time it hit a ball. She had been wondering the same thing for the last ten years. Quex was in the kitchen making coffee and singing 'Back in the High Life Again'. Anna had a headache. In the intervening days there had been too many late nights, too much wine, raised voices, and Selwyn at full-throttle.

She said, 'Do you *have* to sing?'

'I'm happy,' Quex said. There was a sudden hiss and splatter as the water boiled over. 'It's been weeks since I felt like this.'

'Be happy,' Anna muttered, '*don't* sing.'

'What?'

'Be happy,' Anna shouted. Quex came in with two overfilled mugs. Coffee dripped onto the rug.

'It's too bad you're going out,' he said. Anna moved quickly to avoid coffee stains on her grey track suit.

'It's Sunday,' Quex went on. 'You shouldn't be at the beck and call of some old biddy.'

'She isn't an old biddy.'

'She's a client,' Quex said. 'You shouldn't have to play pat-ball on a Sunday.'

'I don't have to,' Anna said. 'I want to.' I want to hit something very hard indeed, she could have continued, I want to run flat out; I don't want to talk to receptionists, telephone operators, suppliers of burglar alarms, and Beryl; I don't want to argue with Bea and Selwyn or listen to them argue with each other; and most of all I don't want to wash the kitchen floor again because you can't keep food on dishes.

But she said nothing. Quex went on, 'You wasted most of yesterday on estate agents.'

'I'd better be off,' Anna said, standing and reaching for her bag.

'It's completely unnecessary.' He towered over her, oblivious to his dripping mug.

'Traffic on Chelsea Bridge,' she murmured, edging round him to the door.

'I mean in a few weeks my flat will be free again and we can move in there.'

'Can we talk about it when I get back?' she asked, and escaped onto the landing.

'How long will you be?' Quex called after her.

'Don't know,' she called back. 'Maybe lunchtime.' She took the stairs two at a time.

Out on the street the sharp autumn air cooled her cheeks. She unlocked the car, a white, nearly new Peugeot 205, dumped racket, balls and bag in the back, and turned the key. The engine turned over sweetly. It always did. There was no coughing or protesting from the Peugeot, no time wasted drying plugs. It was one of the benefits of a more prosperous life. Inside was the usual Londoner's tangle of petrol receipts, parking tickets, maps and peppermints.

In spite of what she had said, traffic on Chelsea Bridge was thin. She parked by the river. High ragged cloud was building up in the west and there was a smell of rain in the air. The river at low tide smelled too.

Battersea Park looked bright and clean in the morning sunlight. Joggers pounded by, sweating virtuously. Anna turned her back to the netting which surrounded the tennis court and faced the sun. In spite of the regulations a white police van had pulled up on the path a few yards away. A policeman was training a giant schnauzer. The dog, young and undisciplined, treated the training session as a game and bounded clumsily. Patiently the man threw a car tyre. The schnauzer galloped after it barking loudly. The dog would get bored long before the policeman.

'Hi!'

Anna turned and saw Lara on the other side of the netting. She wore a pink and cream warm-up suit. Anna made her way to the gate feeling dowdy — a London sparrow about to face a peacock.

'Let's hit,' Lara said without preamble and took the end facing away from the sun. They played with Lara's bright yellow balls.

Lara warmed up slowly. She said her shoulder was stiff but after a few minutes Anna realised that, although she looked like a birthday cake, she knew how to play tennis.

After a while Lara came to the net. She said, 'You want to try a set?'

Anna took off her jacket and laid it next to Lara's big sports bag. Lara said, 'You ever tried a newer racket?'

'No,' Anna said, looking enviously at Lara's white oversized Kneisel.

'I've got a Prince in my bag,' Lara said. 'You want to try that?'

Under a neat pile of clean shirts and Diet Coke cans was a Prince Pro racket. It looked as if it had been strung with different shades of bubblegum. The grip was covered with apricot-coloured suede.

'It'll help your game,' Lara said. 'There's a bigger sweet-spot.'

A prince with a big sweet-spot, Anna thought, nearly laughing. But the racket nestled in her hand, perfectly balanced, and when she hit the ball the strings thwonged and her shot flew long.

'Put a little top-spin on till you get the hang of it,' Lara advised. 'You're over-hitting.'

With the extra power provided by the new racket Anna felt she had an unfair advantage: she was taller, faster and younger than Lara. It was an advantage which lasted just until they began to play the set. Lara served first and won the game after two deuces.

They changed ends and Anna served. Her service was faster than Lara's but Lara returned easily. Lara in fact returned everything. She won the game after two deuces.

At five–love Anna wiped the sweat out of her eyes with the sleeve of her discarded jacket. Lara had a fluffy yellow towel but she didn't need it. Her springy gold hair was still immaculate and she had not yet removed the pink sweater.

Anna considered the situation. It seemed hopeless. There was nothing in Lara's game which Anna couldn't beat, except perhaps her desire to win. That appeared to be unassailable. Lara used all the tricks – the drop shot followed by an ugly lob, the soft childish stroke that gave Anna no pace to feed on. She was slowly but surely wrecking Anna's more straightforward game.

It was time to ignore the fact that Lara was short and over fifty. It was time to ignore the fact that she was a client. It was time to play, if not to win, at least to avoid humiliation. Anna did not want to lose the first set six–love.

She served to Lara's backhand – tossing the ball further ahead of her and leaning into it. Lara returned it high, giving Anna an easy volley from mid-court. She punched the ball away to Lara's forehead. Fifteen–love. Lara regarded Anna speculatively. She blinked her baby-blue eyes and changed sides. She seemed to be limping.

Anna hardened herself against the eyes and the limp and served again. Thirty–love. Lara retied her shoelace. There followed a scrappy but determined nine stroke rally which Anna won by sacrificing style to guile. Lara removed the pink sweater. Anna's next serve clipped the centre line. Game.

She lost the set six-four, and regretted starting so late. She won the next set but the score went to fifteen–thirteen. At three–all in the last it began to rain.

Chapter 12

THEY SAT IN Lara's chocolate-brown Mercedes, facing the river while rain drummed on the roof. Lara snapped open a can of Diet Coke and handed it to Anna.

'Good match,' she said non-committally.

'Interesting,' Anna replied, wiping sweat and rain from her face.

'You ever read a book called *The Mental Game*?'

'No.'

'I thought not. It isn't wise to ignore the mental game.'

'Is that what you were playing?'

'You thought it was just tennis?' Lara laughed briefly. 'It's never just tennis.'

'I don't take it that seriously,' Anna said.

'It's your whole attitude to life,' Lara went on as if Anna had not spoken. 'See, you've got some good strokes, you're quick, you're persistent, but you let me beat you.'

'It was a draw,' Anna protested.

'You should have won,' Lara said, 'so you let me beat you. It won't always rain at three–all.'

'This is England,' Anna said, somewhat offended. 'You're lucky to play at all.' But she didn't think Lara was talking about the weather.

'This is England,' Lara echoed. 'And I guess you may be thinking, "Well, we had a good close game, honours even." Right? "What's the woman griping about?" Right?'

'Sort of.'

'You don't mind if I talk to you like this?' Lara asked belatedly, and went on without giving Anna a chance to reply. 'Take it from me, honours were not even. Sure, it was a good game – but that is not enough.'

'No?'

'And sure, I enjoyed it . . .'

'Well, stripe me pink,' Anna interrupted, 'if I'd known this was going to be war I'd've had raw meat for breakfast.'

Lara sighed and Anna sat quietly for a moment contemplating her attitude to games. The car was misting up and she was beginning to feel cold.

'Maybe I'm too assertive,' Lara said, and sighed again. 'Anyway, I want you to do a job for me.'

'What sort of job?' Anna had been on the brink of making her excuses and going home for a hot bath. She turned to look at Lara. But Lara was rubbing a painful shoulder and staring across the river at the terraced elegance of Cheyne Walk. It was a few seconds before she said, 'It's a business thing. There's a guy – I want to know his background.'

'Have you spoken to Mr Brierly?' Anna asked.

'I thought we could do this privately,' Lara said. 'I didn't admire your boss too much. Don't you take private work?'

'Not normally.' Normally Anna wasn't asked. 'You see, privately, I wouldn't be able to give you much time. And I wouldn't be able to use agency facilities – or if I did I could get fired for it. The firm doesn't take too kindly to moonlighting.'

'What about vacations?' Lara asked. 'Are you getting any time off soon?'

'I've got three weeks leave owing, but . . .'

'Are you married?'

'No.'

'Good. Have you got a passport?'

'Yes,' Anna said. 'Why?'

'Well, I'm going to think about it,' Lara said. 'I'll let you know.'

'I'd be delighted to work for you,' Anna said, feeling that a little formality was called for. 'But it would be best if you went through the firm. You don't have to tell Mr Brierly everything, you know, and nor do I.'

'You're right,' Lara smiled wanly. For the first time she looked tired as well as small and fifty. 'Look, I shouldn't always assume . . . Anyway, I will think about it and I *will* be in touch.'

Chapter 13

ON MONDAY MORNING it was still raining and in the night the temperature had plummeted. Anna discovered that William Herridge owed a South London garage for a set of radial tyres and his credit with most of the hire purchase firms had been stopped. This was peculiar because by all other accounts he was a careful man who did not spend over his limit.

At eleven o'clock she went with Sean to Mrs Stratford-Parker's flat to install window locks. Installation was not normally part of the job but such was Mrs Stratford-Parker's fear of being mugged in her fifth floor service flat that she had refused entry to the carpenter Brierly Security recommended. The carpenter was an old-fashioned gentleman who always wore a hat with a pencil tucked into the band, and he was mortally offended by the mistrust. So by the time Beryl had soothed Mrs Stratford-Parker's fear to the point where she would admit the carpenter, the carpenter had adamantly refused to do the job.

The flat was a model of its kind. The front door was fitted with a spy-hole, a mortice lock, two dead locks, two chains and concealed hinges. The door frames were made of steel. It took a long time even for expected and welcome guests to get in. Once, on a previous visit, Anna had cautioned the old lady about fire, but Mrs Stratford-Parker was absolutely sure of what frightened her, and it wasn't fire.

Once inside Anna slipped off her jacket and got down to work. The old lady wanted her to start in the bedroom.

'You won't mind working alone here, will you?' Mrs Stratford-Parker asked. 'I'm not sure that I quite like the idea of strangers in my bedroom. You do understand, don't you dear? I'll show the young man the dining room.'

Five minutes later she was back, saying, 'And if you don't mind,

37

dear, I'd prefer it if you attended to my bathroom personally. A lady has a very delicate relationship with her bathroom.'

After ten minutes she pottered in with an old pillow slip and said, 'I brought you this because I know you won't want to put your feet on the paintwork, and the chairs belonged to my aunt from Scotland.'

Anna was already using Mrs Stratford-Parker's aluminium steps but she smiled politely and laid the pillow slip on the window ledge.

The old lady said, 'I'm putting the kettle on for a nice cup of coffee. I'll call you when it's ready. I'm sure the young man would like a chocolate digestive biscuit, wouldn't he?'

But when Anna had finished the bedroom and the bathroom and the coffee had not materialized she went to the kitchen to find Sean on his second cup being charming to Mrs Stratford-Parker.

Anna finished the dining room for him. She did the kitchen and the living room without assistance too. Mrs Stratford-Parker inspected the job and said, 'Such a neat worker, my dear – so like a woman to clear up after herself. I do congratulate you. And such a nice young man you brought along with you. He advises me to have a set of extra keys for these window locks.'

Anna gritted her teeth. Each of the locks already had a key although one key would open all of them. A spare set would require another visit.

'Well, *I'm* not bloody going back,' Sean said, on their way down in the lift. 'The old bat wants to show me her husband's samurai swords.'

'Customer relations,' Anna remarked bitterly. 'It's your own fault about the keys. You should know when to keep your charming little mouth shut.'

'She can stuff her sodding keys,' Sean said, 'I've had enough customer relations with her to last a lifetime. Look, Anna, you do it, will you? I'll pay you back.'

'It's you she wants – she said so.'

'I know, but she'll keep me there all day, silly old cow.'

'Such a *nice* young man!' Anna said. But on the way back to the office she stopped at a phone box to call the estate agent and he had a flat for her to look at in Barons Court; if she went to the locksmith first she could wangle a long lunch-break before returning to Mrs Stratford-Parker.

'You won't be sorry,' Sean said gratefully.

'I know I won't,' Anna replied, 'because you are going to follow up a credit check for me.'

'Sure,' Sean said.

'This afternoon.'

'Well, I was going to . . .'

'This afternoon or I'll mention it to Beryl about Mrs S-P wanting you specifically.'

'Tim's right,' Sean said, 'you *are* a hard woman.'

'And you are a lazy sod,' Anna retorted. 'You didn't do a stroke this morning.'

'Customer relations,' Sean said smugly.

Chapter 14

THE FLAT TURNED out to be a cramped, dark, damp base-
ment with a coalhole which had been converted to a bathroom over thirty years ago. Anna found out from a neighbouring
shopkeeper that the last tenant had died of hypothermia and that
the whole row was due for renovation. The lease therefore would
only run for two years. She did not, in any case, feel that she
could survive for two years with so little light: fifteen minutes of
poking dry rot in the skirting boards was depressing enough. It
would not do.

She spent a fruitless hour with Mrs Stratford-Parker and returned to the office to find two memos on her desk. The first read:
'A. Lee to Mr Brierly's office 16.30 sharp. BD.' The second was
from Sean. 'Re: credit check,' he wrote. 'Amount outstanding.
Non-payment. The guy is a no-no.'

Anna picked up the memo and marched into Sean's cubicle.
Sean was poring over a hi-fi catalogue and as his door flew open
he slid a security brochure over it.

Anna said, 'What's this Sean?' And put the memo down in
front of him.

'Your little job,' Sean said. 'I rang the credit reference agency.
How was old Mrs S-P?'

'You are a total and absolute wilf, Sean,' Anna said slowly.
'You have simply repeated back to me the information I asked
you to confirm.'

'Well it's right then,' Sean said. 'Why bother?'

'You don't confirm a report by asking the same people the
same question twice. Where were you brought up?'

Sean stared at her.

'You didn't ring the garage?' Anna asked.

'Why should I? It was probably the garage who put the block

on the guy in the first place. He's a loser, Anna. Can't pay his debts. Tell the client. Job finished. I'm telling you, Anna, you spend far too long on this stuff. I can get through it in half the time.'

'Of course you can,' Anna said angrily, 'because you're lazy and careless.'

'No need to get huffy,' Sean said. 'You don't understand the way the system works here. You've got to believe what Credit Ref says. Job done – new client – fast turnover – boss pleased – pay rise. That's what it's all about.'

'What it's all about is some poor bugger being shafted through you not doing your job.'

'Want to bet?' Sean asked, pulling the hi-fi catalogue out again. 'A fiver says you're wasting the client's time? Whose side are you on anyway?'

'Rack off, Sean,' Anna said, and went back to her own cubicle. She leafed through the yellow pages until she found F.J.P. Garages. It was a chain with six branches in South London. William Herridge had made his purchase at the Putney branch. She dialled the number.

'Accounts please,' she said when the call was answered. And then, 'I'm doing a credit update on a William Herridge. I believe you filed a red card on him about a year ago.'

'Is that Herridge with or without a D?' the man at the other end asked.

'With.'

'Hold on.'

Anna held. Beryl came to her door, rapped on the glass and beckoned impatiently. The man said, 'I've got something here but I'll have to cross-reference. Would you call back?'

Anna hung up and went to the door. Halfway down the corridor was Beryl's retreating back.

'Four thirty-five,' Beryl called over her shoulder. 'You're late again.'

Short legs and high heels disappeared round the corner. Anna followed, past the reception desk where Jenny gave her a sympathetic wink, and into Beryl's office. There, Beryl gave her attention to an ailing cactus and said, 'What're you waiting for? You'd better go in.'

Anna tapped on the inner door and went in to Martin Brierly's room.

Chapter 15

E VEN WHEN MARTIN Brierly said exactly what Anna would expect him to say she could never imagine what he was thinking. He had been her boss for years. He was bulkier than when she had first met him, but his bland round face, his inappropriate yapping laugh, his meaningless gestures were still impenetrable.

Now he sat as he always did behind his desk with his back to the light and said, 'Take a seat, Miss Lee.' Anna sat and he continued, 'I received a telephone call this morning from a Ms Lara Crowther.' He emphasized the Ms. He didn't like it. Unmarried women were Miss; married, widowed or divorced were Mrs. Why hide behind anything else? 'American woman,' he went on, as if this explained any deviation. 'You have already met her.' He paused and lifted his eyebrows.

'Mr Shomacher's sister,' Anna supplied. She wondered if Lara had mentioned the game in Battersea Park. 'House in Barnes. We did an evaluation and estimate.'

'Correct.' He did not know about Battersea Park, Anna decided, and it was just as well because he would not take it well if he suspected a private approach had been made.

'Apparently you made a good impression and Ms Crowther wants to retain your services. There is, however, a problem. I have been looking over your work sheets and I see that you will be fully occupied until, roughly, the middle of January. Ms Crowther appears to require your undivided attention.'

'Is it urgent?' Anna asked.

'Isn't it always?' He had a contemptuous expression and Anna wondered if Lara mightn't have put his nose out of joint.

'And another thing,' Brierly went on. 'Ms Crowther seems unwilling to confide the full extent of her enquiry to anyone but you. As you know, I am reluctant to expose an employee to unknown risks. I like to know the full ramifications of a problem.'

Anna groaned inwardly. No one ever knew the 'full ramifications'. Lara had certainly offended Martin Brierly and now he was going to make difficulties. Rather than sit there and listen to him make them, Anna said, 'Well, as you say, I'm booked up. Maybe you should recommend another firm.'

'What's booked may be unbooked,' Mr Brierly said perversely. 'On your way out ask Miss Doyle to look at your work sheet with a view to redistributing your cases. That will be all.'

'Sorry?' Anna said. 'You're taking Ms Crowther?'

'Of course,' he said dismissively. 'And you'd better get a move on. She's at Kensington Close Hotel and you won't want to keep her waiting.'

So Lara was just around the corner but had refused to come into the office, Anna thought on her way out; another reason for Mr Brierly to be miffed. He always liked to give his clients the once-over.

Back in her cubicle she looked through her diary and work sheet. There was nothing there she could not leave to someone else – unless the someone else was Sean. Just in case, she jotted down all the relevant details of Mr Kemal's enquiry about William Herridge on a loose piece of paper before taking everything along to Beryl.

On her way back to pick up bag and jacket Phil waved from his cubicle. 'I've got a right prat here,' he said. 'The geezer's a real-ale, bake-your-own-bread type. Wants to run a full security system off a sort of wind turbine. Any ideas?'

'How about solar panels?' Anna asked. 'There's a firm makes intruder lights that run off solar panels. I've got a brochure somewhere. Maybe you could adapt something.'

'T'rrific,' Phil said gloomily. 'Can you look it out for me?'

'If you come now,' Anna said. 'I'm on my way out.'

Phil followed her into her office and sat on the edge of the desk while she rummaged in the box file which held all the advertising brochures.

'Is the bloke a vegetarian?' she asked.

'I expect so. Why?'

'Well, if he isn't, what about that place in Bedford that trains attack-dogs?'

'There's a thought,' Phil said. 'But he's the type as'd want to feed a dog birdseed.'

'Then what about an attack-parrot?' Anna found the leaflet she was looking for. She said, 'Also, there's this firm that manufactures recordings of alsatian dogs barking which you can attach to your doorbell.'

'Christ,' Phil said, 'do you keep all that rubbish? Mine goes straight in the out-tray.'

'Geese!' Anna cried, suddenly inspired.

'Duck off,' said Phil, looking depressed.

Chapter 16

'I'M GOING TO tell you a story,' Lara said. She had secured a reasonably private nook in the hotel dining room and was wielding a silver teapot with the expertise of one who had spent many afternoons with the British.

Anna held her cup between the palms of her hands and waited. But Lara took her time. She wore a rose and indigo knitted suit and her expression was securely organized.

'I told you I buy clothes for stores back home?' she began. 'I see a lot of people, and over the years I've made one or two friends. I specialize in knitwear, some of it I buy straight from the designers. I go around the small stores here keeping an eye out for new names, new talent. If I find something I think will sell, sometimes I'll look up the designer – visit him or her, cultivate the talent.'

She paused for a moment to finger the cuff of her jacket.

Anna watched the hands, the plucking fingers. Calm face, nervous hands. 'Just watch and listen,' Bernie used to say at the beginning. 'Don't make up your mind what's important, what's not.'

'This is one of Penny Garden's designs,' Lara said, and Anna stared at the intricate pattern of rose and ink coloured stitches that made up first a design of leaves and branches and then the shape of Lara's jacket.

'I first met Penny fifteen years ago. She'd left college a couple of years before and had a little girl. She had a husband too in those days. They were trying to live off what she knitted herself – all the talent in the world but no business sense whatever.

'I helped her organise. You know, out-workers and all that, so she could concentrate on what she did best. Design. The market for designer knitwear wasn't as big as it is now, but she did all

46

right. I got her work into some of the classiest stores in the States. And after a while she found outlets in Japan and Germany too.

'Now this is the important bit. Four years ago she opened a little shop. Not far from here. I warned her. Having a shop just for your own lines is an expensive game. But there were things on her mind. She wanted something for the husband to do. I hadn't realised it but he was bored and restless. He wanted them all to move into London. From out near Oxford. Did I say? She lives and works in Oakleigh, near Oxford. Of course, she couldn't move. Finding the sort of space she needed at a price she could afford in London would be next to impossible. But the husband wanted London. Male menopause or something.'

Anna heard the way she said 'the husband', and said nothing.

'Then there were the out-workers,' Lara went on. 'Over the years she had developed this whole network of good knitters near where she lives. I can't begin to tell you how important that is. What Penny does isn't straight knitting. It isn't even just wool. Sometimes she used silk, sometimes cotton. Sometimes she'd want a texture so complex she'd have to invent the stitches. Or a pattern you'd need a degree in algebra to follow. So when she found a good out-worker she hung on to her. She had to.

'No, Penny Garden couldn't move. So she got the shop and the little flat above it for the husband. He was supposed to run things, stay in the flat during the week, come home weekends.

'Of course it was the shop that broke her,' Lara said flatly. 'I knew it would. But there wasn't a damn thing I could do to prevent it. Too much outlay, too many overheads.'

And although she was silent for a few moments Anna heard her say, 'The biggest overhead of all was the husband.'

'Penny went bankrupt,' Lara said. 'The shop and her limited company – both called Garden Party – went into liquidation. The husband took a powder. That was early last year. To begin with Penny and some friends clubbed together in an attempt to buy the stock back. It was all she had, you see. But the liquidator wouldn't have it. He said he had to maximize the company's assets in order to pay off the creditors – that he had received better offers. Penny lost her entire year's work.'

From beneath the restaurant table Lara drew a bag which was neither a handbag nor a briefcase although it had the characteristics of both. Inside was a plastic folder. Lara placed the folder on the table in front of her. It was as if she were at a board meeting. Exhibits would be displayed only at the proper time, in the proper sequence.

'Now,' Lara said, back straight, hands on either side of the folder, 'in order to peg her offer at a reasonable rate Penny had to find out how much Garden Party owed its creditors. Easy, you might say. Except that the husband had kept the books, and she couldn't find him. The liquidator would not tell her: he wouldn't even return her calls. Someone advised her to make a company search, and she discovered that there had been no annual returns for three years. She made her offer anyway, and as I say, it was rejected.'

Anna interrupted. 'Were you one of the friends?' she asked. 'Who clubbed together?'

Lara gave her a surprisingly defensive look but said, 'Sure I was. I believe in Penny's talent. It is not in my interest to see her go under.'

The hands, Anna noticed, were jumping again.

'Then a month or so ago,' Lara continued, 'I saw, on the streets of New York, a woman wearing one of Penny's designs. It was one of her limited summer lines – a silk knit wrap-around top. Now I know Penny's work. I know what I bought for the States, and I know that top was a new item. There were only about forty ever made and they were in a batch available only through the shop. Either this top was bought before the shop went bust or it was supplied by whoever bought the bankrupt stock.

'I accosted this woman.' Lara smiled briefly. 'She was pretty flustered but she talked to me anyway. It seems she was on vacation in London and she was doing the markets. It's one of her hobbies: every couple of years or so she goes to London and does the markets looking for Victorian jewellery. Well this time, in Portobello Road, she got sidetracked by a stall selling discontinued French designer lines, seconds, you know, garments with a small fault in them. She let me see the label, and it said "Lalaine".

'Now you may not know it but "Lalaine" is a very, very exclusive French label. The woman thought she had a bargain. But the wrap-around was Penny's. I know it. I more than know it.

'I came back here and talked to Penny. I didn't tell her about the phony label because I didn't want to upset her. She's easily upset these days. But I got from her the name of the bank – the major creditor – and I called up. You'd think that if the liquidator had managed to sell off some of Garden Party's stock the bank would be the first he'd pay off. The bank had received nothing.'

Lara leaned forward and rested her chin on her fist. 'Okay,' she said. 'You've heard what I know. What do you think has happened?'

Anna cleared her throat. 'Rough guess?' she asked.

'As rough as you like,' Lara said.

'Very rough,' Anna warned. 'One: the husband, knowing the business was going bust, walked off with some of the stock before the company went into receivership.'

Lara smiled a broad satisfied smile. 'That's what I thought,' she said. 'Now prove it.'

'Two,' Anna went on, 'the liquidator did a deal with an old mate.'

Lara's smile vanished. 'What do you mean?' she asked uncertainly.

'The liquidator takes a backhander from someone he knows who then buys the stock at a knockdown price. If the liquidator accepts Penny Garden's offer he has to pass most of the money on to the creditors. If he sells cheaply to a mate he gets most for himself.'

'You're kidding,' said Lara.

'It's one of those well-known facts that are more or less impossible to prove. Even if a liquidator is strictly legit, he can charge so much for his time, phone bills, meetings, etcetera that only a small percentage of what he realises finds its way back to the creditors. Some people think being a liquidator is like having a licence to mint gelt.'

The organised expression disappeared from Lara's face, leaving her soft and uncertain.

She wants it to be the husband, Anna thought, but she's a fair woman and now she doesn't know what to tell me to do. She said, 'Have you asked the liquidator directly if he's sold the stock?'

'He doesn't answer any of my calls either.' Lara fiddled with a corner of the folder, bending it back and forth as if she wanted to break it off. 'He's away on business, he's out of the country, that sort of thing. I leave messages but he doesn't call me back.'

Suddenly decisive again she snapped open her bag and slid the folder back in. 'I want you to meet Penny Garden,' she said. 'Pick me up here at eight tomorrow morning and we'll talk on the way down.'

Giving you time to be uncertain in private, Anna thought. You won't let me see you making up your mind; you'll just present me with your conclusions. On the whole, Anna approved.

Chapter 17

AT HOME, NORTH of Holland Park, Anna walked into a domestic row of gigantic proportions. All the lights in the house blazed. The television was on in the Prices' flat but the shouting came from upstairs in Anna's front room. Bea and Selwyn stood nose to nose in the middle of the Turkish carpet.

'You selfish, opinionated, destructive bastard,' Bea was yelling as Anna opened her door. She had a rolled-up copy of the *Kensington Chronicle* in her hand, and at every adjective she whacked Selwyn on the arm. His arm was protecting his left ear.

'. . . Bourgeois, small-minded . . . sneaking behind my back . . . undermining my position . . .' Selwyn thundered at the same time.

'. . . in the bloody papers, the bloody newspaper.' Whack. 'I've never had my name dragged into the press.' Whack. 'This is the last straw.'

In the background was the unlikely sight of a huge man trying to look inconspicuous: Quex sat in the corner of the sofa pretending to read.

'Home sweet home,' Anna said, but nobody noticed.

'You've no right.' Whack. 'To draw on that account.' Whack. 'That's the house account.' Whack. 'And I'll need every penny . . .'

'I'm not moving to a poky bloody hole in Potters Bar. You're trying to castrate me, woman . . .'

'Bleeding shut up!' Anna shouted.

'I'm stopping the cheque!' Bea screamed. 'I'm *warning* you!' Whack.

'You're on your own!' bellowed Selwyn. 'What you want is a pet poodle with a pay packet.'

'Not in here!' Anna said at the top of her voice. 'If you want to beat each other up, do it *downstairs!*'

That was heard. Quex lumbered to his feet saying, 'Hello, sweetie.'

Selwyn said, 'Sorry, Leo, but this woman's bloody impossible.'

Bea simply turned away and marched out. As she went she threw Anna a look filled with such hurt and fury that if Anna had not been tired and angry herself she would have gone after her. Instead she stomped into the kitchen to fill the kettle. Quex sauntered in after her.

'Bit of a fracas,' he said, rubbing the back of his neck. 'Selwyn got a reporter round here yesterday when Bea was out, and today there's a paragraph or two about this plucky couple standing up to property giants.'

'Part of the campaign,' Selwyn said, and leaned against the fridge with his arms folded looking self-satisfied. 'There's a chap coming soon to put in the window bars and the steel-plated front door.'

'You gave him the cheque Bea was on about?' Anna asked and Selwyn nodded.

'You're changing the front door without consulting me?'

'You can chip in half,' Selwyn said. 'In fact that's a good idea. It might cool Bea out about the house account.'

Anna stared at him, speechless. Quex said, 'Come on, old chap, why not go downstairs and make it up with Bea?'

'Let her stew,' Selwyn said grumpily. 'She's not going to get me to apologise. She hit me! Did you see? If I'd hit her, Leo, you'd have been up in arms.'

'Selwyn!' Anna found her voice. 'Just piss off downstairs or you'll find out things about domestic violence you never even imagined.'

'You're on *her* side!' Selwyn sounded incredulous.

'This isn't a game,' Anna said. 'Did you look at her face? She's not messing around like you.'

'Messing around?' Selwyn cried. 'I like that! You're the one who isn't taking this seriously. Just you watch out, Leo. They'll cut your balls off too. You'll end up on his estate in Ireland keeping house for the aunts and bringing up snotty-nosed brats.'

Quex spun round and took Selwyn by the elbow. 'Too far, old chap,' he said mildly. 'Downstairs now. Double quick, eh? You don't want to lose *all* your friends in one fell swoop, do you?'

With Quex propelling him from behind Selwyn seemed to melt away. Anna carefully warmed the teapot and added two spoons of tea. The kettle boiled.

Quex came back saying, 'And Bea, without Selwyn's agreement, has put down the deposit on that place in Potters Bar.'

Anna stared at him. 'It's *all* gone a bit far,' she said. 'A bit bloody far.'

'Steak and fried spuds?' Quex asked, casually opening the fridge. 'I did some shopping this morning.'

Anna woke at three in the morning. She was sweating and Quex's arm, thrown carelessly across her shoulders, pinned her to the bed. She got up, careful not to wake him, and went to the bathroom. Sitting on the edge of the bath with the window open, she breathed deeply. Dream pictures ran through her mind, a spider's web of rose and indigo wool stretching like a security trellis over the only window of a dark room, and a man, crouched in the centre of the web, waiting. She spent the rest of the night on the living-room sofa.

Chapter 18

AT SEVEN-THIRTY she crept out leaving last night's dishes unwashed and breakfast uneaten. On the landing at the top of the stairs she put on her shoes and discovered an envelope addressed to her in Bea's handwriting. The note read, 'I'm so sorry about last night. I know you hate a row. Whatever happens I'm moving to Potters Bar and I want you to know you would be welcome until you can find a place of your own. Remember, you've got less than eight weeks. Love, Bea.'

Anna folded the note back into its envelope and stuck it in her pocket. It was so like Bea – the generous offer coupled with the nannyish reminder.

The Peugeot had collected a fine coat of London grime. She spent a few minutes cleaning the windows before starting off. Clients liked to be able to see out of windows. The fruit stall on the corner of Abingdon Road and Kensington High Street provided two bananas for breakfast.

At eight she found Lara in a fawn trench coat waiting on the steps of the hotel. She had slept well, her make-up was fresh, her slacks had creases sharp enough to slice ham.

'Hi,' she said, when she opened the passenger door. 'We'll take the M40 out of London.'

No sooner were they back on the High Street heading towards Hammersmith than she said, 'I've thought about what you said yesterday and it would seem sensible to start with the liquidator.'

'Agreed,' Anna said. 'He's in the middle whichever way you slice it. Just what is it you want me to find out?'

'Yeah,' Lara murmured thoughtfully. 'Good question. Initially, you see, I thought it was the husband. It still might be. At any rate, he's the one who brought Penny down. It was his extravagance and poor management which bankrupted the business. And then the way he walked out – just upped and vanished when Penny needed him most. It's been preying on her mind, see. Unhealthy. She can't work, and she's on some pills her doctor gave her. I thought if you could come up with something – like he pulled a fast one and walked with the stock – we might have a chance to recover some of it. At least it would prove to her what a low-life he was – you know, that she's better off without him. Her self-image has taken a terrible beating.'

'And if it wasn't the husband?' Anna asked.

'That's the good question. From what you say, even if the liquidator took a bribe, the sale of stock would be legal. Legal on paper, that is. And you'd never prove otherwise. All the same, I'd like to know. Maybe we could get him disbarred or whatever it is you call it.'

'Mmm,' Anna said.

'You don't think so?' Lara asked.

'Tricky. You could waste a lot of time and money trying.'

'See, that's what I like about you,' Lara said suddenly. 'You don't give me any B.S. about "everything's possible". You just tell me what's practical. Can you move these seats? I have to be careful with my back.'

Anna told her how to adjust the seat, and Lara pushed hers back so that she was almost stretched out. She said, 'I do a lot of travelling, so I know the value of a comfortable trip. Even a short one. Look, I just want a rough idea of what's happened. Maybe when you see Penny you'll appreciate why. I'd like to get that gal back on her feet again. I hate wasted talent.'

If Anna had any questions about what made it Lara's business and why she was prepared to hire a private investigator on Penny Garden's behalf she kept them to herself.

Chapter 19

OAKLEIGH SAT SNUG in a shallow valley. The old part was built of Cotswold stone, its narrow streets like clogged arteries against the force of twentieth-century traffic. On the outskirts of the old town and just before the brick and cement outer ring of new buildings was Penny Garden's house.

Lara opened the door without knocking and led the way down a cold passage to the kitchen at the back.

'Oh, honey,' she said as she entered, 'you shouldn't let the fire go out.'

A pale moon-face looked up at them, and wide-apart grey eyes blinked sleepily. The straight hair was dark and fine, and there was only a little white in it.

'Is it cold?' Penny Garden asked.

'Honey, it's freezing.' Lara picked up one of the placid hands and chafed it gently. 'I'll get the beast lit. You make the coffee.' Lara bustled around the huge Aga as if she knew it intimately.

'I wanted you to meet Anna Lee,' she said, over her shoulder. 'You didn't forget we were coming, did you?'

'No,' Penny said. But clearly she had. She stood arrested at the sink with the electric kettle in her hand.

'Coffee, honey,' Lara reminded her, and she slowly came back to life.

It should have been a warm, friendly kitchen with its oak dresser, flagstones and spice boxes, but there was something about it that reminded Anna of Sleeping Beauty's castle. The owner had been asleep for too long to care for it. The windows were still dim and smeared with summer flyblow, and dust lay on shelves and crockery which should have been bright with use. At the top of the back door was a perfect spider's web.

They sat at a heavy pine table. In the centre was a large pottery bowl containing just two withered apples.

'I haven't heard anything,' Penny said. 'Not a letter or a phone call or . . .' The sentence trailed away.

'Never mind,' Lara replied. 'That's what I've brought Anna in for. She's going to sort it all out for you.'

Anna felt the weight of Penny's unfocused hope and glanced sharply at Lara. Lara made a tiny, calming motion with her fingers and said, 'I don't want you to worry about a thing. It's all in hand. You just get back to work and everything else will fall into place.'

'Will it?' Penny asked. 'I mean, everything's *gone*. They've taken *everything*. I've been waiting and waiting and now it's winter again.'

'That's right,' Lara said. 'So now it's time to take action. Why don't you show Anna your studio, hon?'

'Oh, there's nothing to see.'

'Yes there is,' said Lara briskly. 'And she has to be able to recognise your work if she's to get it back. Isn't that right, Anna?'

'That's right,' Anna said, adopting Lara's optimistic tone.

'Well, if you really want to.' Penny got to her feet and started to walk to the back door. She was big, wide-hipped and graceful, but she moved as if she were carrying lead. She opened the door. The wind rippled the web but left it intact.

The studio was over the garage, and the three women reached it by way of a wrought-iron staircase. Lara opened the door and they walked into a blaze of colour. Skeins of dyed yarn hung from wooden pegs driven into the beams. Yarn wound onto huge spools lay in ranks on the shelves. Tacked to the walls were knitted samples, fashion posters and painted designs. A large stone sink was splattered with coloured dyes like an expressionist painting. There were poster paints and jars of coloured pencils, crayons and felt-tipped pens on the desk.

'Terrific!' Anna exclaimed, her optimism suddenly quite unforced.

Chapter 20

Anna sat on the sofa with Penny and Lara on either side of her. In front of them were the contents of Penny's portfolio, catalogues and some thirty samples.

'How's your visual memory?' Lara asked.

'There's a lot here,' Anna said.

'You can take the printed stuff, if that'd help,' Lara said. 'But Penny won't want any designs or samples out of her reach.'

'Oh, she can have them,' Penny said dully. 'I don't need them any more.'

'Yes, you do.'

'Oh, well maybe . . .'

'No maybes about it,' Lara said forcefully. 'You complain about everything going and then you start giving it all away yourself. You've got to hang on to what you've got and rebuild. You've got this God-given talent – so use it.'

Anna, looking at photographs of Penny's God-given talent, could not suppress the envious thought that she herself would not be able to afford any examples of it. Penny designed knitwear to make most women's mouth water, but not many women could shop at the exclusive boutiques that sold it.

The photos and texture samples Lara had sorted out for her were of the missing stock, and she concentrated on learning the shapes and colours. Penny and Lara went over to the desk and Anna heard Lara say, 'But, honey, this is *good*.'

'No it isn't,' Penny replied with more clarity than Anna had heard from her yet. 'My hands shake so much I can scarcely hold a pencil. And, Larry, you need *zest* for this sort of thing. I'm dead. Colours don't vibrate and sing any more.'

What Anna was looking at had zest.

Lara said, 'What's wrong with subtlety?'

'This isn't subtle,' Penny answered. 'It's dead.'

She seemed to know her mind where her work was concerned, Anna thought. Whether she was right or not was another matter.

Later, back in the kitchen, when Lara returned to the theme of work as a cure for all ills, Penny turned to Anna and said, 'Larry's had four husbands. Did you know that?'

'So I know what I'm talking about,' Lara protested. 'If every time a man let me down I sat around and moped, I'd be finished. A man is like a pair of shoes. You find one to suit you and then your feet grow, or you buy a new dress. Then the shoes pinch and are the wrong colour. What are you going to do? You can't walk around with your feet hurting for years, can you?'

It was the closest they came to discussing 'the husband'. Penny had another, more immediate, problem: her cat. The cat had needed worming. It was a job Penny usually did with someone called Cyn. But with Cyn gone, Penny had put off the job until she was sure the cat was riddled with worms. And then the cat disappeared. In her sad, slow way Penny worried obsessively over it. Had it starved to death because of the worms? Had one of the neighbours lured it away? Maybe the cat, like Penny herself, was depressed in a cold and empty house.

Anna wondered if Cyn was the daughter nobody mentioned. Furtively, she looked at her watch under the kitchen table. It was nearly lunchtime. What was she doing, listening to vague, uneasy speculations about a cat. Did they expect her to go out and find it? She wondered if Penny even knew she was a professional investigator. After all, they had never been properly introduced.

Penny took two or three tablets and swallowed them down with cold coffee. She seemed exhausted. Anna glanced at Lara, and Lara said, 'I think I'll stay on here for a while. Hadn't you better be getting back to London?'

'Yes,' Anna said, trying not to look too keen.

Lara came out to the car. 'She's got to stop taking that medication,' she said. 'It's doing her more harm than good. I told her to speak to her doctor, but I'm sure she hasn't. What do you think?'

'I don't know.' Anna fiddled impatiently with her keys. 'I'm not a social worker.'

'Of course not.' Lara looked offended. 'I thought you might have an opinion, that's all. I read someplace that anti-depressants cause dependency.'

'Yes,' Anna said.

'So she should get off them, right?'

'Yes.'

'But that's not your problem, right?' Lara thought for a moment and sighed. 'Look,' she said, 'I left all the information you need in that blue folder on the back seat. Call me at the hotel if you need anything else. I'm leaving for the States in a couple of days, but my New York number is in there, just let me know what you turn up.'

'Right,' Anna said and got into the car.

Chapter 21

WITH QUEX AT home Anna thought it best to go straight to the office. Jenny, red-haired and sly-eyed, stopped her as she passed the reception desk. She said, 'There's a couple of messages. A Mr Smith from F.J.P. Garages wants you to call. And your fiancé rang.'

'I haven't got a fiancé,' Anna said, taking the pink memo-slips.

'Boyfriend then.' Jenny twirled her own engagement ring and looked superior.

'Happen to know who got my cases?' Anna asked.

'Sean, I think,' Jenny said. 'You can't put me off. He sounds really nice.'

'Sean?'

'Your boyfriend.'

Anna pulled a hideous face and went to her cubicle. Without stopping to take off her coat she picked up the phone and rang F.J.P. Garages. The telephonist said, 'Sorry, Mr Smith's out of the office. Can I take a message?'

Anna left her number and rang off. She went across the corridor, but Sean was out. The Herridge file was on his desk with half a dozen others. It did not look as if it had been opened.

She went back to her side of the corridor and tipped the contents of Lara's blue folder onto the desk. She pinned the pictures to the board, anarchic splashes of colour which blotted out the dreary memos and homilies from Beryl and Martin Brierly. What else? Some sketchy information about the liquidator: name, address, telephone number; detailed information about 'the husband'. So convinced was Lara of his guilt that she had amassed several sheets of facts and gossip about him.

Chris Garden. His last known addresses had been, of course, the shop and the house in Oakleigh. But Lara had dug up three extra-marital relationships – her words – one in Oxford and two in London. There were some old bank statements, and a few photocopies of Garden Party statements which purported to prove that Chris had drawn money from Garden Party. Anna would have been very surprised if he had not. After all, he both managed and was employed by the company.

Even if she took Lara's word for it, the evidence only pointed Anna to the feeling that Chris Garden was unfaithful and slightly feckless. There was nothing to support Lara's conviction that he had stolen from Garden Party. But he was missing, and Anna wondered if Lara had tried to find him or if her interest was solely in blackening his reputation.

And if so, why? The oddest aspect of the case remained Lara's interest in it. Looking at the carefully ordered detritus, Anna thought it went beyond friendship. There was something obsessive about it. Who on earth would go around questioning the neighbours about the infidelities of her friend's husband? A detective would. But Lara hadn't employed a detective until she hired Anna.

She had the feeling that she was being lured into something which was not on the menu. Perhaps Lara wanted her to look after Penny while she was away. She had seemed let down when Anna curtly evaded questions about Penny's health. But if that were the case, it would be cheaper and simpler to hire a nurse.

Sticking strictly to the job, Anna picked up the phone and dialled the liquidator's number: Mr David Stamp at an address near Archway. The number rang twenty times, but there was no answer.

Bernie signalled to her through the glass, making the tea sign. Anna nodded and put the phone down. Immediately, it rang, and Quex said, 'Hello, sweet thing. Will you be home for supper?'

'I should think so,' Anna said. Bernie grinned and pointed along the corridor to the rec-room. She nodded again.

Quex said, 'Only you skipped out so quietly this morning. I never even felt you get up.'

'I was late,' Anna lied. 'I was meeting a client early. Didn't want to disturb you.'

'Long day.' Quex remarked. 'Well, don't worry about food – I'm taking you out.'

Anna put the phone down. She left the office quickly and joined Bernie in the rec-room. He gave her a mug and said, 'What's up, young Anna. You look like the mother of four toddlers at teatime.'

Anna laughed. 'That bad?' she said.

'Frayed.' Bernie sat comfortably.

'Nobody answers the phone.' Anna counted on her fingers. 'Bloody Beryl's given my cases to Sean, who will cock at least one of them up something rotten. My client wants me to social work her friend. What else? Oh yes, and we have to be out of our house in seven weeks.'

'Visit – don't phone,' Bernie replied easily. 'Get someone to sit on Sean's tail. Tell your client to stuff herself. Come and stay with Syl and me. Anything else worrying you?'

'Not a thing,' Anna said, laughing again.

'Straight up about your flat?' Bernie asked, more seriously. 'Mr and Mrs Price, too?'

'Straight up,' Anna said. 'The house has been sold. Selwyn's all for sitting-in and pulling up the drawbridge. Bea's put down the deposit on a place in Potters Bar. There've been ructions.'

'And you're looking for somewhere else?'

'Right.'

'Well, well,' Bernie said. 'The kids' rooms are both vacant – until the first divorce, that is. Syl would love to have you, if you need a stepping stone.'

'Thanks, Bernie,' Anna said, touched.

'Think about it.'

'Okay.'

The phone in the rec-room buzzed. Bernie leaned over and answered it. He said, 'She's here,' and handed it to Anna.

'I've told you before about personal calls,' Beryl said. 'The Commander wants to know about your meeting with Mrs Crowther.'

'Yes,' said Anna.

'Well?'

63

'It's just as she described over the phone,' Anna said. 'He knows.'

'Oh.' Beryl, for once, was stymied. 'He wants it on paper,' she said, with a flash of inspiration.

'All right,' Anna said, and hung up. Mr Brierly didn't know a thing. But if there was one thing he hated more than ignorance, it was admitting to it. She could keep him clueless for weeks just by saying, 'The job is exactly as described.'

'Don't you look smug,' Bernie said. 'Watch it or the wind might change.'

Chapter 22

A ROW OF SHOPS — Kiddy Klothes, Paper Weight, Zunwin's Deli and a tobacconist — were on street level. Above them, on the first floor, windows wore painted signs in black and gold — surveyors, secretarial services and, in the middle, David Stamp — Accountant. It was like Brierly Securities, only this was Archway.

Anna climbed the stairs to a dark landing shared by all three offices. She knew even before she knocked at David Stamp's door that there would be no answer: the ribbed glass was dusty and there was no light behind it.

She turned sideways and went into A.C. Secretarial Services instead. A counter, just a yard inside the door, brought her up short. Behind it was a copier and shelves, running from floor to ceiling, filled with paper, ribbon cassettes, paperclips, staples, cardboard folders, elastic bands and all sorts of office supplies in no particular order. A voice from an inner room said, 'Be with you in a minute.'

Tacked to the wall were price lists for copying, a telex and a fax service. Anna read them while she waited.

A grey-haired woman came through. She looked dusty, a bit like a school teacher, in a grey pleated skirt and what Anna's recently educated eye recognized as a mass-produced cardigan.

Anna said, 'Sorry to bother you, but I'm trying to get in touch with Mr Stamp next door.'

'He's away,' the woman said with authority. 'Why don't you telephone on Wednesday morning?'

'Will he be back then?'

'I don't know,' the woman said. 'But the telephone will be answered.'

'It is rather urgent.'

'I'm afraid I can't help you. Ring on Wednesday.' The dry lips folded primly around the last word and the woman turned away.

Anna said, 'I'm from the Official Receiver's office, and there have been one or two complaints.'

The woman turned back. 'Official?' she said. The mouth stretched in an ingratiating smile. 'Our arrangement with Mr Stamp only means that one of us, my partner usually, answers the phone for him on Wednesday mornings. We take messages, you see, and leave them for his collection. Since his illness, he only comes in once a week. He does all his business from home.'

'Home?' Anna produced an official-looking notebook from her bag. 'Perhaps you could give me his home address?'

The woman gave it quickly. Anna said, 'How long has he been ill?'

'It's hard to say, really. It's his kidneys, he told Sonia. At first he had to go in to hospital for dialysis, but now he's got a machine at home. He's waiting for a transplant.'

'Oh,' said Anna, trying to come to terms with interviewing, and perhaps giving a hard time to, someone who was plugged into a dialysis machine. It wasn't easy. 'When does he come in for his mail?' she asked.

'Well, it must be Wednesday night,' the woman told her. 'I don't know, because I haven't seen him for ages. Sonia says it's because he's gone a funny colour.'

'What?'

'He's embarrassed,' the woman said, as if she were making complete sense. 'Apparently, he's gone all yellow and he's afraid of getting caught in traffic jams.'

'Sorry?'

'He doesn't like to be parted from his machine,' the woman said. 'Oh, don't ask me. I hate the whole idea – cutting up people for spare parts – it isn't natural. When I was young you just died like everyone else. None of this waiting around for someone else to die for you.'

'Um, er,' Anna said, fighting a sudden urge to run for the door. 'Well, thank you for the information. Have you a business card? I'll probably want to talk to your partner.'

'Sonia? She's off with the flu.' The woman sniffed, and added with a malicious smile. 'I'll give you her home address too, if you like.' She jotted something in her own notebook, tore out the page, folded it and gave it to Anna.

Chapter 23

SALISBURY MANSIONS WAS an old block of flats with a porter's lodge guarding the rear from trespassing car parkers. The front entrance was barred by a heavy plate-glass door reinforced with steel bars. It was the kind of security Anna approved of – in theory. In practice it meant she could not walk in and knock on David Stamp's door. She pressed the bell with his name on it and waited. Nothing happened. There was an entry phone by the row of bells. Anna rang again and leaned close to it in case the noise of the traffic had blotted out David Stamp's voice. Not a whisper.

She picked another bell at random and pressed it. Almost immediately a voice asked who was there.

'Delivery,' Anna said.

'What?'

'Intercounty,' Anna said. 'Delivery.'

'We're not expecting anything,' the voice said. The door remained tightly shut.

Anna looked at her watch. It was after six and Quex would be waiting. Home-bound traffic crawled down both sides of the road. She pressed another button.

'Who is it?'

'Anna,' Anna said. 'I'm awfully sorry but I've locked myself out.'

'Who?'

'Anna. You know me. I live just under you and I locked myself . . .'

'I heard,' the tinny, asexual voice answered. 'But I live on the ground floor and the only thing under me is the boiler room. So fuck off, or I'll call the police.'

'Thanks a bundle,' Anna said, and made quickly for her car.

Twenty minutes later she was outside Sonia's home. This time it was easy to get to the front door by a maze of brick outside staircases which made the block look like stacks of cottages built on a hill. The front door, when it opened, led straight into a tiny kitchen. A man stood in the doorway. He was dishevelled, hair sticking out in spikes, glasses knocked sideways on his cheek, a large damp patch on the front of his shirt. He carried a huge baby in his arms. The baby was bundled untidily into a bath towel. It screamed lustily and banged with plump fists on the side of the man's head.

'What is it?' he yelled, trying to be heard over the roaring baby.

'Sonia,' Anna yelled back. 'Can I speak to Sonia, please?'

'Oh God!' he shouted. 'Come in a minute – it's freezing with the door open.'

Inside, there was hardly anywhere to stand. Baby equipment – high chair, walker, pedal car – took up nearly all the space. The baby stopped screaming, smiled blissfully at Anna and threw up on the man's sopping shirt.

'Oh God!' the man said. 'Oh buggeration. Sorry, I'll have to . . . you'll have to . . .'

He thrust the baby into Anna's arms and stumbled from the room. The baby started to roar. It grasped two handfuls of Anna's hair and pulled down while it struggled to stand up in her arms.

She sat down on the only available chair, squashing a box of disposable nappies as she did so. Then she rearranged the towel, swaddling the infant so that its arms were wedged against its body.

'Listen, gnome,' she hissed, 'behave yourself. I'm trained in thirty-five methods of self-defence and I can make life very tough for you. I specialize in controlling hooligans, ferret fart, and if you don't shut up I'll dismantle your stroller and feed you the bits – sideways.'

The baby stared at her, goggle-eyed. Anna warmed to her theme. 'Talk, you little lout,' she said. 'Where's your mum, eh? It's no use holding out on me, bouncing babies is what I do best. I had red meat for lunch, so watch it! I know your type – you act rough and tough with anyone you think you can knock about – but you're mush, just mush . . .'

The man appeared again, buttoning up a clean but unironed shirt. He made no move to reclaim his baby and sat down on the other side of the kitchen table.

'You're not the health visitor by any chance?' he asked hopefully.

'I just wanted a quick word with Sonia.' The baby squirmed restlessly as soon as she turned her attention elsewhere.

'Quiet!' she warned. 'One peep out of you and I'll hide your teething ring.'

'He's been giving me hell all day,' the man said. 'This is the first moment I've had . . .'

'He seems to like threats and insults,' Anna said. 'Don't you, bird brain?' The baby blew a sleepy raspberry. 'Is Sonia in?'

'No, she isn't,' the man said. 'She's never in.' His face looked like a fallen soufflé. There was a story behind it which Anna didn't want to hear.

She said, 'I thought she had flu.'

'Flu?' He smiled bitterly. 'She's at her Paul Newman Marathon. She always says she has flu but she's never sick.'

'She's where?' Anna asked, not quite believing her ears.

'You wouldn't do me a big favour, would you?' the man said. 'You wouldn't put Mark Two down in his cot for me, please. He's been up since six this morning and this is the first time he's dropped off. I couldn't bear it if I took him and he woke up.'

Anna followed the man, who was evidently Mark One, through a jumbled living room to the baby's room.

'Okay, big boy,' she said as she laid him in his cot. 'Get your ugly mug on that pillow. If I hear anything but snores out of you, you'll get what-for.' The baby didn't answer.

'Have a drink?' Mark One asked, when they were back in the kitchen. 'I can't tell you how grateful I am. He winds me up and winds me up so I don't know if I'm coming or going.'

He poured himself half a tumbler of gin and added a splash of Mark Two's orange juice. Anna refused.

'He's teething,' he added, sucking his drink through his own teeth. 'Oh Christ, that temperament and teeth too!'

'What's a Paul Newman Marathon?'

'Unbelievable, isn't it? They hire a suite at the White Hotel, Swiss Cottage. Between them they've got videos of all Paul Newman's films and they have a forty-eight hour binge. I'm not expecting her back till tomorrow. And then she'll sleep till the evening.'

'Maybe you've got it all wrong,' Anna suggested. '*You* should pig out on Paul Newman and give the baby the gin.'

'I've certainly got something wrong,' Mark One said miserably.

Chapter 24

THE CARLTON SUITE at the White Hotel had been furnished for the occasion with sofas, divans and easy chairs all in matching plum and peach coverings. The light was dim, but three brilliant monitors showed Paul Newman and Patricia Neal sparring with each other in a bedroom. Paul Newman was saying, 'You're a good cook, you're a good laundress. What else you good at?' He was holding a daisy and looking as if he knew he was irresistible.

Anna nearly sat down on the nearest chair to watch. Instead she looked around the room. Probably two-thirds of the people there were women, but there were several couples too, and a smattering of single men. Anna went over to the buffet where three women were helping themselves to French bread and pâté.

She said, 'Do you know where Sonia is?'

One of the women held a finger to her lips.

Paul Newman said, 'Man like that sounds no better than a heel.'

'Aren't you all?' replied Patricia Neal lazily, and Anna noticed that the woman was silently mouthing the dialogue.

Paul Newman said, 'Honey, don't go shooting *all* the dogs 'cause one of 'em's got fleas.'

The woman expelled her breath in a long sigh. 'God, I love that line,' she said, and looked at Anna with dreamer's eyes. 'Now, what was it you wanted?'

'Sonia,' Anna said. 'Sonia Casey.'

The woman pointed to a door. 'She went in there,' she said. 'But I wouldn't . . .' She paused, half smiled and went on. 'She went in there.'

Anna stared at her.

'What's the matter?' the woman asked. 'Have I got spinach on my teeth?'

'No,' Anna said hurriedly. 'I was just admiring your sweater.'

It was made of fine wool – a sunset design in green, pink and gold. It was one of Penny Garden's. Anna had looked at a picture of it just that morning.

'It's lovely,' Anna said truthfully. 'Do you mind me asking where you got it?'

'For sale by private treaty,' the woman said, twitching her shoulders and glancing self-consciously down at her own chest. 'Actually, Sonia brought some tonight. Apparently, it's bankrupt stock, although how anyone selling stuff like this could go bankrupt I'll never know.'

'I wonder if she has any left,' Anna murmured.

'Shouldn't think so. They were going like hot cakes before the evening started, and she only brought a few.'

With her eyes now used to the dim light, Anna could pick out what the women were wearing. Among the figures lounging round the monitors she counted four who were wearing Penny Garden knitwear, and two possibles.

There was a feeling in her chest, a rapid two-beat pump of the heart. Something was happening. The case was really a case. It was alive – like an animal she could track, tame and maybe, eventually, ride. She had expected hours, days, weeks, of chasing down pieces of paper, checking where stock went, whether or not creditors had been paid any money. She had not expected to run into someone selling the bankrupt stock on her first day. Life wasn't like that – at least Anna's wasn't.

She went to the door the woman had pointed to, opened it and went in. The room was lit only by the TV monitor and the same film was on the screen. Coats and bags were piled on a chair and on the floor to make room for the couple on the bed. The woman was on top, her face blueish and flickering like the film. She was staring fixedly at the screen, riding. Paul Newman was carrying someone up a staircase, saying, 'One of the cows cuddled up to him.' Sonia, if it was Sonia, did not notice Anna. It was not an occasion when Anna would expect to be noticed. She backed out of the room.

There are some things even the most inquisitive detective does not interrupt, and one of them is a Paul Newman movie. Anna left the White Hotel with a sense of frustration clearly not shared by the woman she wanted to interview. She felt let down and stupid.

Chapter 25

I T WAS SO quiet when Anna got home that she could almost believe she had the place to herself again. But Quex was sitting in the corner of the sofa. He looked strange, and it was a moment before she realised that he had shaved off his beard and was wearing his best suit. His black, curly hair had been rigorously brushed down, but one curl was loose on his forehead. A bottle of Red Label stood on the small table by his side. It was either half full or half empty.

He said, rather thickly, 'You didn't ring.'

'You shaved!' she exclaimed.

'You noticed!' he said. 'Clearly, obviously, apparently, visibly, I have shaved. I am no longer hairy. I have skin under my mouth. And you noticed. But then you are a trained observer, aren't you? – trained to observe the state of a man's chin, if not the state of a man's soul.'

The bottle, Anna decided, was half empty.

'What's up?' she asked.

'You didn't ring.'

'I know. I'm sorry. But what's the matter with you?'

'You did *not* ring.'

Anna stared at him. He had a muscular neck, a good jaw and a strong mouth. But he didn't look like the same man. Quex did not look like Quex.

He said, 'Bea has left. Selwyn is rat-arsed. I've just finished putting him to bed. And you didn't ring. How was *your* day?'

'Long.'

'Clearly, obviously and apparently, it was long. Quite correct. I had the same impression. We think alike. We, you and me. Long.'

He got up, staggering slightly, and held out his hand. 'Now come to bed.'

Anna said, 'I'll make some tea. What happened with Bea and Selwyn?'

'No,' he said. 'I don't even want to think about Bea and Selwyn. And tea would choke me.'

Later, he said, 'I'm sorry.'

'It was my fault,' Anna said. 'I should have rung.'

'I didn't mean that,' he said. He seemed a long, long way away.

Chapter 26

IN THE MORNING Anna went back to the White Hotel. She felt
feverish and a little shaky. She thought she might be coming
down with flu. It was that time of year. Everyone on the bus was
bundled up with scarves and thick coats. They looked pale and
miserable.

In the Carlton Suite, however, nothing had changed but the
film. Thick curtains were closed against the morning and Anna
slipped in as if she were slipping back in time. Paul Newman was
saying, 'Lay down and die by yourself – don't take me with you.'

Another man said, 'Just like that?'

'Yeah,' said Paul. 'Just like that.'

Anna narrowed her eyes and tried to pick out faces in the
gloom. They were the same faces as last night, although some
had changed clothes.

The man said, 'Thanks for the drink, Eddie's girl,' and exited.

Anna caught sight of Sonia Casey, stretched out on the floor,
her back against a sofa. She made her way across the room
towards her.

Paul Newman said, 'Boy, everybody – everybody wants a piece
of me!'

He did not seem to have the insouciance of the night before.
Nor did Anna. A woman on the sofa moved her legs, and
Anna sat on the floor beside Sonia. She leaned close to her and
whispered, 'I didn't like to intrude last night because I could see
you were busy, but I would like to talk to you about your stock
of bankrupt knitwear.'

'I'm busy now,' Sonia said.

'Not *that* busy.'

Sonia turned to look at Anna. In the half-light her eyes were
long and lazy. She turned back to the screen.

Paul Newman was reading from a sheet of paper. 'What's this supposed to mean?' he said. '"We have a contract of depravity . . ."'

'You are selling Garden Party knitwear,' Anna persisted. 'Where did you get it?'

'Not now,' Sonia hissed. 'Mind your own business.'

'It is my business.'

Sonia twisted to look for someone else in the room. Anna followed her eyes, but all she could see were the legs of the women on the sofa. Sonia turned back.

'Who are you?'

'Anna Lee.'

'I mean, what makes it your business?'

Someone on the sofa said, 'Shsh!'

'Let's go somewhere we can talk,' Anna suggested.

'Do you have any right to be here?' Sonia asked. 'Did you pay for the privilege? I mean, this *is* a private function.'

'And there's no law against private acts at private functions,' Anna whispered. 'You're quite right. I didn't pay. Why don't I just go and wait for you to come home. I met Marks One and Two last night. I'm sure they'll be pleased to see me again.'

Sonia scrambled to her feet. She had been sitting in the same position too long, and she was not graceful.

'Sit down!' someone said. 'I can't see.'

Sonia made for the door. She was searching for reinforcements, Anna thought, as she followed. But she didn't find any, and Paul Newman was getting his thumbs broken as she left the suite.

Sonia closed the door carefully behind her and said, 'Look Miss Whatsyourname, I just brought a few sweaters to sell for a friend. They're nice sweaters and I knew people here would like them. What's wrong with that?'

'You tell me,' Anna said. 'You work next door to, and *for* David Stamp, who is very difficult to contact, and who just happens to be liquidating the company that makes those nice sweaters.'

'So?' Sonia shifted her weight onto one leg and stuck a hand on her hip. 'It's perfectly legal to buy and sell bankrupt stock.'

'Did you buy it?'

'No, I did not.' Sonia had come out without her shoes and her stockinged feet made a soft noise on the carpet. 'I'm just doing a favour for a friend,' she went on. 'Selling last year's fashion isn't always easy, you know.'

'Who's the friend?' Anna asked. 'Who is the legal owner of the stock?'

There was a pause. An Asian woman trundling a cleaning cart down the corridor glanced curiously at them. Anna watched Sonia and tried to sum her up. She already had a weapon, but it was not one she particularly wanted to use. Sonia had been up all night, well, nearly all night. She should have been showing signs of wear and tear, but if you ignored the fact that she had no shoes she looked remarkably fresh.

A small wave of rage broke over Anna. Was everything, she thought, going to depend on what the night before had been like? Sonia had had a good one, and she looked smug and in control.

Quickly Anna said, 'I am acting on behalf of a creditor. There have been complaints, and the implication is that the liquidation of a certain company has not been handled correctly.'

'Is this an official enquiry?' Sonia asked calmly.

'It certainly will be,' Anna said, 'if I don't get some satisfactory answers.'

'What was the question again?'

'Why are you making such a meal of this?' Anna asked. 'All I want to know is where you got the goods you're selling.'

'And all I want to know,' Sonia snapped back, 'is what right you have to ask.'

'I told you.'

'You told me nothing.'

At that moment Anna could have cheerfully strangled Sonia with one of Penny Garden's beautiful long-sleeved sweaters. She could have done the same to Quex. It was his fault that she was being pressed to explain herself, when it should have been the other way round. Emotional outbursts were bad for work. Quex did not have to work so he could afford them. As she saw it then, his self-indulgence was costing Anna her ability to control this interview.

She gritted her teeth and said, 'Creditors, if they think a liquidation is being improperly conducted, have a perfect right to appoint a representative.'

'And you're it?' Sonia threw back her head and laughed.

'Okay,' Anna said, turning away, 'if that's the way you want it. Just remember, you're in the front line. I know you. I know where you live. When the axe falls, Mrs Casey, it'll fall on you.'

Sonia let her retreat about five paces before she said, 'I tell you what I'll do. Give me your card, and I'll have the owner of the goods get in touch with you. He's away on a business trip at the moment, but as soon as he gets back I know he'll want to sort this out.'

She sounded like a telephone answering machine. Anna gave her a card. The one with just her name and two phone numbers on it, and as she went down in the lift she thought about how impenetrable Sonia was. She was perfect. If David Stamp had picked her to keep enquirers at arm's length, he couldn't have picked better. No wonder Lara had been so frustrated.

Outside the hotel, Anna looked carefully at the lie of the land. She wished she had brought her car although there was nowhere convenient to park. In the end she chose a spot with a decent view of both the hotel entrance and the ramp up from the garage.

The taxi was more difficult. Two drivers were not prepared to wait for an indefinite time. The third said, 'It's your money, mate,' and settled down to read the racing pages.

He was not a talker, for which Anna was very grateful. It's hard enough to keep your concentration when nothing is happening and being talked to makes it virtually impossible. Good observation is the art of concentrating steadily on nothing in particular. When Anna first started in police work she had found it very hard. She was always hoping for something to happen in the first five minutes, and when it didn't she became first impatient, and then bored stiff. She used to think that there must be a trick to it: a way of keeping the image of what you were waiting for in your head while letting the rest of your mind run free. But if there was such a trick, she had never mastered it. The only thing that counted was patience.

Chapter 27

AN HOUR AND forty minutes later Anna began to see people she recognized from the Paul Newman marathon emerge, blinking, onto the hotel steps. She leaned forward and told the driver, 'Any minute now.' He grunted and folded up his paper.

Another ten minutes went by before she saw Sonia, in a red Cavalier, come up the ramp. As the taxi driver pulled out after her, he said, 'I don't think I'll be much good at this, love. I came out without me specs.'

'Oh, terrific!' Anna snarled.

'Didn't ask, did you?' the driver said. 'If I'd known, I'd've brought me junior MI5 kit.'

He followed Sonia so closely that had she braked suddenly there would have been an accident.

'Drop back,' Anna said.

'Don't want to do that,' he said. 'Some bugger'll get in between.' That was precisely what Anna wanted to happen, but her driver edged even closer, and when Sonia turned off the Finchley Road the two cars almost turned as one.

'Piece of cake!' the driver exclaimed, and Anna fought an urge to belt him on the back with her handbag.

They were so close that she could see Sonia was not alone. There was a man beside her, and his arm was across the back of the seat, his hand nestling at the back of her neck under her hair.

Sonia was heading away from her home. She was talking animatedly to her companion and not attending very closely to the road. Anna prayed she was not attending to her mirror either.

'Wotchit!' the driver cried, slamming on his brakes, and dumping Anna onto the floor. 'What's she doing of now?'

'She's stopping,' Anna said through gritted teeth. 'Overtake!'

'Overtake?'

'Quickly!'

'Women drivers!' he said, swinging the cab out around the Cavalier with a sickening lurch. 'Didn't signal or nothing.'

Anna scrambled up onto the seat and twisted to look through the rear window. The Cavalier was parked at a bus stop and the passenger door was open.

'Stop!' she said.

'What, here?'

'Here.'

'If you say so,' the driver grumbled. 'I s'pose you know what you're up to.' He pulled in to the kerb. 'No waiting,' he said. 'Double yellow lines.'

'Right,' Anna said, getting out. 'What's the damage?'

'Blimey!' he said. 'You got money to burn, or what? We ain't done quarter of a mile.'

Anna paid him an astronomical sum, knowing she would happily double it rather than go an inch further in his cab.

'Oh, I get it,' he said. 'It's her bleeding boyfriend you're after, innit?'

'Don't tell anyone,' she said. 'Forget you ever saw me.'

'Mum's the word.' He fumbled behind the seat and produced a dog-eared card. 'Got any more jobs like this, give me a shout. I'd say I'd got the knack, know what I mean?'

Anna walked briskly back towards the Cavalier and then turned into a shop doorway. Sonia and her man were still talking. There was only a feeling to go on. It was when Anna had mentioned Garden Party and Sonia had looked for support from someone already in the room. Would she have looked for someone who was simply her boyfriend? Anna didn't know. She might have if she were a soft, dependent sort of woman but Anna knew she wasn't.

She glanced over at the car. The couple were still talking earnestly. They could be discussing what to do about the stranger investigating a liquidation or they could be arranging their next date. Or maybe it was the greenhouse effect, or the price of pork chops.

Sonia's car pulled away leaving the man at the bus stop. A few more people joined the queue and Anna walked over to stand behind them. She studied the man's back.

He was tall – over six foot, his hair was light-brown, his haircut looked expensive. So did his coat and shoes. The back of his neck was tanned. That looked expensive too.

A pair of women in the queue, obviously friends, nudged each other, glancing sideways at him. Sonia's feller was a hunk. He did not look as if he belonged on a bus in cold, damp, windy London.

But a bus came, and he got on. He sat at the front, looking out of the window. Anna went to the back. She found herself dreaming about Rome and the south of France.

Chapter 28

THE 31 BUS is famous in some circles. It runs from Camden Town at the northerly end of its route to World's End in Chelsea. It likes its own kind. 31s come in bunches. People say you can wait for hours for one and then three turn up at once. They say that while you are waiting the weather *always* turns nasty. You have to be philosophical about it — feast or famine.

Anna had plenty of time to be philosophical as they zigged and zagged through Kilburn, Carlton Vale, Westbourne Park and into the home territory of Notting Hill Gate and Kensington High Street. Sonia's man did not get off, and as she sailed past the Brierly Security office Anna had time to wonder what sort of mess Sean was making of her cases. She worried briefly about William Herridge and whether or not his career was to be blighted for the price of four radial tyres. And then the bus turned south down the Earl's Court Road and her thoughts turned with it to Sonia and the man she was following.

In less than twenty-four hours she had seen Sonia's partner, her husband and child, her unclothed body, and her lover. It was a lot to see of a woman she knew nothing about.

Yesterday she had been looking for an elusive liquidator. She hadn't found him and it seemed as though Sonia had stepped in to fill the breach. Now she'd lost Sonia and she was following her lover instead.

There was something random about the route she was taking. It was ruled by negatives. Anna considered this. She was on a 31 bus because she did not want to be in a taxi. She had gone to the White Hotel because she had not wanted to spend the time and energy on David Stamp — and also because she had not wanted to go home. She was working for Lara Crowther because, fundamentally, she did not want to work for Martin Brierly.

Chapter 29

S ONIA'S MAN GOT off at the King's Road. He walked east —
a brisk athletic walk. Anna admired it for about half a mile
and then, abruptly, he turned in to a Greek taverna. He stayed
there for nearly an hour. Anna crossed the road and munched
slowly through an egg salad roll at a sandwich bar which gave
her a clear view of the restaurant door.

When he came out she had her first look at his face. He was
older than he seemed from behind, but just as good looking. She
left a can of lemonade unfinished on the counter. They continued
walking east. He never looked back. He was taller than almost
everyone else. There were plenty of people about. It was easy. He
was not window shopping: he knew where he was going.

There was a wide doorway between two shop windows displaying a medley of ultra modern and sub-fetishist garments. He
disappeared into it. Steps led down into a cavern of different stalls
selling every conceivable style of street fashion. Anna closed the
distance between them. He threaded his way quickly between
racks of hanging dresses, leather jackets, rubber, neo-hippy chic,
to a broad staircase at the back.

Up he went to a mezzanine, slightly better lit, where the stalls
looked more expensive and more conservative. Jazz-rock seeped
out of hidden speakers. Shoppers wandered from rack to rack.
Bare fingers sampled fabric. Truant schoolgirls in twos and threes
giggled and sighed at price tags.

Sonia's man led Anna to a bay fitted with steel and mirrors
where woman-shaped silk, wool and polyester, reflected a hundred times, marched into a false infinity. The bay was tended by
two very young girls.

Anna went on to a rack of antique clothes and hid herself
behind rows of Victorian nightgowns. Sonia's man spoke to one

of the girls. She blushed. The other one handed him a red ledger. He flipped through the pages. She opened the till and took out what seemed to be wedges of notes. He counted, handed some back, pocketed the rest. He spoke again. Both girls looked confused. Then one of them knelt on the floor and started to pull clear-wrapped sweaters from a pile stacked beneath the hanging garments. The other opened plain carrier bags. They stuffed four bags and handed them to Sonia's man. He patted the younger girl's cheek. She blushed. He walked away. Anna followed.

She followed him down the stairs, through the crowded cavern and out again onto the street. He crossed the road and entered a bank. Ten minutes passed and when he came out he walked five doors east and went into a travel agent's.

After twenty minutes Anna, feet numb and hands freezing, risked peeping through the window. Behind the joyful posters advertising winter breaks and sunny beaches, Sonia's man was haranguing a pimply youth. The lad was pink with humiliation and fumbling through papers, his fingers trembling. At last he found what he wanted, jammed it into an envelope and handed it to the tall, handsome man.

Sonia's man walked out. He stood for a moment looking around. Then he simply dropped the white plastic bags on a pile of boxes left out for collection. There was a faint smile on his face as he stepped to the kerb and raised a leather-gloved hand. A taxi stopped as if it had been cruising all day waiting for just this opportunity. The man got in and was carried away. There were no other free taxis.

Anna watched him go, and when his cab was out of sight she rescued the bags from the rubbish pile. The bags contained Penny Garden sweaters. The labels read 'Fortissimo' but the sweaters were, without question, Penny's. Anna felt slightly disappointed: it was too easy, too careless. No questions had been answered.

Quickly, before he could forget his blush, she went to see the lad in the travel agent's.

Two women in perky red blazers looked up as she came through the door. They both had phones, like permanent deformities, glued to their ears. The lad with the pimples kept his head down. Anna went to his desk and sat down.

She said, very quietly, 'Excuse me, but could you tell me who that man was?'

He glanced up, puzzled and blushing again, then looked away.

Anna said, 'I wouldn't ask, only he's the man who ripped my mother off after my father died. He said his name was Martin Brierly, but I know it isn't.'

The lad met her eyes steadily then.

She went on, 'It's one of those silly stories. When my dad died it was in the papers, and that . . . man, calling himself Martin Brierly, came to see my mum, you know, asking if she wanted to sell anything for a bit of spare cash, you know, to tide herself over. Well, she didn't really need the money, but she was in a panic, all upset, and she thought she did.'

'I've read about that sort of thing,' the lad said.

'Yes. I suppose even my mum had,' Anna agreed. 'But she was at a really low point, and she didn't ever think it'd happen to *her*.'

'What did he take?'

'Well, she had some nice china figurines, and all that. She'd been collecting them all her life. And he said they weren't worth anything, but he gave her twenty quid for the lot. Only they were the real McCoy, worth thousands.'

'The bastard,' the lad said with enjoyment. 'Well, he's not Martin Brierly, he's Hugh Fellows. Are you going to get the police onto him?'

'Well, I'm not sure what he did was a real crime . . .'

'Oh, you must!' He was pink with excitement now. 'You should report it, y'know, stop it happening to anyone else. Slimy bastard!'

'Well . . .' Anna said, reluctantly.

'Go on. I'll give you his address and phone number. I know it's the right one because we've sent tickets there. He only came in this time because he wants to change his flight.' While he was speaking he scribbled furiously on a pad in front of him.

'He doesn't give a shit how difficult it is this time of year. If *he*

88

wants to fly tomorrow he thinks someone'll give up their seat and say, "Oh, you first."'

'Where's he going?' Anna asked.

'Tampa, Florida.' He tore off the top page from his pad and handed it to her. 'Tomorrow. Piedmont out of Gatwick. Business class, of course.'

'Some people have all the luck,' Anna said.

'I wouldn't call that luck, not after what you've told me,' the lad said.

'When's he coming back?'

'Not for eight weeks, so if you want to do something . . .'

'Better step on it,' Anna finished for him.

'Don't say it was me told you,' he said, suddenly anxious.

Chapter 30

ANNA STOOD IN a piss-reeking phone box at Sloane Square. She was talking to Lara Crowther.

'That's fantastic,' Lara said. 'You've got them with you now?'

The carrier bags were open at Anna's feet. She said, 'Well, there's only a couple of dozen . . .'

'Unbelievable!'

'So I still don't know what's happened but it can't be kosher or this chap wouldn't have moved them out and just dumped them.'

'Right,' Lara said. 'Right, right, right. Who is the guy? Do you know?'

Anna looked at the page the lad from the travel agent had given her. She said, 'His name is Hugh Fellows, and . . .'

'Oh, my God!' said Lara.

'What's up?'

Two container trucks carrying chilled meat roared past. Anna pressed a finger to her free ear and said, 'What? I can't hear.'

Lara said, 'Listen – I've got to talk to Penny. Where can I reach you?' She sounded overwrought. 'No, wait a minute. Don't go to your office. Don't say anything to your boss. I'll call you at home. When can you be there?'

'Half an hour.'

'Okay,' Lara said. 'I'll call when I can. Don't do anything till I call.' She hung up.

Anna pressed the receiver button and then dialled her own number. The phone rang and rang which meant Quex had gone out without switching on the answering machine.

On the tube between Sloane Square and Notting Hill Gate she thought about Lara's reaction. She couldn't make anything of it: there was too much she hadn't been told. Well, Lara would have to tell her something now – either that or drop the job completely. She hoped it would not be the latter. It was the first interesting piece of work she had done in two years.

And after she left the tube and was walking down Holland Park Avenue it struck her that working for Martin Brierly and finding a new place to live were both parts of the same decision. She thought too about Selwyn and his rebellion against Potters Bar. She wasn't like Selwyn, she knew that. But the idea of working forever as a security rep in order to pay a mortgage or rent on some overpriced chicken coop suddenly revolted her.

When she arrived at her house she was greeted by the dismaying sight of two workmen and no front door. The old one with the glass panels had disappeared and the new one, a great solid slab, leaned against the front of the house. The workmen had ripped out the wooden door-frame and installed steel instead. The hall was icy and stank of sawdust and metal filings. Selwyn's door was shut tight against the draught, and the sound of Nat King Cole at top volume seeped through to compete with the workmen's drills.

One of the workmen stopped drilling long enough to say, 'You'll be safe enough in here, darlin', safe as houses.' He laughed. 'Don't want uninvited guests disturbing your beauty sleep, eh?'

'What about keys?' Anna asked, eyeing the pile of bolts waiting to be fitted.

'Don't you worry,' he said. 'We'll let *you* out, won't we – if you're good.'

Upstairs, in her own flat, she lit the gas fire and put on the kettle. Quex had made the bed and tidied the kitchen but his books and newspapers were all around the living room. He had been writing in a red spiral notebook which had been left open on the coffee table. Anna wondered if she was meant to read it. She went to the phone and called the office. Although she asked to speak to Bernie, Jenny put her straight through to Beryl.

Beryl said, 'Well! So you deigned to check in at last. The commander is still waiting for your report.'

'I'm doing it now,' Anna told her, fingers crossed. 'Had a busy day. I just called in to see how Sean was getting on with Mr Kemal's job.'

'It's not your business now,' Beryl said, satisfaction oozing along the phone line. 'But if you must know, his report is in front of me now. Some people don't keep clients hanging around.'

'Some people don't follow up properly either,' Anna said. 'What were his recommendations?'

'An agent's recommendations are strictly confidential,' Beryl said joyfully. 'I would've expected you to know that by now. And I'll expect your report first thing in the morning.'

Anna asked to be transferred back to the switchboard, but the line went dead. She bottled up a stream of foul language and went to make the tea.

With a hot mug in her hand she went back to the phone and punched out David Stamp's home number. It rang twenty times. Quex came in behind her and said, 'You're home early.'

Anna replaced the receiver and at once started to punch another number. She said, 'There's fresh tea in the pot.'

Sonia's partner answered on the second ring.

Anna said, 'Is Sonia Casey there?'

'I'm afraid she's out of the office at the moment. Can I take a message?'

'In that case, would you take a message for David Stamp?'

'I'm sorry,' Sonia's partner said, 'you have the wrong number.'

'But you do take messages for him,' Anna snapped in her official receiver's voice. 'So will you tell him, please, that Anna Lee – you know who I am – wishes to speak to him. Urgently. Will you tell him it is about the Garden Party liquidation, and that if he is to avoid proceedings,' Anna lingered on the word, 'he should contact me immediately.'

She hung up.

Quex was looking at the white carrier bags. 'Been shopping?' he asked.

'No.' Anna began dialling the office number again. 'That's evidence.'

Mistake. She shouldn't have phoned Sonia's partner. There was no need to call the office again either.

Jenny answered, and Anna asked to speak to Bernie. She wanted to be busy. Wrong. She wanted to look busy. She heard the internal phone ring in Bernie's cubicle. Nobody picked it up. Jenny came back on the line.

'I think he went out,' she said. 'Actually, now I think about it he said he had an appointment at the doctor's. He went home early.'

'Right,' Anna said, drumming her fingers on the phone table. 'Would you ask him to ring me in the morning?'

Why did Bernie want to see a doctor? Bernie was never ill. She crossed the room to her table and cleared a space among Quex's books for the typewriter. She sat down and began to type, 'Regarding my conversation with Mrs L. Crowther, it is . . .'

Quex said, 'Look, Titch, we really must talk. I know you don't want to, but we must.'

Chapter 31

H E STARTED SLOWLY. 'You avoid things,' he said.
'No, I don't.' She was thinking how odd he looked. It was
like talking to a stranger. This Quex, with his clean jaw and
strong mouth, was serious. It was as if he had put on a suit and
become grown-up.

'You do,' he said, firmly. 'You bury yourself in work. You meet
that head-on. You face the grind of everyday life, like working
on your car or repointing the Prices' kitchen extension. You go
to work every day of your life – no matter how tedious it is. What
you won't face is exactly how you feel about things.'

Anna almost said, 'What things?' but she didn't want to deal
with the answer. With a sense of rising anger she thought, 'I'm
on my back foot again.' How many times had she been caught
on the back foot already today? She said quietly, 'Is this what
you call a talk? Attacking me for the way I am? I'm still in the
middle of a working day, you know. Maybe you can afford to
waste your energy on emotional scenes, but I can't.'

'I'm not attacking you,' he said gently. 'You think I am, and
the way you said the word "emotional" tells me why.'

'Oh, bollocks!' She laughed and finished the tea in her mug. It
was too hot and her eyes watered. 'Haven't you had enough
emotion from Selwyn in the last few days?'

'I don't want it from Selwyn,' he said.

'Good thing too.'

'There you go again.'

'There I go what?'

'Hell,' he said. 'Let's forget about emotion. What I wanted to
say was, since I moved in here you've been avoiding me.'

Anna shook her head.

'Oh, yes you have. I mean, even when we're here together you

94

sort of turn things aside. This moving house for example. I take it you aren't going to play Selwyn's silly game, which means you'll have to move. We've never actually talked about it. I know you're being sent bumf by estate agents. So you're looking for somewhere. Meanwhile I have an enormous flat in Fulham we can move into in a few weeks. Why, whenever I mention it, do we always end up talking about something else?'

The phone rang and Anna got up to answer it. Quex caught her hand as she went by.

'Leave it,' he said. 'This is important.'

'I can't.' She pulled away and he let go. 'I'm expecting a call from a client. I can't leave it.'

She picked up the receiver and Lara said, 'Meet me at Oakleigh. We have to talk.'

'All right,' Anna said. 'When?'

'Soon as you can get there. And, hey, you say that guy was in a travel agent's?'

'Yes.'

'You happen to know why?'

'He was changing a flight. He's off to Tampa tomorrow.'

'Jesus!' Lara said. 'We'll have to pull the stops out. Tampa, Florida?'

'Yes.'

'I'll think of something,' Lara said. 'See you later.'

'Okay,' Anna said and hung up.

Quex sighed. 'You're going out,' he said. It was not a question.

'I've got to.'

'Of course.'

Anna scrambled into her coat and wound a scarf round her neck. She said, 'Look, you've had your say. I'm not avoiding you. It's just there's an emergency and I really do have to go.'

'I know,' Quex said patiently. 'But remember, me having my say is not the same as us talking about it.'

Downstairs a saxophone wailed like an unhappy child and the workmen were hanging the new door.

The evening air was cold and damp. Anna gulped it down, standing with her face turned into the wind.

Chapter 32

THE AGA WAS toasty warm and the kitchen lit by a low-hanging lamp over the table. In the soft light the place looked better, but there was still a cobweb across the corner of the back door. A fat woman, who looked like half a ton of potatoes in a lilac-coloured sack, dished up bowls of thick chicken soup and cut large slices of grainy brown bread.

Anna had not been introduced, and the woman left as soon as she had served up, saying, 'Cheerybye, Mrs Garden. See you tomorrow.' Lara watched her critically, and when she had gone said, 'There, Penny, isn't that better?'

'Oh, I don't know,' Penny sighed. 'I'm not sure I like having a stranger in the house.'

'She's a neighbour, honey,' Lara said.

'It's good soup,' Anna remarked. She hadn't expected supper and was grateful.

Penny reached for the salt and stirred her soup doubtfully.

'We had to do something,' Lara said, but she looked doubtful too. They ate in silence, and Lara waited until Penny had nearly finished before she said, 'Penny, Anna here has seen Hughie Fellows.'

Penny gave a little gasp and dropped her spoon. Lara caught her wrist and said, 'Honey, we have got to talk about it.'

Penny moaned. She looked at Anna with watery eyes. 'Where did you see him? What did he look like? Did you . . .'

'Just a minute,' Lara interrupted. 'He's going to the States tomorrow and we should decide what to do. I think Anna here should go with him. Kind of follow him, see where he's at.'

'Wait a minute,' Anna exclaimed, almost dropping her spoon too. 'That just isn't practical.'

'Why not?'

'Well, suppose by some lucky chance I manage to get a seat on the same flight, what then? I don't know the ground. Suppose he's picked up? I'd have to hire a car or whatever. I've never been to the States. I'd be lost before I started.'

'You're right,' Lara said. 'I'll go.'

'No.'

'Why?'

'Same thing. It isn't practical.'

'But, Larry,' Penny wailed, 'we can't let him get away. I've got to know where he's living now.'

Lara looked hard at Anna.

Anna said, 'You need someone to pick him up at Tampa, follow him to his destination and then tell you where that is. You need a local.'

'How do I find one?' Lara asked.

'You phone Mr Brierly,' Anna said. 'It'll be bloody expensive, but he can give you the name of someone who'll take care of Tampa.'

'I've got a better idea,' Lara said, looking cheerful and in charge again. 'My New York lawyer. She'll arrange it.'

She got up briskly and left the room. Anna was not accustomed to clients with enough money to arrange stringers in Tampa by way of a transatlantic phone call. She looked at Penny, but Penny was sunk in isolated depression.

'Who the hell is Lara?' Anna asked, eventually.

Penny looked up. 'She's been a good friend to me,' she said.

'Interfering old cow,' she added under her breath.

'What?' Anna thought she had misheard.

Penny said, 'Have you ever been depressed?'

Anna stared at her. 'Not the way you are.'

'Is there another way?' Penny looked at her hands. They were broad and pale like the rest of her. The wedding ring looked countersunk. 'I don't know,' she said at last. 'I don't seem to want to do anything. Larry thinks all it takes is a little will power.'

'Gutted,' Anna said.

'Gutless?' Penny asked, without the energy to be angry.

'No, *gutted*. Different thing.'

'Oh. Right. Thank you.' Penny started to cry.

Lara came in snapping the clasp of her personal organiser and saying, 'Well, that was easy.' She saw Penny crying and said, 'Hey, honey, what's the matter?'

'She understands,' Penny sobbed. 'She really understands.'

Lara glared at Anna who lifted her arms in bewilderment.

Lara said, 'Ethan Callow of Florida-Technics is calling in about ten minutes. He'll want some information.'

'Where's the phone?' Anna asked.

'Down the passage, second door on the left,' Lara said coldly, and Anna went, feeling nothing but relief.

The phone was on an antique desk in a small office. A single lukewarm radiator failed to compete with the draught from a badly fitting window. There was a two-seater sofa with a plaid blanket disguising hollows and lumps, and a shelf bowed under the weight of dusty box files. This had probably been 'the husband's' office, Anna thought, as she reached for the phone.

First she rang directory enquiries and then Piedmont Airlines. Then she waited for a couple of minutes until the phone rang. She picked it up.

A man said, 'Ethan Callow, Florida-Technics, for Ms Crowther.'

'Anna Lee,' she said. 'I'm acting for Ms Crowther.'

'I understand she has an assignment.'

'Yes,' Anna said. 'A pick-up at Tampa Airport. Hugh Fellows.' She spelled it. 'British Passport, coming in on Piedmont PI1161 via Charlotte. Arriving 1900 hours local time.'

'Okay, got that,' Ethan Callow said and in a flat voice repeated back everything she had said, adding, 'You want to fax me a photograph?'

'Um, fax?' Anna said. 'Well, possible but not probable.'

'Shit,' said Ethan Callow, sounding human for the first time. 'Give me the number anyway and I'll see what I can do.'

Ethan Callow gave her his fax number, phone number and Telex number in exchange for a description of Hugh Fellows. It was a lot of numbers. He said he would be in touch when Hugh Fellows got where he was going to. He told Anna to have a nice day and then he hung up.

Anna put the phone down and immediately started to search the desk. She found out-of-date Garden Party ledgers, a two-year-old business diary, a book of customers, a book of suppliers, a shipping folder, reams of headed notepaper, thousands of With Compliments slips, half a bottle of Vodka, a snake's nest of elastic bands and a family photograph.

Time had stood still in that little office: nothing was dated later than two years ago. And time stood still for the family group. Penny was in the centre, her broad face transformed by shining eyes. 'The husband', a slim, neatly-made man, had a greedy mouth, and the daughter, Cyn, was wild-haired and sulky-eyed.

'Sanity begins at home,' Anna thought, and replaced the photo where she had found it.

The only interesting thing she learned, as she flipped through the list of customers, was that Crowther was the name of the chain of stores Lara claimed she was buying for. This did not surprise Anna in the least.

In the kitchen, Lara and Penny were drinking coffee. Lara said, 'Well?' She hadn't quite forgiven Anna for understanding Penny.

Anna said, 'Well, I gave him what details I have. He wants a photograph. I should go to Gatwick anyway to check Hugh Fellows is actually on his flight, so I might be able to take one then. After that all I need is a fax machine.'

'There's one at my hotel,' Lara said. 'I use it all the time.'

'Fine. It's a seven-hour flight, so there'll be plenty of time.'

'Well,' Lara said, with a satisfied smile. 'That's that, for now.'

'Is it?' Anna asked. She had no idea what a faxed photograph would look like. She had never dealt with American operatives before. She had spoken glibly on the phone but she felt out of her depth. It was a far cry from chasing down a seedy liquidator in Archway. This was the American business world of television, where you picked up a phone and things magically got done thousands of miles away. It seemed like make-believe. She scratched her head and tried to look as if it was all commonplace.

Lara said, 'I expect you want to know who Hugh Fellows is.'

Chapter 33

'WE MET HIM about five years ago,' Penny began. 'We. Isn't it queer, Larry? I still say we. Was there ever really an us, do you think? Those are take-it-for-granted words — we and us. There was him and there was me and there was Cyn. I thought us, but it wasn't us, was it, Larry? It was just Chris, Penny and Cynthia.'

'I'll tell it,' Lara said soothingly. 'It was my fault in the first place.' She turned to Anna. 'Hugh Fellows was my agent in the UK. I try to keep in touch with everyone personally, but five or six years ago I decided to take on some help. Hugh Fellows was the salesman for a group of West Country knitters and weavers. He knew a lot of people and I liked his style . . .'

'Public school smarmy,' Penny put in unexpectedly. 'Charming, smooth. He could talk the hind leg off a donkey.'

'Yeah,' Lara agreed. 'Anyway, it didn't work out, so I let him go. But, of course, he was in the trade, so he kept his connections with the people I dealt with. I mean, he suggested at one time that he become your agent, didn't he Penny?'

'Except Chris handled the business,' Penny said, 'so I didn't need one. But Chris and Hughie stayed friends. They played squash sometimes. Or golf. They were quite alike in a way, weren't they Larry?'

Lara nodded. 'I guess they had the same sort of background.'

'So, if he turns up with Garden Party stock, you shouldn't be too surprised,' Anna suggested.

Penny and Lara exchanged a long look, and then Penny said, 'I'm shattered. It's dreadful.'

Lara reached over and patted her hand. Penny said, 'I need some pills, Larry. Honestly. I think I'm going crazy.'

'No, you're not,' Lara said. 'But take one if you have to. Just one. I'll make some more coffee.'

Penny took a pill. She held it up between thumb and forefinger for Lara to see. Anna wondered if she was being sarcastic, but if she was Lara didn't seem to notice.

'It's awful, just horrible,' Penny said to Anna. 'Because, you see, Cyn . . . my daughter, Cyn, ran away with Hughie Fellows. He more or less abducted her and . . .'

'Come on, Penny,' Lara said, 'It wasn't that way.'

'It was!' Penny insisted. 'She was sixteen and he was thirty something. Forty? I don't know. He's perverted. And, don't you see, Larry, if he's still in this country, still meddling in Garden Party, then Chris must know about it. Chris is condoning it.'

'Steady,' Lara said.

'Hughie seduced Cyn,' Penny shouted. 'And he's still living off my work. It's disgusting, Larry. And it's as if Chris was his daughter's pimp.'

'Just hold it right there,' Lara said. 'You're running away. You don't know any of this.' She turned to Anna and explained. 'It's because everything happened at once. The company folded, the husband left, the daughter ran away. She's making connections.'

'You said it yourself,' Penny argued. 'You said you bet Chris kept his hands on the stock. I couldn't believe it of him. But I've come round to your point of view. And if Hugh's selling it, then Chris must be supplying him. Don't you see what it all means?'

'Hang on,' Anna said. 'It doesn't have to be that bad. You're forgetting about the liquidator. As far as I know, Hugh Fellows is connected to the liquidator only by way of his friendship with the woman who works as his secretary. There may have been some wheeling and dealing but your husband needn't be involved at all.'

'There,' Lara said. 'See?'

'What does *she* know?' Penny said tiredly.

'Not a lot,' Anna admitted. 'But what connections there are have not involved your husband yet.'

'Then where is he?' Penny asked in a small voice. 'Why has he never come to see me? Why did he let it all fall on my head and not once come back and help?'

'Some men just can't cope with trouble,' Lara said. 'They just run away like little boys from a broken window.'

'Do they?'

'Mine seem to, sure enough,' Lara said. 'First they break the window, honey, then they run away.'

And some of them break the window while escaping through it, Anna thought, and wondered how easy Lara Crowther was to live with; or how many hurts had gone into her easy generalisations about the iniquities of men. But the idea that it was all men, rather than specifically Chris, who betrayed seemed to comfort Penny, and she closed her eyes wearily while Lara stroked her hand.

Chapter 34

THE ROAD BACK from Oakleigh to London was almost deserted – just an hour's drive between the inky dark of the country to the permanent yellow glow of the city. It was like returning to her own climate – even the temperature was warmer, and there was always something to do, somewhere to go if she didn't want to sleep.

Tonight, however, she did want to sleep, but when she arrived home she found the new door firmly locked against her. There were lights on in the house, but when she rang, first her own and then Selwyn's bell, no one came to let her in. She banged on the door with her fist. She kicked it. She threw pennies at the window. No one came. She phoned from the nearest call box. No one answered.

She retired to the Peugeot and curled up, cold, on the back seat. At first she couldn't sleep for the anger which flowed like electricity through every nerve. She could imagine Quex and Selwyn drowning their moronic sorrows and fulminating, as only articulate men can, about the bitches they were tied to. She could imagine Selwyn, at least, plotting petty revenge.

Later, after she had remembered the travelling rug she kept in the boot, she began to doze. It was like being on a swing – backwards into dreams and warmth, forwards into angry thoughts and a cold car. Backwards, forwards.

Someone tapped on the window and she jerked awake. Quex said, 'Oh Christ, Leo, I'm really sorry.'

'Piss off!' she shouted. 'Leave me the keys and just piss off out of here.'

'I forgot you didn't have any keys,' he said. 'I'm sorry.'

His fingers were resting on the open edge of the car window. Anna tried to amputate them. He jumped back.

'Selwyn's in hospital,' he said, 'I've just come back from St Mary's, Leo. I didn't *mean* to leave you out in the cold.'

She unlocked the car door and he opened it. 'God, Leo, you look terrible,' he said. 'I could shoot myself.'

'Don't bother.' She crawled stiffly off the back seat. 'I'm going to do it for you.'

It took three keys to unlock the front door. Anna waited in stony silence.

'This had better be good,' she said as they went upstairs. But her flat was warm and Quex made a pot of tea.

'After you went out,' he began, 'and after those chaps had finished with the door, Selwyn came up. He was in a funny mood.'

'He's always in a funny mood these days.'

'Yes. Anyway he gave me his "monstrous regiment of women" speech: the usual cobblers about domesticity being the enemy of genius, and when that was over he suggested we do a bit of pubbing and clubbing.'

'Free the wild, manly spirit from the chains that bind it?' Anna quoted.

'Exactly.' Quex grinned ruefully. 'Except I'd freed my manly spirit the night before and I still had a headache, so he went out on his own. I've no idea where he went, but when he came back, about eleven-thirty, he had a woman with him.'

'Gordon Bennett!' Anna exclaimed. This was new. 'How do you know?'

'Because he called me down as a witness to how wild and manly he was being.' Quex rubbed his face to mask another grin. 'Actually, she was very nice. Quiet; not young or glamorous. Just a nice, ordinary soul who was a bit lonely. But of course Selwyn was besotted with his own daring and . . .'

'Legless.'

'Well, he certainly wasn't sober. Anyway, I had a quick drink with them and left them to it.'

'It?' Anna asked, warming both hands on her steaming mug.

'Well, that's the point,' Quex said. 'I don't know what happened then. I mean, I felt pretty awkward. Bea's a friend too, isn't she? I just came up here and had a bath. I was waiting for you. But, oh, I don't know, about twelve-thirty, the phone rang and it was Bea. She wanted to talk to you but she made do with me instead. Apparently, Selwyn phoned her and told her about this woman.'

'What?'

'Yes. Except she was in such a paddy she told him to enjoy himself, *if he could*, and hung up on him.'

'She didn't!'

'She did. And then Selwyn phoned her back, full of apologies, saying nothing had happened, and that she – Bea – was the only woman who could straighten him out, and how could she leave him to destroy himself. She hung up on him again. So he rang a third time, and told her he was ending it all.'

'Poor Bea.'

'Right. She's pretty sensible, so she told him not to make a mess of it. But she was worried enough to call you.'

'And?'

'And I went down to make sure the silly sod was all right. All the lights were on, the door was open and the woman was gone. Selwyn was spark-out on the bathroom floor with two empty bottles of aspirin clutched in his hot little hand. I couldn't rouse him so I called the ambulance. When they pumped him out all they could find was seven tablets. The rest was the usual carrot and alcohol soup.'

'Bleeding hell,' Anna said disgustedly. 'He's really blown it this time.'

'The note was a gem.' Quex yawned hugely. 'You must read it some time.'

'No, thanks.' She was almost too tired to think about it. 'What're we going to do?' she asked. 'Everything's going from bad to worse. All Selwyn's dramas are turning nasty.'

'I know. We tend not to take him seriously because he's such a . . .'

'Plonker?' Anna supplied.

'Yes, but even plonkers come to the end of their rope.' He was yawning almost continuously. 'Let's get some sleep.'

Chapter 35

THE MORNING WAS bright and Gatwick Airport was crowded. Anna carried a bag and a coat and mingled with the scrum around the check-in counters. Her camera was not out of place.

The queue for Piedmont Airlines flight 1161 grew and then slowly dwindled. Hugh Fellows did not show up until the last minute. By that time Anna had put her bag on a luggage trolley and was sitting among a party of skiers with her back to the light. The camera was loaded and ready to go. She shot off half a dozen frames as he crossed the hall. Someone in the ski party followed her example and began to take pictures too.

Hugh Fellows checked in. As he turned away from the counter and towards her, she shot off four more frames and then turned the camera on to a little girl who was sitting nearby cuddling a giant panda. He passed close to her and then he was gone.

She retrieved her car from the car park and drove back to London and the one-hour developing service Brierly Security used. While she waited she jotted down a description of what Hugh Fellows had been wearing. For all she knew it might be more useful than the photographs.

Of the ten pictures there were four – two profiles, one three-quarter face and one full face – which looked as if they might be all right. Lara, though, was grumpy and ready to find fault with everything.

'You should have got closer,' she said. 'The only decent shot is the kid with the bear.' But she took the four Anna had chosen down to the hotel office. Anna stayed in the bedroom to phone Florida-Technics and confirm yesterday's arrangements.

As English hotel rooms went, it was big and well equipped. Anna did not really mean to spy on her employer. She was not looking for anything in particular. If challenged, she might have said it was simply habit. More probably she was looking for a way to assert control over circumstances which appeared to be decidedly random. But she would never have said so. What she did wonder was if Hugh Fellows was so crucial to her client's problems why had he not been mentioned before yesterday? And, if she hadn't more or less stumbled over him by accident, would he ever have been mentioned? The brief, the way Lara presented it, was about a bankrupt company. It was not, until now, about a runaway daughter.

Now there were two investigations – one on either side of the Atlantic. Would either one be dropped, she wondered as she quickly scanned the contents of Lara's bathroom cabinet. Not that there was anything to be discovered there except large quantities of antacid and some stuff called Ban-Doze. People tend not to take the revealing personal minutae of their lives away with them to foreign hotel rooms. Lara certainly didn't unless it was in her handbag. But her handbag was on her arm when she came back.

'Well, that's done,' she said briskly. 'Now maybe we'll get some answers. Look, I didn't say it yesterday because your phone call came as quite a surprise, but thanks anyway for recovering those sweaters. It's kind of symbolic, and it meant a lot to Penny.'

'There must be more,' Anna said.

'Not that many. Not now.' Lara sat in the armchair by the telephone. 'They are not mass produced.'

'I know,' Anna said. 'But what I didn't tell you yesterday, because things took such an unexpected turn, is that the woman who is David Stamp's secretary was selling the sweaters to friends.'

'Yeah? This woman, is she one of Hugh's friends?'

'You might say so,' Anna said cautiously.

'How old is she?'

'Late twenties, early thirties. Why?'

Lara sighed. 'I was thinking of Cyn, I guess. The man is an animal.' She stared past Anna at a landscape on the wall. She looked tired, and Anna wondered if she had spent the night at Oakleigh. 'What's she like?' Lara said at last.

'Sonia?' Anna was surprised. 'I don't know at all. So far, she seems to be a liar, a cheat, a brilliant stone-waller and a bad driver with a liking for Paul Newman. Her partner looks after the business and her husband takes care of the baby.'

'She has a baby?'

'Yes.'

Lara sighed again.

Anna said, 'Look, where exactly do you want this enquiry to go?'

'Where?'

'Yes,' Anna said, hiding impatience. 'It seems to me, we could get more *facts* if I chased this liquidator down. Do you still want me to do that?'

'Sure,' Lara said without much interest. 'See, Anna, I was hoping you'd tell me the husband . . . Oh I don't know. What I want is for Penny to make a clean break with the past and get on with her life. The husband is a worthless . . . well, you know what. And Cyn . . . You see, Garden Party *was* Penny. Everything rested on her getting out those designs – Spring, Summer, Autumn. New ideas regular as clockwork. Those two, the husband and Cyn, were never any more than a drain on her energy. But she just couldn't see it.'

'They were her family,' Anna protested.

'Some family! You know, Anna, I can't understand why creative people bother with families. If I had any talent at all, I sure as hell wouldn't waste my energy on men and babies.'

'You can't work in a vacuum,' Anna said, slightly appalled. 'I mean talented people need love and, well, family life too.'

'In my experience,' Lara said tartly, 'love and family life do not go together at all. Business and family life don't work together either. And when you have a husband like Chris Garden or a daughter like Cyn the result is destructive both of talent and business.'

'Surely it was losing them which was destructive.'

'That's what Penny says.' Lara looked disgusted. 'Well, I guess, one way or another, we've got to find them for her. When we do I hope she'll reject them for herself. Maybe that was the destructive thing: they rejected her.'

'Why?' Anna asked. 'I mean, why do *you* have to find them for her?' It came out blunt, nearly rude.

Lara raised her eyebrows. 'I told you,' she said, almost haughtily. 'Penny is a friend.'

Anna said nothing. She had asked her question, now she prepared to leave. She stood up.

'Wait,' Lara said. She fiddled with her handbag and stared at Anna. 'I guess you must be asking yourself why I'm taking all this trouble. I have other friends, other designers. Right?'

Anna watched the unquiet hands.

'What I haven't told you,' Lara went on, 'is that Penny designs an exclusive line for me, personally. It comes out under my own label and is only sold in my stores. This is a trade secret I'm telling you. You must never, *never* pass it on.'

'Your own label?' Anna asked.

'That's right,' Lara said. 'I haven't a creative bone in my body. It's one of the great sorrows of my life. When I met Penny I saw she could do the sort of things I'd want to do if I only had the talent. Now, she does it for me. Or did. So you see, my reputation and her problems are sort of handcuffed together. Do you understand?'

Anna nodded.

'And you have got to promise never to reveal what I've told you,' Lara continued. 'This must not become gossip. Ever.'

Anna promised.

Chapter 36

'IT MAY BE a mistake to play this one too close to the chest,' Bernie said. He was rocking gently in his office chair. Anna, perched on the corner of his desk, drew a face on her thumbnail with one of his fibre-tipped pens.

'I know you like having one over on the Lord of the Flies,' he went on, 'but fair's fair. If you want to use the facilities you'll have to come a bit clean.'

The face, on the clean pink dome of her thumb, looked rather like Martin Brierly's. She said, 'Oh well, it was nice while it lasted.'

In fact she had already typed a report which, while vague, described most of the relevant points. It was just that she had not yet given it to Beryl. She added a moustache and a pair of horns to the face, and said, 'It's getting more and more like giving in homework.'

'You can't get away from the paper,' Bernie said. 'You were on the force once – you ought to know that.'

'I do know that,' Anna agreed. 'Bernie, why did you go to the doctor's yesterday?'

'Regular check-up,' Bernie said, smiling. 'Sensible thing to do at my age.'

'At your age!' Anna snorted.

'The old order fadeth,' Bernie said, 'and this old order intends to fade in good health, thanks very much.'

'Don't talk soft.'

'Soft?' he asked. 'You think flat feet's the worst that can happen to an old copper?'

'Yes.' She licked a piece of tissue and wiped the face off her nail.

'You're acting very childish,' he said, eyes twinkling under plump lids. 'Here, give us that name. I'll have a go at your David Stamp if you'll be your age and tell the old fart what he wants to know.'

'Okay,' Anna said, brightening. She went back to her own cubicle and stapled the report into it's regulation buff folder. Childishly, she placed the staples where they would cause maximum difficulty for anyone turning the pages.

Beryl was not at her desk so Anna hid her report, two down, in a pile of similar folders. While she was at it she searched for and found Sean's report to Mr Kemal. As she had feared he had not followed up her enquiries to the South London garage and had simply recommended that William Herridge should be given no further responsibility. Beryl had rubber-stamped the bottom of it. The old fart had accepted Sean's work without question.

'Cobblers!' Anna said under her breath. She stole the file and concealed it behind Beryl's floppy disk box. Beryl's hairy pink cardigan hung like a doppelganger over the back of her chair and Anna, in a fit of malice stapled it to the seat.

'Now that really *is* childish,' she whispered and left the room suffocating with silent laughter.

Bernie was putting down the phone when she came into his cubicle.

'Well,' he said. 'Your David Stamp.'

'Yes?'

'Dead.'

'What?'

'It's what the geezer said,' Bernie told her. 'Kidney failure, about six months ago, at the . . .' He looked at his notes. '. . . at the Royal Free Hospital.'

'What geezer?' Anna asked, Beryl's cardigan instantly forgotten. 'That's not right. People are still doing business with him.'

'Are they?' Bernie looked up at her. 'I did the simplest thing and rang the porter's lodge at the flats where he lives. Said I had a personal delivery, when would I catch him? And the geezer said,

"You won't, mate. He's brown bread." He said the flat was empty. As far as he knew Mr Stamp's heirs had just left things as they were.'

'I'd better check with the Royal Free,' Anna said.

'You do that.' Bernie nodded. 'Someone's been having you on.'

Anna checked with the Royal Free and, although they called in 'renal failure', the message was the same. David Stamp had died six months ago. She rang Lara Crowther.

'But that's unbelievable,' Lara said. 'I mean I haven't spoken to the guy personally — that was one of the reasons I employed you — but I know the bank had a letter or something. The bank seemed perfectly satisfied.'

'Was this before six months ago?' Anna asked.

'I don't know,' Lara admitted. 'I'll check with them.'

'Wait,' Anna said. 'If you check and find the letter was written after he died, then it was written fraudulently, and the bank'll have no choice but to tell the police.'

'Sure.'

'Well, but who's the letter writer? Pound to a penny it's Sonia Casey — who is selling Garden Party clobber, and is nesting with Hugh Fellows who's selling the same stuff.'

'Shake the goddam tree,' Lara said.

'Yes, but do you want Hugh Fellows not coming back to England? Because if we shake the tree and Sonia falls out, chances are Hugh will too. And if Sonia warns Hugh, then chances are he'll stay in the States, and if he does, so will Cyn.'

'If they are still together,' Lara mused. 'Yeah. Well maybe I can talk to the bank without letting on the liquidator is dead.'

'Sounds like a good idea,' Anna said. 'If someone's been pulling strokes . . .'

'Pulling what?'

'Doing a naughty. I mean, if it turns out there's been a fraud or something criminal you'll have to tell the bank and other creditors because they may want the police in on it. At the very least a new liquidator should be approached as soon as possible. But if you don't want Hugh Fellows to go to ground . . ?'

'Yeah,' Lara interrupted. 'Sit on the information till we know where we are.'

'Right.'

'Right' said Lara, and broke the connection.

Chapter 37

ANNA BOUGHT A doughnut on the way home. The powdered sugar stuck to her lips and seemed to rasp against them in the cold wind. The new steel-reinforced front door turned a blank face to the street. It made the house ugly and impenetrable.

Selwyn had been sent home during the day, and Anna looked in long enough to tell him he was a prat. To her dismay he looked proud of himself. He felt he had made a grand gesture. Quex was downstairs with him, and he had been talking quietly and seriously which added to Selwyn's sense of self-importance.

Upstairs, the red light on the answerphone glowed in the dark. Anna switched on a lamp and played back the message. A clipped woman's voice said, 'This is Sonia Casey. Regarding our conversation yesterday, if you require further information meet me for a drink at the Deerbourne Arms, Englands Avenue. I'll wait for you until seven o'clock.'

Anna looked at her watch. She had forty minutes to get there. There was some cheese in the fridge, and she hastily assembled a sandwich. Quex would have to fend for himself. She began a note to him. 'Gone to Belsize Park – sudden call-out. See you . . .' but Quex came in while she was writing it.

'Bill Blake's blue beard, what a day!' he said. But when he saw what she was writing, he bit something back and said only, 'Ah well, the perfect ending to the perfect day. Take care, Leo. See you later.'

Anna said, 'Look, I'm sorry. The job I'm on has taken off a bit.'

'So I gather,' he said ruefully. 'But so has real life.' He reached out a large hand and ruffled her hair. 'Get along with you. We'll talk when you come home.'

Anna went.

The Deerbourne Arms was a modern conversion which had been disguised as old elegance with dark wood and crimson plush. Fake gas lights illuminated cosy booths, and Anna found Sonia chatting to a salesman type in one of them. The man had obviously bought her a drink and was trying to capitalize on his generosity. Sonia dismissed him with an airy wave and a 'business before pleasure' remark. She crossed her fine legs and immediately looked businesslike.

'I'm so glad you could come,' she said formally. 'I was tired when you approached me yesterday – not too friendly. I do apologise. Of course, when I stopped to think about it I realised I should have cleared up any misunderstanding straightaway.'

She had dressed, Anna decided, especially for this occasion: a charcoal-grey wool suit with a ruffled white shirt underneath. The look was what women's magazines would describe as suitable for that special business meeting while preserving femininity – competence with a dash of allure.

Anna, who now had reasons of her own to tread softly, said, 'Yes, we got off to a bad start. It was just that with so many unanswered letters and telephone calls my principals were beginning to worry about Mr Stamp's ability.'

'I am only a part-time employee of Mr Stamp,' Sonia said, her clear slate-grey eyes seeking Anna's. 'And as such I have little or nothing to do with liquidations. I can tell you, though, that he is extremely unwell.'

'So I gather.' If Sonia could come out with such nonsense without batting an eyelid so could Anna.

'Nor am I directly involved with the company selling the knitwear you were interested in yesterday. However, as I told you I would, I got in touch with the friend who is Managing Director of the company which legally purchased the goods in question.'

'Thank you for being so quick about it,' Anna murmured.

'My pleasure.' Sonia sipped her drink and coolly replaced her glass in the exact centre of a beer mat. 'Anyway, he is in New

Zealand at the moment, but he has authorised me to show you the purchase documents. I took the liberty of preparing copies of all the relevant papers as I'm sure you will want to give them to your principals.'

'Very thoughtful,' Anna said appreciatively.

Sonia leaned forward and picked up a black leather document-case which she placed on the seat beside her.

She opened it and drew out a sheaf of papers.

'I can't let you keep the originals,' she said. 'But you might like to look at them anyway.'

Anna looked and saw that, as far as she could tell, they were genuine bills of sale, stamped at a date when David Stamp had been alive. They did not appear to have been tampered with. The purchasing company was named neutrally as C and H Fashions.

She said, 'Yes. It looks as if C and H got a good deal.'

'I don't know how the price was arrived at,' Sonia said calmly. 'As I say, I am no more than a friend of the director. But I do know that things move fast in fashion. A garment which might be very expensive to begin with is often worth nothing by next year.'

'That's not my bailiwick either,' Anna said. 'I only want to know that the goods you were selling yesterday had been properly acquired.'

'I hope these invoices are satisfactory proof.' Sonia's expression was calm and just a little smug.

Anna said, 'Oh, I'm sure they will be. And thank you again for getting back to me so quickly.' She handed back the originals. 'And would you tell, er, what is his name? Your friend?'

'Mr Fellows.'

'Yes, would you tell Mr Fellows we appreciate his co-operation?'

'Of course.' Sonia zipped up her document case and got to her feet. She held out her hand and Anna solemnly shook it. She genuinely admired Sonia's clear, frank gaze.

Several heads turned as Sonia left the Deerbourne Arms – she looked so fresh, feminine and, above all, in command.

'New Zealand!' Anna said under her breath. Was Sonia lying

to Anna? Or had Hugh lied to Sonia? Anna's money was on Sonia, each way, and all the way. She finished her tonic water. If lying were an Olympic event, Sonia would be a gold medallist.

Chapter 38

BEFORE SHE WENT to bed that night Anna searched for and found her old black tracksuit, a thick navy sweater and black basketball boots. To be on the safe side she also changed the batteries in her torch. She would have preferred to keep these preparations secret but the flat was too small and Quex was at her shoulder all the time.

Earlier she had brought back a couple of American Hot pizzas. American Hot was Quex's favourite and he devoured all of his own and half of Anna's in record time. She had also brought a Four Seasons for Selwyn but Quex explained that Selwyn had gone to bed early with a tranquillizer. He ate a large chunk of the Four Seasons too and put the rest away in the fridge for breakfast. Quex's breakfast was something Anna did not like to witness.

There were things he didn't like to witness either.

'What are you doing?' he asked as she slid a canvas rolled collection of tools into the inside pocket of her jacket. 'Where are you going?'

'Don't ask,' Anna said lightly. 'Think of it as a night shift. I'll try not to wake you.'

'I don't care if you bloody wake me!' he protested. 'I just want to know where you're going and what you're up to.'

'It's this job.'

'I know it's this bloody job! What's so special about this one? You don't usually go out in the dead of night dressed like a bloody mugger.'

'It's been known.'

'Not by me it hasn't.' Quex sat on the edge of the bed staring at her. 'Who's going with you?' he asked. And when she didn't reply, 'Does your Mr Brierly know about this?'

'Don't be a pain,' Anna said. 'I don't interfere with what you do.'

'Maybe you don't care what I do.'

'Quex,' Anna said suddenly, 'this isn't working.'

'What isn't?'

'You. Here.'

'Yes it is,' he said. 'At least it could if you didn't take every opportunity to avoid issues. You aren't giving me a chance.'

The phone rang. Anna went to answer it leaving Quex in the bedroom.

Lara said, 'Hi. The guy from Florida-Technics just called. Hugh Fellows drove south to Sarasota. He checked into a motel. The guy says he'll keep an eye on him till he's stationary. I asked him if Hugh was met at the airport but the guy says he wasn't. He says he didn't see a woman, or anyone with him at all.' She sounded excited.

Anna said, 'Right. Well, if Cynthia's around she'll probably show up soon enough. Meanwhile, I've got copies of the bills and receipts proving that David Stamp, on behalf of Garden Party, sold goods to a company called C and H Fashions. They seem kosher but I think you ought to look them over.'

'C and H Fashions?' Lara asked. 'Never heard of them.'

'One of the directors is Hugh Fellows. H for Hugh, maybe?'

'And maybe C for Chris.' Lara sighed. 'I see what you're getting at. Okay, bring them over.'

'When?'

'Now.'

Anna glanced at the bedroom door.

Chapter 39

Lara was drinking milk and making faces. Sunk deep in a wing chair in the hotel lounge she looked like a dowager. All she needed was a cashmere shawl and a *petit point* footstool.

'They got the stock cheap,' she said, glancing at Anna over the top of her reading glasses. 'But not cheap enough to be outrageous.'

'I was wondering,' Anna said tentatively, 'if David Stamp's paperwork and these receipts actually matched.'

Lara looked up again. 'You mean he might have falsified his own records?'

'Well,' Anna began slowly. 'He can pay himself for his own time – time spent on Garden Party business. If he can show that the stock only sold for, say, a thousand pounds, but his time and effort were worth a thousand, he wouldn't have to pay the creditors anything, would he? If anyone asks, all he has to do is prove that income and expenses are just about equal. But what he shows in his records and what he actually receives in hard cash might be quite different.'

'But the guy's dead,' Lara pointed out.

'Yes, but this little deal was completed before he died.'

'So how are you going to find out?'

'Perhaps there's nothing to find,' Anna said. 'But it's worth a look.'

'His office?'

'Yes.'

'Tonight?' Lara removed her glasses and rubbed her eyes. 'Is it worth it?' she asked.

'It might be. Garden Party couldn't have been the only liquidation he was handling. I want to know why no one was informed about his death. I want to know if someone is taking care of business under his name.'

'Why? I'm only interested in Garden Party.'

'And C and H Fashions,' Anna reminded her. 'Suppose Garden Party is only the tip of the iceberg. Suppose Hugh, Chris and Sonia Casey are cleaning up on all his old liquidations. I was going to suggest anyway that we do a company search on C and H.'

'I'll go for that,' Lara said. 'But I don't want you pushing the liquidation side.'

They looked at each other for a few moments before Lara went on. 'Of course it would be interesting to know if Hugh, Chris and Sonia were – what did you call it? – pulling a stroke. But if you are thinking of breaking into the liquidator's office I'm bailing out. How risky is it?'

'I don't know yet,' Anna admitted.

'Don't do it,' Lara said decisively. 'I'm not paying you to do anything illegal. No way. Got that?'

'Yes.'

Lara grinned at Anna over her glass of milk. 'Well, good luck then,' she said.

It was good to be out alone at night. There were only a few cars moving through the wet streets, windscreen wipers working hard, tyres sloshing through puddles in clogged gutters.

Anna parked the car among other parked cars and waited. She could just see the doorway set back between the delicatessen and tobacconist. Neither of the two shop fronts was lit and the nearest street lamp was yards away. She had already looked for a back entrance, but there wasn't one.

She opened the car window an inch to prevent the glass fogging and settled down to watch the street. Rain fell and showed no sign of letting up. Only six cars passed in fifteen minutes. Nothing stirred on the pavement.

It was getting colder. Anna left her Peugeot and ran through the rain to the doorway. It was an old door. Good. It had warped away from the door frame. Good. There were two locks. Bad. One was a spring lock. Good. The other a deadlock. Bad. No burglar alarm.

The deadlock took five minutes; the spring lock, five seconds. Anna slipped inside. Her pulse was racing and her hands were slippery with sweat. It suddenly occurred to her that she was enjoying herself.

She switched her torch on, covering the glass with her hand, and went softly upstairs. There was a sick, fluttering pleasure to be had from doing what should not be done. Secretly. It was the zenith of personal freedom. Why stop at breaking in? Break one rule – you might as well break them all.

Crouching on the floor in front of David Stamp's office door with her tools on the carpet beside her, Anna experienced a swirling sense of vertigo. It was as if she were about to cut all the cords that tied her to decency.

She stopped.

'Don't be so bleeding wet,' she muttered to herself. She was only opening a door. She had been through forbidden doors before. She pushed the sensation aside and concentrated on the lock. The trick was to leave everything unbroken and unmarked. It's easy to break into a place when damage doesn't count. But Anna wanted to leave no noticeable trace.

When the door opened she found herself in a cramped lobby with two plastic chairs and a tiny coffee table between them. It smelled of dust and disuse. Beyond that was David Stamp's office. Anna went in.

She switched the torch off and went straight to the window. There were Venetian blinds which looked as if they hadn't been touched in a year. They were closed, fortunately, and Anna had to part the slats to look down on the road. A car passed without stopping. No one was walking in the heavy rain. There were no lighted windows in the row of shops and flats opposite.

Anna stood for a minute to collect her thoughts and adjust her ears to the sounds of the building. It was a perfect place: a dead man's office, small but well-equipped, right next door to Sonia's own. There was even a day bed left over perhaps from the days when David Stamp had needed a rest in the afternoons.

The desk was tidy and had been dusted recently. Everything was in good working order. Someone was paying the rent, phone and electricity bills. Anna looked for a chequebook but couldn't find one. She started carefully on the files, but although they were kept neatly in alphabetical order she found nothing which referred to Garden Party.

Back at the desk in an old box file she found an index. Garden Party was mentioned in that, with dates and a file number. But nothing else. At random, she picked a name from the index, Avalon, and there on the shelves she found Avalon's file. Avalon had traded in patio furniture and had gone bust five years ago. The next one she looked for, Fantasy Packaging, was missing. She began, systematically, to check the names on the index against the files on the shelves. In all, four, including Garden Party, were missing from a list of sixteen names. She jotted the names in her notebook.

She looked at her watch: ten to five. Unreasonably, she felt she had been there too long. Instead of searching further into the desk and files she began to check that everything she had touched was back in place. She had just reached up to align a box with its neighbour's when a sound made her hand fly to the torch. She switched it off.

It was an electronic beep, like a wristwatch alarm. Anna stood stock-still in the dark. It sounded four times. A machine in the office had been activated. Sweat trickled down over her ribs. The beeps were followed by a soft mechanical whirr which lasted for about sixty seconds. Then there were four more beeps. And silence.

Anna held her breath, but nothing more followed. When she had begun to feel silly standing like a statue in the pitch-black she switched the torch on again. Nothing in the office appeared to have changed.

Anxiously she searched the corners where the ceiling met the walls but there was nothing. If there had been any surveillance equipment, surely she would have found it on her first sweep of the room.

What she had overlooked was the fax machine. She found it on a knee-high plastic stand tucked between the desk and the wall, a neat cream-coloured device with a tongue of paper sticking out at her.

The message read: 'SONNY IS HOT STUFF. Hi darling. Good times, what? I was thinking about it on the flight and I agree it would be sensible to cool out until you are quite sure the heat is off. Let me know if you pulled it off with the lady in question. It seems a pity to junk good gear, but better safe than sorry. You are so wise, my sweet. I rely on you for everything. Make sure all is well in Milan and I will be back before you have had time to miss me.'

It was carelessly typed with several mistakes in spacing. Anna copied all of it into her note book. Then she left, laboriously locking each door behind her.

She had got away with it. She skipped to the Peugeot, with nothing on her conscience, almost laughing out loud. The little car whizzed along the empty streets making the journey seem like nothing at all. It was surprising therefore to find that, as soon as she reached home, fatigue and depression fell on her like rain, and she could scarcely drag herself upstairs to bed.

Chapter 40

QUEX SHOOK HER awake at eight-thirty.

'Phone,' he said. 'Your esteemed client.'

'What?' She was giddy from a dream of flying.

'Phone,' he said again. 'Come on!' He was rumpled and blue-chinned.

Anna stumbled to the phone to hear Lara's voice saying, 'Dammit, they lost him. Can you believe that? This is a firm my lawyer recommends, they're supposed to be hot potatoes and they lost him. What in hell were they playing at? It's only a two-bit town. How can you lose someone in Sarasota?'

She pronounced it 'Sour Soda'. Anna rubbed her eyes and tried to concentrate.

'What happened?' she asked.

'The guy saw him check into a motel. He waited a while and then the dumb bastard went for something to eat. When he got back Hugh's car was gone from the parking lot.'

Quex appeared at the bedroom door. He had a towel around his waist and did not look in a good humour.

'Now what do we do?' Lara said.

Quex padded across the living room into the kitchen and Anna heard him filling the kettle.

'Did Hugh know he was being followed?' she asked.

'The guy swears he didn't,' Lara said. 'But if that's so, how come he took off?'

'Let's hope it was just a lumpy mattress,' Anna said. 'Maybe he just didn't like his room.' Her jacket was where she had left it a couple of hours earlier, slung carelessly over the back of the sofa. Her notebook was poking out of the pocket.

'Hold on,' she said, and went to get the notebook. Quex padded back to the bathroom. He avoided looking at her.

At the phone she said, 'Just before midnight, USA time, Hugh sent a fax message to Sonia Casey. Can your guy trace a fax number?'

'He'd better,' Lara said grimly, and when Anna had given it she added, 'Thank God for that,' and hung up.

'Don't mention it,' Anna said as she put the phone down. She was getting used to Lara's abrupt telephone manner.

The kettle was boiling so she made the tea and left it to brew. She plugged the phone in next to the bed, got in, and waited for Lara to ring back. She could hear Quex splashing in the bath. He was not singing. She fell asleep with the phone cradled in her arms.

Quex woke her with a cup of tea. Shaved and dressed, he looked in a better humour. He sat on the end of the bed and grinned at her.

'Drink up, chicken,' he said. 'You're going to be late for work. No excuses. Three hours sleep is more than enough for a growing girl.'

'Eat maggots,' Anna said. The tea was strong and bitter from having brewed too long.

'That's my girl,' Quex said. 'A trooper. Is she grateful for tea in bed when she could've woken up in choky? Not on your life. "Eat maggots"! Actually, I'm having breakfast with friend Selwyn and if that doesn't blunt my appetite for life, I'll be out for the rest of the day, so don't cook and don't wait up.' He left and Anna went to sleep again.

When Lara rang back it was eleven-thirty. She said, 'Comcheck will be ringing you in a couple of hours.'

'Who?' Anna tried to keep the muzziness out of her voice.

'Comcheck,' Lara said. 'I use them all the time. Company search. C and H Fashions. Anything you want to know: registered offices, shareholders, holding company, turnover. They'll tell you, okay?'

'Okay.' Anna squeezed her eyes shut and tried to feel alert.

'Anything urgent you want to tell me?' Lara asked. 'Because I am at Heathrow so I'll be out of touch for today.'

'You're going home?'

'Sure,' Lara said. 'I told you, didn't I?'

Anna couldn't remember.

Lara said, 'Ethan Callow at Florida-Technics has your number too. And the letter the bank received from David Stamp was written only four months ago. I think that's all. My flight has been called. Gotta go.' And she went.

Anna brushed her teeth as the bath was filling. She had the sensation that she was moving very slowly while outside events were racing. But a long hot bath made her feel better.

Her flat, which always struck her as much too small when Quex was there, assumed its proper size, and the house was silent. She played a Sting cassette while boiling two eggs.

When your brain has fused, Anna decided, the best thing to do is to make a list: things to do, questions to ask. She opened her notebook and made a heading: Hugh Fellows, C and H Fashions, and then stopped. Suppose C and H Fashions was not a proper company? If it wasn't, it would not turn up in a company search. Never mind. She wrote, address? And then remembered the lad at the travel agent. He had already given her an address and telephone number. She leafed back and found it. Parson's Green.

She wrote, 'Liquidity?' and stopped again. What did she really want to know? Shareholders. That was it. Were Sonia Casey and Chris Garden either directors or shareholders? No. Forget Sonia. Anna knew where to find Sonia and her interest was getting too personal. It was becoming like a game Anna wanted to win. The one she was supposed to be looking for was Chris Garden.

'Stick to the point,' she muttered, and the phone rang.

A man said, 'Anna Lee? Mrs Crowther has authorized me to pass on to you a company status report on, ah, C and H Fashions. Ready? Yes? C and H Fashions is a private company, incorporated on 21 March 1985. Registered office at 85A Lumbley Road, Parson's Green, London. Company secretary, H. Fellows. Latest annual return, last year. Nominal capital, one thousand pounds divided into one thousand ordinary shares of one pound each. Issued for cash, five ordinary. Holding company, none.'

'Hold on!' Anna said, her fingers cramped around the pencil.

'Going too fast, am I?' the man said, sounding happy. He went on as if talking to a severely retarded child. 'Names of directors, H. Fellows and C. Garden.'

'Bingo!' Anna yelped.

'Pardon?'

'Nothing. Go on.'

'Names of principal shareholders, H. Fellows – two, C. Garden – two, S. Casey – one. Particulars of charges or debentures registered, none. Amount outstanding . . .'

'Hold on,' Anna interrupted again. 'Have you got C. Garden's address?'

'Pardon?'

'Director and principal shareholder,' Anna said. 'C. Garden. His address.'

'Oh,' the man said. 'Mrs Crowther just asked for a company status report.'

'She told me you'd give me whatever information I required.'

'Well, all right,' he said grudgingly. 'I'll ring you back.'

There were people, Anna thought contentedly, who had jobs even more boring than her own – people who worked for companies whose sole object was the retrieval of information about other companies. It made giving advice about security look like a playground. She opened a carton of mango and papaya yoghurt.

The man from Comcheck rang back with the information that C. Garden's address was the same as the company's registered office, or at least it had been at the date of incorporation and there had been no change of address filed since then. This was interesting because in 1985 Chris Garden was actually living in Oakleigh and still married to Penny. It was disappointing because Anna did not believe that Chris would be sharing a place to live with Hugh. Maybe it was only an address of convenience for both of them.

She asked him if there was a trading address different from the registered office. He said he had no such information. She asked if either C. Garden or H. Fellows were associated with foreign companies particularly in Sarasota, Florida and Milan, Italy. He said he would crosscheck but it would take time. He would have to clear such an expensive search with Mrs Crowther.

When he asked, rather plaintively, if Anna wanted the rest of the status report that he had already prepared, she asked for a print out. She didn't say so, but the gobbledegook about charges and debentures meant nothing to her and she wanted it in a form she could give to someone else for analysis. Talking to the man from Comcheck was like talking to Dial-a-Recipe: there wasn't a lot of give and take.

She grabbed her coat and escaped before anyone else could ring up with a mass of information she didn't understand.

Chapter 41

L UMBLEY ROAD HAD been taken over by developers. It was held up by scaffolding and patched together with For Sale signs. Number 85 looked as if it had been recently renovated, but the one next door had its windows boarded over. The boards were used for local advertisements and graffiti. In neat girlish handwriting someone had penned, 'My name is Jill. I'm on the Pill. If you buy me a drink I will . . .' Underneath was, 'My name is Bill. I had my fill of dirty Jill. And now I'm ill.' There were posters for rock concerts, action groups and public meetings. In spray paint someone else asked, 'Jill who? Bill who?' And a helpful soul replied with the telephone number of the AID's unit at St Stephen's Hospital.

Number 85 had three doorbells. Anna rang all of them but no one replied. She walked down to the paper shop at the end of the street but the woman behind the counter said she did not deliver papers to number 85 and besides she had a poor memory for names and faces. She also had thick glasses and a hearing aid. She said that all her regular customers had moved away in the past two years. Anna did not ask how she could tell.

The obvious answer was in the telephone book, and Anna wondered why she hadn't thought of it before leaving home. At the nearest telephone box she looked up first Chris Garden and then, in the yellow pages, C and H Fashions. There were several C. Gardens, but only one C and H Fashions. It was in Wandsworth, just across the river. Worth a look, Anna thought. She jumped into the car and headed south.

The developers hadn't reached Bedwick Street yet. A second-hand car dealer took up a third of an acre. Hondas and Toyotas were crammed side by side so there was hardly enough room to open the doors. Yellow plastic bunting fluttered in the hard cold air, and tangled in the wire netting. Next door a cracked building, upper storeys condemned, housed a take-away kebab shop. It was garbage collection day, and all down the street black plastic bags formed heaps around the lamp posts.

On the other side of the second-hand car dealer was a small warehouse. At eye level on the wide garage door C and H FASHIONS had been painted in black and red letters. But above that, only partially scraped away, were the words, Fantasy Packaging.

Anna got out of the car and walked across the narrow forecourt. The goods entrance was closed, but round the side was a door into an office. Beyond, a passage led into the warehouse. Someone was singing, 'Girls just wanna have fu-hun,' along with the radio. The voice, through the thin wall, was reedy and off-key.

Anna peeped round the door and saw an electric-blue overall and a mass of henna-coloured curls stagger towards a pile of boxes. The woman dumped an armful of boxes on top of the pile and turned back for more. The pile collapsed.

'Mega shite on a kite,' the woman said. 'Double mega shite on two kites!'

Anna said, ''Scuse me, I'm looking for Charlotte.'

'Cock off!' the woman said. 'Unless you want to muck in with these effing boxes. I've had it up to here effing about on me own.'

'What're you up to?' Anna asked, coming out from behind the door and looking helpful.

'Modelling Janet Reger underwear,' the woman said. 'What's it look like I'm doing?'

'Modelling Janet Reger underwear,' Anna said, and picked up a box.

'Got yourself a friend for life,' the woman said, and gathered up two boxes. 'This lot's for pick-up teatime.'

The boxes were cardboard cartons, not very heavy, with the legend Cara Cosmetics USA stencilled on them. Each one was addressed to The Style File, Sarasota, Florida. Anna learned the address, including the postcode, off by heart, because there were about seventy packages and they all had to be replaced on a makeshift loading bay near the goods entrance.

'Freight agents are a load of effing dog-dos,' the woman said.

'Every bleeding thing's got to be just crapping so, don't it. And if you aren't ready when they frigging are, it's up yours on a cocking tricycle.' She straightened and flicked one of the corkscrew curls out of her eyes. 'The name's Coral, by the by. You know what? — I haven't talked to a single soul since breakfast, and that was me old man who has about as much conversation of a morning as one of me mixer taps. And you know what? — a year ago come Christmas I was working down Droans — y'know, industrial gloves — and I thought sod this for a lark, I don't want to be a machinist all my life. But I'm telling you for free, this job's the dickingest pile of old moody I ever saw in all me born days.'

'What's wrong with it?' Anna was examining one of the cartons which had split open. It was full of shiny boxes, pink, white and black, containing 'Cara Rejuvenation Gel'.

'What's right with it?' Coral said. She handed Anna one of the brightly coloured boxes. 'Here. You have it. It's crap but it smells nice. Your face'll still look like my aunt Edna's prune tart. Mine does, any road. Or maybe I'm ageing faster than it can rejuvenate.' She scowled as if her face was a personal enemy. Anna couldn't see anything wrong with it.

'This job,' Coral said. 'Well, the wiring machine's on the blow for starters. These cartons are supposed to be wired up in fours. But that dick-head spotty Sam went off sick as soon as he heard Mr farting Fellows wasn't coming in today. So I'm here all on my tod just when there's a consignment going out. All the donkey work and all the pissing paperwork too. Happens all the time. Charlotte who, anyway?'

'What?'

'You said you was after someone called Charlotte.'

'Oh, Charlotte,' Anna said. 'Charlotte Brown. I thought she worked here. Fantasy Packaging, she said.'

'Before the flood, kiddo. Fantasy Packaging went dipsydoodle. This lot took over and used the stock to box up their own goods. Bye-bye Fantasy, bye-bye Charlotte Brown. Couple more days like today and it's bye-bye Coral too. If it's not one thing it's another. Stuff comes in — it gets put in bleeding boxes — out it goes. King Groper's here, then he's not. That other didlow's always on the *Conteenong*, and spotty Sam's about as much use as a chocolate door-knocker. Besides I need someone to talk to.'

'Still,' Anna said, 'it could be worse.' She opened the jar of Rejuvenation Gel and sniffed. 'It could be jellied eels.'

'Doesn't matter what's in the effing boxes.' Coral perched on the loading platform. 'You don't go to work for the screwing product, do you? It's the money and the company, innit? What's your game, anyway?'

'Me?' Anna rubbed some of the jade-green gel into the back of her hand. 'Dispatcher. Mini cabs. I'm on nights this week.'

'There you are then. I wouldn't mind some of that. There's always someone to talk to on the radio, right?'

Anna said, 'This stuff makes your skin tingle.'

'Yeah.' Coral grinned. 'It's a shame to waste it on your face, I always say.'

'You've got a mind like a sewer,' Anna said appreciatively.

'That's what my old man says.' Coral looked surprised. 'As a matter of fact, the product ain't half bad. I've had a go at all the make-up and some of the diet pills. And a few spare frocks and the odd woolly. Some of the gear's worth nicking – you can't say fairer than that, can you? I never had it away with no industrial gloves.'

'Where does all this come from?' Anna asked.

'Italy,' Coral said. 'If you ask me it's cheapo, cheapo gunkola the Italians wouldn't touch with a barge pole. It comes in tatty old crates and we put it in our own pretty boxes, and Bob's your uncle – exclusive cocking Cara Cosmetics specially manufactured for the Yanks. It's amazing what some people fall for. Loads of crap comes through here, discontinued lines, seconds, frigging fake fashion from Korea. Stick it in a pretty box and say it's Frog or Italians and some poor bleeder laps it up.'

'That's packaging for you,' Anna said.

'That's poxy packaging,' Coral agreed. 'Got the right idea has our King Groper – buy crap, sell style. They make a bob or two in the middle. Pity more of it doesn't rub off on me.'

'Just King Groper and his partner?' Anna asked. She wanted to talk about the partner because she was wondering if she had made a mistake. Suppose C. Garden was not Chris. Suppose C. Garden was Cynthia?

'A right pair of fanny addicts,' Coral said, cheerfully. 'King Groper and King Leer. One of 'em looks but don't touch, the other's got faster hands than a gyno . . . gynoc . . . a twat doctor, if you know what I mean.' She sighed. 'Men over forty,' she went on, 'they don't got the juice themselves no more so they're always sniffing it out in us girls. Disgusting, I call it, but you can't half eat well while you're fending them off. I just love middle-aged, middle-class men, don't you? They're such sodding suckers.'

'Family men,' Anna said, encouraging her.

Coral nodded emphatically, ringlets bobbing. 'They're the best,' she said. 'A bit of guilt goes a long way in this game. Not that the Kinky Kings admit to being family men, oh no, but old Christopher Robin, you could see him coming a mile off.'

'Christopher Robin?'

'Yeah. Mr Garden, "Call me Chris", King Leer. He's always good for a steak and chips. Just a bit of fun, mind, so don't tell the old man indoors. But the time comes when they just don't want to be husbands and fathers and *taxpayers* no more. That's the time to catch 'em, take it from me. They haven't had a good time in so frigging long they hardly know how anymore. But they don't mind shelling out a few quid on further education.'

Anna laughed and Coral laughed with her, a deep-down dirty chuckle. 'He's a bit of a wanker, is King Leer, but he's in Italy most of the time so what's the diff? Vino and signorinas. Keeps him happy. The other one's more of a problem. I don't like him one bit. Got gangrene of the heart. I wouldn't drop dead of surprise if it turned out he got his jollies hurting people.'

Chapter 42

A NNA DROVE AROUND the corner and then stopped. She got out her notebook and jotted down some notes. Leafing back, she found 'F.J.P. Garages' and an address scribbled in pencil. She stared at it for a moment and then started the car.

F.J.P. Garages was a sign painter's nightmare. Everything was advertised – windscreen replacement, wheel alignment, MOT, batteries, petrol – in a jumble of conflicting graphic styles. Anna asked at reception for the accounts department and was directed to a backroom behind a pebble glass door. She knocked and went in. A young man was curved like a coat-hanger over a VDU. He rattled at the keyboard for a few seconds before looking up.

'Yes?' he said, gazing at her through watery blue eyes.

'Anna Lee,' Anna said. 'I rang you a while ago about a credit check I'm doing on a William Herridge. You said you might have some information, but you never got back to me.'

'Did I?' he said. 'I mean, didn't I?'

'It was about a set of radial tyres, apparently not paid for. Your firm put the word out to the credit agency.'

'Well,' he said, glancing wistfully at the screen, 'maybe it wasn't me. I mean six people have had this job in the past four years.'

'But it's just a matter of information retrieval,' Anna said. 'I simply want to know what happened.'

'Why?'

'Because it's curious. As I said I've been doing a check on William Herridge. He's up for promotion, and his boss wants to know if he's reliable. Well, he's very reliable. He pays his mortgage, his rates, his tax, his credit card. All bang on time. There's just this one bad debt. It's out of character. It means that half the hire purchase houses in the country won't touch him and it means he won't get promotion.'

'Why don't you talk to the credit company?' Another wistful glance at his screen.

'I have,' Anna said patiently. 'But it's all cut and dried with them. They say F.J.P. Garages reported a risk, and they are acting on it.'

'The thing is,' the man said, scratching at prematurely thinning hair, 'it might take a little time. When you rang last time I probably had the debts programme up.'

'I can wait.'

'Well, the thing is it's after five-thirty now, and my wife's got her cousin and his fiancée coming to dinner. She wants me back early.' He wasn't going to do it.

Anna said, 'You see, it's pretty hard on William Herridge, isn't it?'

'I suppose so,' he said and turned off his VDU.

'I mean, one mistake like that . . .'

'It isn't necessarily a mistake,' he said defensively.

Anna waited.

'Tell you what,' the man said with a sigh, 'I'll call it up first thing tomorrow and ring you back.'

'Great. Thanks,' Anna said. 'Make a note of it, will you? I know how busy you must be.'

'Oh, all right.' His long fingers scrabbled for a pen. He looked out of practice. 'Herridge. Is that with or without a D?'

Chapter 43

J UST AROUND THE corner from the garage and not far from
C and H was an estate agent. Anna parked the car. A few
hours in the neighbourhood had told her that it was seedy
enough to be cheap. And suddenly, upwardly mobile was a
direction she did not want to take. It was a treadmill. She wanted
one of those dirty little pockets of London where you could put
your car up on jacks without the next door neighbours raising
their well-groomed eyebrows. She wanted a pub not a winebar,
a betting shop, and a café where you could get sausage, bacon,
egg and beans with two slices, not tofu and bean sprout flan. She
wanted a local shop where a woman could go for her breakfast
pint of milk in slippers and curlers.

The estate agent said he would put her name on the computer
mailing list. He had hopes for the area. He thought it might be
looking up. Anna sighed and went home.

Quex did not come home until after eleven when Anna was
almost ready for bed. She heard him arguing outside the door
with Selwyn. Selwyn obviously wanted to come in for a nightcap
but Quex wouldn't let him. With relief she heard him say, 'Go to
bed, old son. I'll see you in the morning,' before he opened the
door.

His nose was cold when he kissed her. 'Good day?' he asked
neutrally. 'Get any more sleep?'

While she cleaned her teeth she heard him undressing, and
when she came into the bedroom she saw that for a change he
had hung his clothes up and his shoes were neatly stowed under
the bed. He had replaced the cap on the toothpaste too. Anna
heard alarm bells going off in her head. But nothing happened to
break the spell. Quex was calm and considerate that night: he
did not interrogate her about her intentions or about what she

had been doing during the day. He did not steal her share of the bedding. She relaxed and went to sleep.

At two o'clock in the morning the phone rang.

Anna rolled over and juggled the receiver to her ear. Lara said, 'I want you over here. I've booked your ticket. You can pick it up at the desk. You're on the same flight Hughie took, mid-day from Gatwick.'

'When?' Anna opened her eyes and saw the luminous face of the clock staring at her. 'Where?'

'Sour soda,' Lara said. 'Did I wake you? You said you had a passport, didn't you? Well, go to the bank first thing and get some traveller's cheques. You won't need 'em because I'll be meeting you, but it's best to have some for immigration.'

Quex turned on his bedside lamp and sat bolt upright.

Anna said, 'Hang on a sec. I'm not quite with you.' She sat up too and gazed blankly at the wardrobe.

Lara said, 'What's the matter? If it's your boss you're worried about I'll ring him tomorrow. If it's money, it's all arranged. The ticket's ready for you. All you have to do is get over here.'

'That's ridiculous,' Anna began, 'what you need is a local.'

'I've got a local,' Lara said. 'Now I want you. Look, I'll call back in half an hour. You obviously need time to wake up.'

'Don't . . .' Anna said, but Lara rang off.

'What's going on?' Quex asked.

'Search me. That was Lara Crowther. She wants me in the States.'

'What on earth for?' He knuckled his eyes vigorously. His hair stood on end.

'Dunno,' Anna said. She swung her legs over the side of the bed.

'Where are you going?'

'To plug the phone in the other room. She's ringing back in half an hour. I don't want to disturb you.'

'Leave it. When does she expect you?'

'Dunno,' Anna said. 'It sounded like tomorrow.'

'Tomorrow!' Quex shouted.

Anna jumped.

'That's bloody ridiculous,' he thundered.

'Why?' she asked perversely.

'You're not actually thinking of going?'

'Don't shout at me!'

'I'm not shouting,' he roared.

Anna got up and took the phone into the living room. It was cold. She lit the gas fire and put on her coat. Quex stood shivering in the doorway.

He said, 'Sorry I shouted. Fancy a cup of tea?'

Anna, huddled on the hearth rug in front of the fire with the phone in her lap, said, 'Why don't you go back to bed? There's no need for both of us in here.'

Quex walked barefoot to the kitchen and filled the kettle.

He said quietly, 'How long would you go for?'

Anna took a deep breath, determined not to lose her temper. 'How should I know?' she asked. 'How long *does* a job last, Quex?'

'Don't shout.'

'I'm not shouting, but if I have to go to Sarasota I have to go to Sarasota. I don't know how long for.'

'You don't have to go anywhere,' Quex said.

Anna shrugged and he went back into the kitchen to make the tea. He returned with two mugs and a packet of chocolate digestive biscuits.

'I know this is bad timing,' he said. He ate a biscuit in two bites and munched, almost regretfully, on a second. Anna clasped her mug in both hands and prayed the phone would ring.

Quex sighed. 'I hadn't meant to tell you yet. I don't want to push. But I've been busy, and today – well, I suppose it's yesterday – I came to an agreement with my tenants. They'll be out next week.'

He reached for another biscuit. Anna stared at the pattern on the rug.

'For God's sake, Leo!' he exclaimed. 'I had to do something. Selwyn's going round the twist and you've got your head buried in the sand. It's a big flat. You won't even notice Selwyn.'

'You've got to be joking,' Anna said flatly.

'Listen to me,' Quex said. 'You haven't heard the proposition yet. You've made up your mind without thinking. You say it isn't working, but that's because we don't have enough space. We've never lived together before. What we've been doing is *seeing* each other. I've never been here much. I've been out of the country. Well, that seems to suit you. It certainly suited me. But I wasn't seeing anyone else. I don't know about you and I'm not asking. What I'm saying is that when my father died things changed. Not only does it mean I've finished as an oil man, but I found I wanted to give *us* a chance. We've never had a chance, Leo. We never even thought about it. And we don't have a chance here. It's just too damned small.'

'It's not that simple,' Anna began, although in a way it was that simple: while he was speaking the living room had contracted to the size of a box.

'Of course it isn't,' Quex agreed. 'But look at it this way – I won't be there all the time. The estate in Ireland's going to take a lot of time so you will be on your own a great deal, if that's what you want. And you know what's happening to Selwyn: he's having giant menopausal twitches – that's all. He'll be back with Bea before Christmas, you'll see.'

'I don't think Bea will have him,' Anna said.

Quex looked astonished. 'Of course she will,' he said. 'They've been married for over ten years.'

'Exactly.'

'Why are we talking about Bea and Selwyn?' Quex asked.

'You brought them up.'

'And you're using them so as not to talk about us.'

'I'm not using anything,' Anna snapped. 'I'm just waiting for a phone call. But since you mention it, two o'clock in the morning is a daft time to talk about anything big.'

'But you're going away tomorrow,' Quex said inexorably. 'Look, I'm not asking for an answer. I'm just asking you to think about it. Please.'

'All right.'

Quex sighed. 'I mean, think about it calmly, like you do when you're thinking about someone else's problems.'

The phone rang.

Chapter 44

TAMPA AIRPORT SMELLED of air freshener and oranges. All the British tourists had stripped down to T-shirts in Charlotte, North Carolina, and were standing in defensive huddles around the baggage carousel with overcoats, anoraks and sweaters discarded like skins around them. Everyone looked dazed and vulnerable.

Anna's single bag sailed towards her. She plucked it off the line and limped towards the doors. Her knees were stiff and her feet had puffed up.

People from England are so used to outdoor air being colder by far than indoor air that stepping out of Tampa Airport into the warm milky bath of Florida night turns their world, at a single stroke, inside out. The automatic doors sighed shut leaving Anna stranded in front of a line of shiny big cars, completely at a loss.

'Hi!' Lara said. 'Good trip? I almost didn't recognise you without your coat. Put your bag in the trunk and we'll be off.'

Anna noticed vaguely that the car was a white Mercedes and that Lara herself was a blur of ivory and aquamarine. She was altogether more vivid than she had been in England, her hair was brighter, her accent stronger, and either she was wearing more perfume or the car was fitted with an air freshener too. She pulled smoothly away from the kerb and joined the line of traffic leaving the airport.

'I do it all the time,' Lara was saying, 'so I'm used to it. I find if I can get my back right everything is fine. If my back is wrong, the next couple of days I'm a wreck. You got to drink water all the time if you want to escape jetlag.'

The road climbed over Tampa in a giant switchback.

'Some people say you need the vitamins in orange juice,' Lara said. She didn't seem to be driving at all, just sitting behind the wheel. 'But all you really need is the fluid. I never travel without a big bottle of Evian. And of course my lordosis support cushion.'

Four lanes of traffic swept, without pause, straight out to sea on a long causeway. Black water glittered on either side. It was an amazing road which did not seem to be influenced in its course by land or sea. If the shortest distance between two points is, logically, a straight line, then American engineers, Anna decided, must be frighteningly logical people.

'If you want it, go for it,' Lara agreed. 'You British used to be like that in the last century. But I guess you ran out of steam.'

'Maybe we just ran out of space,' Anna said tiredly.

Lara laughed. 'This is a big country,' she said. 'You'll like it here.'

Anna was inclined to agree. Already, England seemed tiny and cramped and full of impediments, whereas the United States was a place where they built roads straight, even across the ocean, and you didn't have to wait three quarters of an hour for your suitcase to appear at a dirty airport.

'You're probably wondering why I insisted you come out here,' Lara said. 'I told you on the phone we found Hugh. At least, we found where he sent the fax from. It's a company which imports European fashion and cosmetics.'

'The Style File?' Anna asked, encouraged to find that her memory had not deserted her.

'How do you know?'

'I found C and H Fashion and it seems to be just a warehouse where they collect goods, re-package them and then send them on. The way it works apparently is Chris Garden in Italy buying, and Hugh Fellows over here selling. There was a consignment of Italian stuff being shipped to Florida.'

'You should have told me.'

'You only gave me a New York number. I didn't like to leave a message because I didn't know how much you wanted anyone else to know.'

The car slowed down and Anna saw that they were approaching a brightly lit area which looked like a border crossing. Toll booths stretched across six lanes. Lara barely paused. She threw some change into a receptacle and drove on.

She said, 'You will talk to Ethan Callow tomorrow. He's kind of puzzled about what Hugh is doing.'

They were heading out to sea again and the road rose up into a breathless arch topped by two brightly lit sails. The sails turned out to be an optical illusion created by cables attached to two slender masts from which the main spans of the bridge were suspended. Anna had seen nothing like it before. She closed her eyes. It didn't seem possible that she would be able to do anything useful in a country which built bridges like that.

'Are you listening?' Lara asked. 'Look, I can save it for tomorrow if you like.'

'It might be better,' Anna agreed. 'I think I left my brains at Gatwick.'

She dreamed about the bridge that night. Her car, the Peugeot, dwarfed by the soaring cables, stalled just as it got to the top of the main span. It hesitated and then began to roll backwards. She could not find the brake. There were a dozen foot pedals but none of them slowed the car. It gathered speed. She grabbed the handbrake but it came away in her hand. She raced helplessly backwards as if down a mountain.

She woke up, sweating. It was three o'clock in the morning, eight o'clock at home. Time to get up. She turned on the light. The hotel bed seemed to be made of plastic. The under blanket had a rubber backing. The pillow was foam rubber. No wonder she was sweating.

She got up and went to the bathroom to wash. Mirrors surrounded her, and in the fluorescent light she looked pale yellow. Back in the bedroom she turned the air conditioner up a notch. She would never get back to sleep now. She lay on the bed listening to the dull hum of machinery and fell asleep.

Chapter 45

BREAKFAST IN AMERICA, Anna decided as she sipped her freshly squeezed orange juice, was not just a wild traveller's tale. There were pancakes and maple syrup, bacon and eggs, and any amount of weak coffee.

The hotel was hermetically sealed with artificial lighting and artificial fresh air. Lara, colour co-ordinated in lemon and white, sat opposite and drank decaffeinated coffee while Anna ate.

'Here's the plan,' Lara said. 'We're going to put you on Manatee Key. There are three Keys, all connected – San Isabel, Manatee and Coquina. Ethan is ninety-five percent certain Hugh has a place on one of the three. It's all resorts down there. You're a British tourist, right? No problem. A friend of mine has a condo on Manatee, and she's agreed to let me use it. There's a tennis club, pool, restaurant, so you'll be quite comfortable.' She looked at her watch. 'Ethan should be here soon.'

Anna said, 'But what do you actually want me to do?'

'Find Cyn. Get close to her. Persuade her to go home.'

'I don't want to look a gift horse in the mouth,' Anna said, 'but you know her. You know the whole family, and you know Hugh. Wouldn't it be a lot more direct if you . . .'

'Sure it would. But you said it: I know Hugh, and Hugh knows me. He worked for me, and when I let him go he was pretty sore. I don't want to see him. It would not be a positive move to handle this personally. Hugh can be obnoxious and obstructive. He's got a grudge.'

'All right,' Anna said.

'And besides, I've got a business to run. I have to be back in New York by tomorrow morning.'

'How do you want me to play this?' Anna asked. 'I don't know anything about Cyn. I don't know how she got on with her mother . . .'

'Ah,' Lara began and then stopped. A short man in a silky sky-blue windbreaker was approaching the table.

'Hi, Ethan. This is Anna,' Lara said.

Ethan took off his dark glasses to shake hands. He looked like a baby with his hairless plump cheeks and his blue outfit.

'Hi Anna,' he said and pulled out a chair. 'Good trip? I always wanted to go to London. This your first time over here?'

An elderly waitress appeared and Ethan ordered some coffee. The waitress wore a hot-pink dress, and from her side of the table, Anna was suddenly convinced that the three Americans were clothed in birthday wrapping paper. Ethan Callow was not what she had been expecting.

Lara said, 'What's new, Ethan?'

'We took him over Bay Bridge, Ms Crowther,' Ethan said. 'He's used all three approaches to the islands, but that is where he goes. What he does then, see, is he switches automobiles. There's a bar just off the bridge. He drives into the parking lot, goes into the bar, and he doesn't come out. Over back of the bar is a plaza, and I figure he exits that way, picks up another car and that's it. What I don't understand is why this guy is putting on these moves.'

'He must know you are there,' Lara said.

'I swear he doesn't, Ms Crowther. One of the others took him last night and we never use the same vehicle twice. What kind of guy is he?'

'Dodgy,' Anna said.

'Well, he might be into something,' Lara said, almost at the same time. 'He's into something back in London. Anna here has been doing a little research. But that isn't our main concern now. We need to know his home address.'

'And that is what we are working toward,' Ethan said. His coffee came. He stirred some non-dairy cream and non-sugar sweetener into it.

'But it sort of affects the job description,' he went on. 'I wouldn't want any of my team getting into something they aren't prepared for, is all.'

'How can they?' Lara said. 'You aren't going near him. You aren't even going to talk to him. We just want to know where he lives.'

'Okay,' he said. 'As long as we know where we are.'

Lara said, 'I am going to take Anna down to Manatee now. But I want you to stay in touch with her. As soon as you get Hugh's address let us both know, okay?'

'Will do, Ms Crowther.' He finished his coffee. 'Pleasure to meet you, Anna. Anything you need, give me a call.' He pressed a card into Anna's hand and left.

'I wonder about him,' Lara said, doubtfully. 'He's slow.'

'It's only been two days,' Anna suggested. 'He didn't expect the ducking and diving.'

'No,' Lara agreed. 'Come on, let's get you checked out of this place.'

Anna, who did not even know what the weather was like outside, was eager to go.

Nothing disappointed her. The sun was bright, the sea was blue. Small craft bobbed on the water and large clean cars sailed like ships over the long bridge to the Keys. Every second building was a club: The Belvedere Club, The Cottonwood Club, The San Isabel Key Club. They were set far behind lines of palm trees and lawns, with rococo gates and columns. There were golf courses on either side of the road.

'Do you play golf?' Lara asked, and Anna shook her head.

'It's too flat to be interesting,' Lara went on, 'but it's not a bad place to learn. Like it so far?'

'Not half,' Anna assured her. 'It's like every picture postcard I ever drooled over. Maybe you'd better tell me a bit about Cynthia Garden before I forget why I came.'

'Right, Cynthia,' Lara said. The white Mercedes cruised at a steady forty-five miles an hour with scarcely a sound.

'Cyn was a pretty average teenager,' she said at last. 'From what I saw of her, anyway. She didn't seem to me to be exceptionally bright or beautiful. Nice manners with guests. But when she turned fifteen she filled out and got interested in clothes and boys. She used to annoy me somewhat because she always seemed to want something from Penny. It never occurred to her that Penny couldn't drop everything to drive her to movies or discos or the shops. She didn't appreciate it was Penny's work that bought her everything. She was bored living in the country. She said she never got to meet anyone. Just like her father.'

'Not your favourite kid,' Anna said.

'I wasn't crazy about her,' Lara admitted. 'But I never had any of my own, so maybe I just didn't understand. I guess that kind of friction is normal in most families. I was mainly concerned with Penny, you see, and it seemed both the daughter and the husband were making demands she just could not meet.'

'What about when Cyn met Hugh Fellows?'

'That was when I was introducing Hugh round to all my designers. We had tea outside on the lawn. Hugh was very charming, and Penny and the husband got along with him just fine. I don't recall exactly, but I think Cyn came later. She didn't make any special impression.'

'But then?'

'I can't say. Hugh would have gone to Oakleigh several times as my agent. And after that I guess he went whenever he felt like it.'

'What does Penny say?'

'Until it all came apart for her she hardly said a word about him. I didn't know he'd been going there. If I had I might have warned her.'

'Of what?'

Lara didn't answer for a while. The sparse traffic began to bunch up, and finally came to a halt. They had stopped with a bridge just ahead of them. A barrier came down across the road and red lights flashed. Across the bay Anna could see the tall buildings of Sarasota rising up out of the haze. They looked miles away and out of reach. To the right was the Gulf of Mexico and a single yacht proceeding towards the bridge.

Lara said, 'You see, I knew Hugh fooled around. Of course I didn't know he was actually dishonest, but he took short cuts. He wanted to get rich quick – which is okay in itself, I guess. But I've been in business a long time. I've got a reputation to protect.'

She leaned forward and turned the radio on. A man's voice said, 'One day only. Don't miss it. Exceptional furniture savings!' She snapped it off and leaned back. Slowly, the bridge split apart.

Lara said, 'It's all hindsight. Don't you think it's extraordinary how the past always looks somehow inevitable? I mean, anything I could have said to Penny two years ago, would have seemed vague and bitchy. But somehow, when I look back, it's as if I knew it all.'

The yacht chugged straight between the two flaps of the bridge and headed towards Sarasota.

'Penny told me she had no idea. No idea at all,' Lara said. 'When Cyn left she thought she had gone to her father in London. Penny had been working in her studio all day. Cyn had gone to school as usual in the morning. She just never came home that night. And she never came home again. When it came down to it, the school said she had been skipping classes for months. She had told her friends she was seeing an older man and they were going away to Mexico to be married. According to Penny, no one believed her. She went in for self-dramatization as a matter of habit.'

'They're married?' Anna asked. 'You're talking about her as if she's a schoolgirl.'

'I don't know if she's married,' Lara exclaimed. 'I couldn't care less about what they did or didn't do!'

'But if they're married,' Anna said, 'I can't just persuade her to go home. How old is she anyway?'

'Not old enough,' Lara snapped. 'If the girl wants to ruin her life that's up to her. What I can't take is what it's done to Penny.'

Anna twisted sideways to look at her. Nothing showed on the smoothly made-up face. Only the voice was jagged. The two halves of the bridge folded down and the barrier came up. Lara put the car in drive and they moved off.

'I can't stand waiting around for goddammed boats,' Lara said.

What on earth am I doing here? Anna thought. Quex was right. This was a whim of Lara's: she hadn't thought it out properly. She's asking me to interfere in the lives of strangers, and she has no real authority. But Anna had to admit, as they drove in silence through Manatee Key, that if Lara hadn't thought it out properly, she, Anna, hadn't thought it out at all. And in any case, interfering in strangers' lives was what she did for a living.

Surreptitiously she checked in her inside pocket for her passport and the air ticket home. Looking at Lara's unyielding profile she thought it best to have an escape route prepared.

Lara caught the movement and turned her head to look. Anna said, 'It should be easy enough to trace Chris Garden.'

'Who?'

'Chris,' Anna said. 'The husband. According to my source at C and H Fashions he's made his base in Milan.'

'Maybe, when I've dealt with Cyn,' Lara said shortly.

Anna leaned back and looked out of the window.

Lara softened. 'He won't go back to Penny,' she said. 'But he should be made to take some responsibility. He has to get in touch with her – clarify the situation.'

'Don't you think it's strange,' Anna asked, 'that both husband and daughter left without a word? Until I went to C and H and talked to someone who had seen him recently I thought he might have died.'

'Did you?' Lara sounded amused. 'That would certainly clarify the situation.'

Anna glanced at her sharply.

Lara said, 'Look, neither of them, Cyn or the husband, gives a damn. They were out for what they could get, and when the business went bust, and there was no more to be got, they left. It is as simple as that. He was a lousy parent anyway. Any caring done in that home was done by Penny.'

'But it's a bit more than that,' Anna said. 'I mean Chris and Hugh are still selling her old stock. That looks like malice.'

'Could be,' Lara said almost indifferently. 'But maybe it was just meeting the liquidator that put them in mind of another way to make easy money. Look, Anna, forget the liquidation. I got you over here to concentrate on Cyn, and if you don't mind, we'll do just that.'

Chapter 46

MANATEE KEY TENNIS Club was like a village built around a clubhouse and ten tennis courts. There was a central roundabout with a fountain watering banks of crimson poinsettias, and lanes diverged from this to groups of houses. The houses were quite tall and built of cream painted wood. They all looked brand new.

Lara eased the car gently down the lane towards the sea. The house she stopped at was like all the others: there was a mock-Georgian front door set back from a garage, two palm trees shading the front, and two floors on top of the garage. Lara unlocked the door. A small foyer opened onto stairs leading up to the living and dining room. This was dominated by huge sliding glass doors which overlooked the sea.

It was not, as Anna had expected, someone's home – or if it was it had only just been decorated. It looked more like something only seen in magazines: everything matched everything else. The tables were glass, the fabric on the long, low sofa went with the wall paper. The Japanese prints on the walls were picked up by silk flower arrangements on shelves and in corners.

'Neat, huh?' Lara said, surveying the room. 'Over here is your kitchen – everything you need – dishwasher, refrigerator, ice water dispenser, washer and dryer.'

She led the way upstairs. There were two bedrooms and two bathrooms.

'Which one?' Anna asked.

'Whichever.'

'Won't your friend mind?'

'My friend? Oh, no. She only comes now and then. She probably bought this condo to retire to. She has other property.'

Anna chose the bigger of the two, the one which faced the Gulf.

Her bag looked shabby beside the fresh paint and fabrics. Caught unawares in one of the many big mirrors, Anna looked shabby as well.

Lara must have thought so too. She said, 'You should get some sun on your face.'

They went downstairs. Lara was still looking critically at her so Anna sat with her back to the light.

Lara said, 'There's a lot of money on this island.'

This was said almost as a warning. Anna stirred uncomfortably. Lara took a deep breath. 'Look,' she said, 'if you want to fit in here you should maybe play a little tennis and sort of look right. There's a lot of resort wear on sale at the clubhouse. You'll be here a few days, I can't say for how long, but I don't want a lot of people asking questions about you.'

Anna said, 'Hugh Fellows may not even live on this Key. Cynthia may not still be with him.'

'Yeah,' Lara agreed. 'But I got you all the way out here so you might as well acclimatize.' She got up. 'Come on,' she said. 'Let's go look at your car and then I'll take you over and introduce you to the social secretary.'

The car was in the garage. It was a white Ford Tempo with Hertz plates on it. The key was in the ignition.

Lara said, 'If you want something better trade it in.'

It might have been jetlag but Anna was feeling entirely out of control of the situation. Sitting in the Mercedes to drive the few yards back to the clubhouse she almost burst out laughing. She was a passenger, quite passive. The chances of becoming active in the search for Cynthia were slim. How could she look for someone she did not know in a place she did not know either? The fact that Lara seemed to expect her to stay in a luxurious house at a club where she had to meet the social secretary and mix with moneyed people made it even more ludicrous. What did Lara think she was paying for? There was a car in the garage with only three hundred miles on the clock and Anna could 'trade it in' if she didn't like it. She felt herself grinning like an idiot.

The clubhouse was built in the colonial style with a porch that ran all the way round. White garden chairs and tables were grouped in its shade and a few people in tennis whites sat drinking out of cans and paper cups.

Lara led the way up some steps into a cool shop where a passage between racks of sports and leisure clothes opened on to a counter. There were three women behind the counter. One of them, a woman of about sixty came forward.

Lara said, 'I'll wait for Elaine.'

Elaine was talking on the telephone. She had the receiver tucked between her chin and shoulder, and at the same time she was folding a sweater. She said, 'See, if you call Frank, he can tell you directly. If I call Frank, maybe I can't get a hold of him. Or maybe I get a hold of him but then I can't get a hold of you . . . yeah, the court *is* booked . . . eight-thirty tomorrow . . . yeah, I do suggest you call Frank directly . . . 'kay. Bye.' She hung up, opened a big ledger and began to make a note in it. At the same time, almost without looking up she said, 'You must be Ms Crowther. What can I do for you today?'

Lara said, 'I bought Anna Lee over to meet you, she's in seventeen.'

Someone called from behind a rack of warm-up suits, 'Elaine, where are the twelves?'

Elaine said, 'To your right. Hi, Anna, this your first time here?' She was small, dark and spark-eyed. 'She's never a twelve,' she added, almost to herself. 'So you're in seventeen. You'll like it here. You want to play a little tennis?'

Lara said, 'I'd appreciate it if you'd fix Anna up with a couple of games. Also if I could open an account for her here: she'll need some equipment and things.'

'Anything you say, Ms Crowther.' Elaine gave Anna a very brief but piercing look. 'You'll be a size ten, I guess. Anything with a grey label is forty per cent off. What's your rating?'

Lara said, 'They don't do it like that in England, but I guess she's about a three five.'

Anna was feeling exactly as she had when she was a child and went shopping with her mother.

'See, Anna, what we do here,' Elaine began, but an old man in white shorts ambled up to the counter saying, 'Where do you keep the Gripsy, Elaine?'

Anna wondered what the other two women actually did. Watching Elaine was like watching a juggler.

Elaine said, 'See, Anna, because you are living in one of the units you are a member. So I can put you in a game but I don't want to put you in a game where maybe you are a little too strong or even the other way round. So what I'll do is book you in with one of the pros first and he can assess where you'll be most comfortable.'

'That's great,' Lara said. 'Today?'

Elaine opened another ledger. 'We got a cancellation at four. Will that do? Come in at three-thirty so's we can fix you up with a racket etcetera. Okay?'

Anna said, 'Thanks very much.'

Just then the shop started to fill up with men and women, greeting Elaine and fingering the merchandise.

'Changeover,' Lara said. 'Let's get some lunch. I'll have to get back to the mainland soon.'

The restaurant was past the changing rooms and showers, past the sauna, the bar and the offices. Picture windows looked, at one side, onto the pool, and at the other, onto a court. There was no one in the pool.

Lara ordered a spinach and bacon salad. Anna asked for a BLT just to see what it was. She wasn't hungry and her conscience was troubling her.

In the end she said, 'Look, all this must be costing you a fortune, and it isn't at all certain you'll get value for money.'

'It's my decision,' Lara said. 'And in my judgement you are realistic and sensible. If you can't get Cynthia back you can at least tell us how she's doing. It's having no news that's driving Penny crazy. Okay, so a local operator could do that. But Cyn is British and you are British and when it comes to talking to her I'd rather it was you. If we don't succeed, tough. You'll get a good vacation if nothing else.'

'What about the Garden Party stock?' Anna asked. 'Am I still keeping an eye out for that?'

'You could do that,' Lara said, 'just as a matter of interest. But we already established C and H bought it. I don't know how ethical the sale was, but they bought it. Now we've got to concentrate on her damned family.'

'You don't care what Hugh Fellows is up to here?'

'If he's up to anything.'

'Oh, he is,' Anna said. 'Ethan Callow knows it.'

'Well, whatever it is, don't you get involved,' Lara said. 'I don't want you mixed up with the police or anything like that. Your job is purely social.'

'You're the boss,' Anna said. She had been wanting to say it all day. Lara nodded.

The BLT was a bacon, lettuce and tomato sandwich so thick that it had to be pinned together with a toothpick. The sight of it made Anna instantly ravenous. Outside, in the hot sun she could see a lean brown man giving a tennis lesson. By his side was a supermarket trolley filled with yellow balls. Perfect strokes, she thought, and a picture of the hackers in Battersea Park came into her head.

She said, 'What did Mr Brierly say when you told him I was coming here?'

Lara shrugged. 'Someone ought to remind him sometime that whoever pays the piper calls the tune.'

Anna grinned. She wished she could have bugged the call.

Lara said, 'Maybe you should call him yourself, see if he calmed down any.'

Anna stopped grinning.

Chapter 47

T HE SEA LOOKED like a blue ploughed field. Anna sat on the porch to make her phone calls. Sun filtered through the fine mesh screen and warmed her legs.

Mr Brierly said, 'That was irresponsible, Miss Lee, utterly irresponsible. In the final analysis it is I, not Mrs Crowther, who pays your wages. You would do well to remember that. And she would do well to remember the five-hour time gap between our two countries, and not get me out of bed at four in the morning. As to the case itself, as presented to me, it was merely a question of tracing some missing knitwear, not missing persons. Your lack of candour has been quite deplorable.'

What Anna needed to recover from Mr Brierly's broadside was a cup of tea. But the cupboards in the immaculate kitchen were bare. She would have to do something about that. In the meantime she phoned Quex.

He said, 'Thanks for ringing. I was worried.'

'No need,' Anna said. 'You should see here. It's like a palace in paradise.'

'Room for two?' he asked in a tone that was only half humorous.

'Room for two families,' she replied to the humorous half.

'Well, keep in touch,' he said. 'Don't get into trouble.'

'I won't – you know me.'

'I do,' he said, sounding depressed. 'I miss you.'

'Only 'cos you can't throw far enough.' But old jokes didn't make Quex laugh and she couldn't think of any new ones.

She explored the kitchen. Apart from a surfeit of ice cubes, there was nothing edible there at all. Even the matching glass salt and pepper shakers were empty. It looked as if no one had ever lived there. There was nothing to wash or wash up with either.

She extended the search. The sheets on the beds looked as if they had just been bought. The soap was new. But there was nothing with which to clean the bath or shower. She made a list. It was time to test drive the car and find the functional part of the island, if there was one.

Bay Plaza was at the north end of the island just before the bridge over to Coquina and just after another causeway back to the mainland. Acres of parking space fronted acres of shops. The choice was confusing and Anna could have spent hours there if she had not had an appointment at three-thirty. But everything was easy and straightforward and contrasts with London struck her at every turn. The luxury of having somewhere to park was one, the smooth, healthy look of the shoppers was another. There was no queueing. The old people had all their teeth. There were hardly any dogs or babies.

She finished her shopping with the purchase of a map and drove back to Manatee Key Tennis Club. It was time, as Lara put it, to fit in and acclimatize. It was time to be assessed as a club player.

But first she had to look like a club player, which could have been an extremely expensive business without Elaine's help. As it turned out it was only fairly expensive. Elaine looked at her shrewdly, while simultaneously talking on the phone and lacing a stack of Reebok shoes, and pointed her in the direction of all the bargains. There were scarcely any other members about. Sprinklers were raining gently over all the courts except the two closest to the club house.

Anna sat and waited on the west porch of the clubhouse next to a big red drinks dispenser with 'Enjoy Coca-Cola' stencilled up its side. The sun was in her eyes. On the far court a huge blond man with a loud voice was drilling nine children, some of whom looked too small to hold a racket. A group of parents or grandparents stood in the shade of a loggia watching.

There was a lesson coming to an end on Court One. The man with the perfect strokes was saying, 'You been playing a little too much racketball up north, Freddy. We gotta get rid of that wrist while you're here. Otherwise you're in good shape.'

His victim, a middle-aged man with a long body and short legs, muttered something Anna didn't catch and began to pick up balls in a hopper. He did not look in good shape. He looked as if he had just run a marathon in the pouring rain.

Anna went down the grassy slope to the edge of the court. The middle-aged man tipped his hopperful of balls into the supermarket trolley and said, 'Some workout, Lewis.'

Lewis said, 'See you tomorrow.' He turned towards Anna. 'Anna, right?' He extended a hand. It was bone dry, and he looked immaculate.

'You're from London?'

'That's right.'

'I been there a coupla times,' he said. 'Wimbledon, you know. And played a place called Bristol.'

'Where are you from?' Anna asked. It certainly wasn't the USA.

'Ballarat,' he said, and laughed.

'Victoria?' Anna asked. 'Well, that explains it. I was watching you from the restaurant and you reminded me of Ken Rosewall.'

'Yeah?' he said. 'Well, well.' He did not seem displeased. 'Let's hit a few balls.'

Anna had never played with a pro before, and after a self-conscious beginning she started to enjoy it. Lewis could put the ball wherever he wanted and at whatever pace he wanted. He wasn't trying to beat her. And far from trying to upset her rhythm he was setting one. This meant all her mistakes were her own, quite unforced.

The court surface was perfect, her new racket was wonderful, and in the brilliant afternoon sun the balls looked the size of grapefruit. Nothing could have been less like Battersea Park. The only thing which bothered her was the sweat. Until she started moving the humidity had not been noticeable. But after a few minutes she was dripping wet. And when her half hour was up she had a raging thirst and needed another half hour in a tumble dryer. Lewis's hand was still bone dry.

'Okay, Anna,' he said when she had picked the balls up. 'Elaine will fix you up when I've had a chance to talk to her.'

Anna wondered if she should ask what her rating was, but as

he didn't volunteer the information she thought it might be a rude question. It was something she never did find out. Three giant teenage boys were waiting beside the court, jigging up and down as if hormones and excess vitamins were boiling in their veins.

'How did you get on?' Elaine asked, back in the cool of the pro-shop. She was hanging up shorts and shirts. In a corner another big blond man was stringing a racket.

'Great,' Anna said.

'Bit different from England,' the blond man said. 'I was there once and it rained all the time.'

Elaine said, 'You look beat. Half an hour too much for you?' She looked as if she was having a private joke.

'He keeps you busy,' Anna said.

'Lew, he's the best,' Elaine said. 'He's a natural.'

The remark seemed to be directed at the big blond man. He scowled. Even his facial muscles looked over-developed.

'Are you some relative of Ms Crowther's?' Elaine asked.

'Not really,' Anna said.

'I was just wondering.' Elaine slipped a shirt on a hanger.

'Elaine wants to know everything,' the blond man said. 'She never forgets a name or a face. What she doesn't know she wants to find out.'

'Mrs Feiffer's coming for that racket at four-thirty,' Elaine said. 'Hadn't you better get a move on?'

Chapter 48

As Anna stepped out of the shower the phone rang. She took the call in the bedroom.

Elaine said, 'Hi. I've put you in a game with Sabine Mueller, Betsy Hicks and Marcia Gold. Eight-thirty tomorrow morning. 'Kay?'

'So soon?' Anna said, trying to stop her hair dripping on the carpet.

'Carol Biermann is usually in that four but she's going to Naples for the day. You don't mind filling in here and there, do you?'

'Not at all,' Anna said. 'And thanks.'

'Okay. You know, some people think they can get into a regular game right away, but there's a lot of pressure on the courts. Everyone wants to play in the morning and most of the members already have a regular four. But if you don't mind kind of floating I can put you in when someone else drops out. And I got to admit it, there's one or two members nobody likes to play with – they call lines funny – and they drive me crazy wanting to be put in with people who don't want to play with them, so I might now and then ask you to fill in there. But I wouldn't want you to think I was taking advantage. I told Ms Crowther I'd look after you and she packs a heavy punch.'

'Do you know her well?'

'Never saw her before yesterday. But she knows the head of the development corporation that set us up and built this place. I heard she has a bunch of clothing stores up north and a load of property all over, that right?'

'She packs a heavy punch all right,' Anna agreed. 'But she's an okay lady with it. Looks after her friends.'

'That's what I thought,' Elaine said. 'I wouldn't want her to think I was taking advantage.'

'She won't. Not from me.'

'Okay. See you tomorrow, eight-thirty. And don't worry, this is a *nice* game.'

'Thanks,' Anna said and hung up. Immediately, the phone rang again. This time it was Ethan Callow.

'I want to cover all the bridges to the Keys,' he said. 'If we don't we could pussyfoot around for days and I figure Ms Crowther wants us to wrap this up a.s.a.p. I am a little stretched on the personnel side but if you could help out we could maybe finish this tonight.'

'What do you want me to do?' Anna asked. 'Just remember I don't know this place at all.'

'Yeah. I thought I could put you where Hugh Fellows switched cars last night. So far he hasn't pulled the same stunt twice running, so there's little chance you'll have anything to do. But I want it covered anyway.'

'All right.'

'Okay. Here's what you do. Bay Bridge is at the north end of Manatee Key. Just off the bridge is a bar called Gulf Tides, and behind that is the parking lot of a shopping mall called Bay Plaza.'

'I went there this afternoon,' Anna put in.

'Yeah? Well, good. Put yourself in the northeast section of the parking lot. That's right near the back of Gulf Tides. If the guy comes out the back of the bar and crosses into the Plaza lot you'll see him. Right? He doesn't know you, does he?'

'No.'

'What are you driving?'

Anna told him.

'Okay,' Ethan said. 'Be at Bay Plaza from, say, six o'clock on, and stay there till I come. You don't have a phone in your car do you?'

'No.'

'Because it might be a long wait.'

'I don't mind,' Anna said, glad there was something she could do other than play tennis and acclimatize.

'I mean, you don't work for me,' Ethan said. 'I'm just supposed to supply you with certain information. But I don't think Ms Crowther realised what she was asking.'

Anna dried her hair, dressed and transferred her tennis clothes from the washing machine to the dryer. She wasn't hungry but she grabbed a packet of Cape Cod Potato chips to eat in the car.

It was early but she wanted time to drive around and find her sense of direction. The sun was going down and the sky on the gulf side was turning spectacular shades of yellow and turquoise. She drove north, past Bay Plaza, and saw on her left Gulf Tides, a low clapboard building with a big car park of its own. A sign said, 'Steak and Ale. Lobster special. Happy Hour 5–6. Appearing Tues–Sat Royal Shaft.'

She crossed the bridge to Coquina Key and found herself on a narrow strip from which she could see both the Gulf of Mexico and Sarasota Bay. She pulled off the road onto a sandy expanse where a few campers and cars were parked under some Casuarina pines.

She walked onto the beach. It was low tide and the pale wet sand stretched away from her. The sun was a huge orange ball low in the sky. A couple of pelicans flapped lazily away to the south, their great heads looking like prehistoric throwbacks, silhouetted against the light. Fishermen hung over the rails on the approach to the bridge.

It was a moment to share with a lover. Anna walked quickly back to the car, did a U-turn and drove to Bay Plaza.

While she waited she studied the map. On the radio Marty Robbins sang, 'Down in the west Texas town of El Paso . . .' It was a country music station, and when Tammy Wynette began to sing D-I-V-O-R-C-E, Anna switched over and heard Aretha Franklin sing R-E-S-P-E-C-T. She grinned and went back to the map.

The three Keys were all long and narrow. One main road ran from the south of San Isabel all the way to the northernmost point of Coquina. San Isabel looked to be the least populated. It was where most of the golf courses and boat clubs were. There were more residential and commercial developments on Manatee but they seemed planned and well spaced out. By contrast, Co-quina looked quite untidy with roads running higgledy-piggledy. It was the only Key which advertised public beaches.

As it grew dark the lights in the car park came on. The small shops closed and all the traffic gathered in front of the supermarkets. The area where Anna was became deserted.

At ten to seven, when Anna had finished most of the potato chips, a figure detached itself from the shadows at the back of Gulf Tides, and pushed through the hedge between the two car parks. It was Ethan Callow. Anna opened the passenger door for him and he got in.

He said, 'The guy appears to be on the road to Tampa so he won't be coming this way for quite a while. You want a drink while we wait?'

They entered Gulf Tides the back way. There was a long horseshoe bar. On one side there were tables and a dance floor. The other was more like a lounge. Food was being served in a separate room. All around the bar television sets were showing a basketball game and the commentary could only just be heard above the noise of conversation and country music.

'That guy sure gets around,' Ethan said. He ordered two club sodas. 'You mind telling me what he's into in London?'

'Didn't Ms Crowther tell you?'

'She said Hugh Fellows ran away with a girl she wants traced. That right?'

'Yes.'

'See, she's always on the move,' Ethan said. 'She's never around to talk to. I talked to her attorney in New York and she says, basically, whatever Ms Crowther wants she gets. She says Ms Crowther wouldn't be mixed up with anything messy.'

'That's the impression I get too,' Anna said. 'But Hugh Fellows used to work for her a few years ago, and he's mixed up with messy things.'

'You want to tell me what?' Ethan asked. 'I'm asking because I'm thinking of seriously calling a time-out here.'

'It's like this,' Anna began, wondering how much to tell him. 'He has two partners and they run a company called C and H

Fashions. They seem to buy up bankrupt stock for a song and then sell it on.'

'This C and H is linked to the Style File?'

'That's right,' Anna said. 'When I was at C and H there was a consignment of cosmetics being shipped to the Style File.'

'That fax number you gave Ms Crowther belongs to the Style File. That's how we picked the guy up after we lost him the first time. So what is wrong?'

'Well,' Anna said. 'Fraud. How they get their stock isn't quite kosher. They're acting through a liquidator who was probably bent in the first place. But now he's dead, and they're carrying on business in his name.'

'Is that all?'

'As far as I know.'

'That's not so bad,' Ethan said, rubbing his baby face with a plump hand. 'Man. I'll tell you, it is not just fraud here. Soon as I met the plane I knew. First he makes like he's headed toward Lakeland, then he doubles back. He moves around in heavy traffic, sort of uses other vehicles as screens, like it's second nature to him. This is one paranoid guy. He comes back south to Sarasota, checks into a motel. I thought I had him. But soon as I turn around, he's gone. The motel had him as Mr Colin Dredge, British tourist. What's so funny?'

'Colin Dredge is an English cricketer.'

'Is that so?' Ethan looked offended. 'Has he any sporting connections in London?'

'Not that I know of,' Anna said, wondering if he would count Sonia Casey as a sporting connection. Probably not.

'Because he has some here,' Ethan said. 'A man went to see him yesterday. Suarez swears he was the assistant coach of the Bradenton Bucks. That's a local college team. Football.'

'Suarez?'

'Rule Suarez. Works for me.' Ethan looked at his watch. 'I should call him.' He got up and eased his plump thighs round the table. He was gone for about five minutes. There was swampbuggy racing on the television, but no one seemed to be watching. On the other side of the bar a band was tuning up.

Ethan came back and said, 'No action tonight. He took a flight to Miami. We have someone on the plane.'

'He jumps around like a bloody flea,' Anna grumbled, rising to her feet. She followed Ethan out through the back door.

He said, 'You sure he doesn't deal in sports equipment?'

'No I'm not sure,' Anna said. She felt very tired all of a sudden. 'He might deal in rhinoceros horns for all I know. But I only saw woollies and rejuvenation gel.'

'You say the darnedest things,' Ethan remarked, as they went out into the warm night air. 'Stay in touch now.'

Chapter 49

AGAIN IT WAS at three in the morning when Anna woke up, her heart pumping and sweat rolling off her body. She opened the window and heard the sea sighing and slushing. The walls seemed to pulse with heat and a nameless anxiety. She washed in the tiled, mirrored bathroom and padded barefoot downstairs to make some tea. The moon seemed closer than home.

But at eight-thirty she was on court with three middle-aged women trying to serve into the sun. On the next court four old men, each of them wearing surgical supports on knees, ankles and elbows played loudly. Not one of them looked to be under seventy-five but their faces were brown and boyish. There were tennis players as far as the eye could see and all the parking bays were filled with long sleek cars.

The three women in Anna's game knew each other well. She was glad she had played with Lara in the park because it had given her the ability to recognise both the friendliness and determination to be on the winning side. The women were there to have some fun and exercise, but it was taken for granted that winning was fun and losing was not. The idea that a game was fun in itself did not seem to be part of the equation. Whenever they changed ends the talk around the water fountain was about dinner parties or redecorating bedrooms, but on court they took no prisoners.

Anna concentrated on not making a fool of herself. What she lacked in experience of club doubles she made up for in leg work.

Nobody seemed particularly curious about her except once, at the water fountain, Marcia Gold said, 'I gather you are in the clothing business, Anna.'

'Not really,' Anna said, getting ready to lie.

But it wasn't necessary. The subject had only come up because the women were talking about clothes and not because they were interested in Anna.

Not everyone was so incurious. On her way back to shower and change the blond man she had last seen stringing a racket stopped her. He was spraying insecticide on the flower borders round the courts.

'I was watching you,' he said, lowering the gauze mask protecting his nose and mouth. 'You'll run your legs off if you aren't careful. That would be too bad.'

The blond was a bleach job, Anna decided. It went with the muscles and cut off jeans.

'We don't see too many like you here,' he went on. 'This place is for the newly weds or nearly deads. Which are you?'

'Nearly wed,' Anna said loftily.

'No kidding,' he said. 'Well let me know if you get lonely. There are a couple of night spots I could show you.'

'Thanks,' Anna said. 'But I'm not lonely.' She was drenched with sweat and the only thing on her mind was a shower.

When she got upstairs however the phone was ringing.

'Hi, Anna,' Elaine said. 'Those women want to play with you again tomorrow. Can you make it?'

'Okay,' Anna said. 'Thanks. It was a good game.'

'Didn't I tell you? Anyway, they asked for you so I guess they like you.' She paused. 'Tony thinks you're kind of cute too.'

'Who's Tony?' Anna couldn't have felt less cute.

'You were talking to him just now.'

'He didn't say what his name was,' Anna said, thinking that Elaine must have X-ray vision. The conversation had taken place out of sight of the clubhouse.

'He has a reputation,' Elaine informed her. 'Seeing as you're a friend of Ms Crowther's I just thought I'd tell you.'

'What sort of reputation?'

'Just a reputation,' Elaine said. 'But it's up to you. I don't want to interfere.'

'Nothing to interfere with,' Anna said.

'Okay. Eight-thirty tomorrow then?' Elaine rang off.

After her shower Anna went out to the beach. She left the windows open so that she could hear the phone if it rang. There were a few sunbeds close to the concrete sea wall, and Anna lay down on one. Her calf muscles were cramping slightly and she wondered how much salt she was losing with all the sweat.

There was a small breeze from the gulf and the palm fronds clattered lightly. A flock of sandpipers tiptoed by, and on a breakwater a cormorant stood drying its wings.

Anna wondered if the sea was warm enough to swim in. In a while, she thought, she would jump off the sea wall and test it for temperature. Meanwhile she closed her eyes and turned her face to the sun.

A cold shadow fell across the sunbed. She looked up and saw a man standing there.

He said, 'You don't want to sleep in the sun – not till you're used to it.'

'I wasn't sleeping.' But she looked at her watch and found that over an hour had passed. She sat up, dazed. The man was a black shape against the sun. The sky was dazzling.

'Rule Suarez,' the man said. 'I work for Ethan Callow.' He held out his hand. 'Ethan said you'd like to know where Hugh Fellows is.'

Chapter 50

THEY WENT IN Rule's Buick. He drove at the statutory forty-five miles an hour, very relaxed, with his left elbow leaning on the window frame. They went north, across the bridge to Coquina. The road was lined with motels, bars and shops. There was more traffic.

'It's a house on Pier Drive,' Rule said. 'North of the island, right on the beach.'

'I thought he went to Miami last night,' Anna said. She glanced at his profile. He was solidly built, like an athlete, with black wavy hair and a moustache. His skin looked more weathered than tanned.

'He went and then he came back,' he told her shortly. 'This morning. I guess he's tired – he wasn't too hard to keep up with this time.'

'Were you on the flight with him?' she asked.

'I was not,' he said and drove on in silence. He seemed perfectly at ease. Anna wondered what he would be like to work with. Not a chatterer, that was for sure.

At the northern tip of the Key the road came to a T-junction. Opposite, a wooden pier stretched out a couple of hundred yards into the bay. At the end of it, perched lonely on the water, was a restaurant. 'Bad Billy's', the sign read, 'Coffee, Seafood, Chowder, Beer. Live and Frozen Bait'. The pier was dotted with fishermen and pelicans.

Rule turned left and followed the coast road. There were houses on either side, most of them quite old. Some of them had For Sale or For Rent signs on them. Some were overgrown with broadleafed trailing vines, some were trim and well kept.

Rule slowed down and jerked his thumb towards the window on Anna's side. The house he pointed to was made of cedar boards and built on stilts. Through them she could see an expanse of sand dunes. A Thunderbird was parked under the house. There was no one about. They cruised slowly past. The road curved and on the curve was a white TV repair van. Rule pulled in on the other side of it, out of sight of the house.

Ethan Callow got out of the van and came to Rule's window. He said, 'He's in there. Nobody has been in close. We're just discussing that now.' He was wearing a sky-blue leisure suit today. He went on, 'There's a path to the beach down there.' He pointed. 'You can get in back of the house that way. Did you tell her about Miami?'

'Not yet,' Rule said.

'Well, tell her. See what she has to say.'

Rule moved the car further down the lane and parked in the shade of a spreading pine tree. He took a pair of binoculars and a small radio transceiver from the glove compartment. Before he shut the compartment Anna saw a short black handgun. She began to feel very uneasy.

He locked the car and they walked up the pathway. It was like a tunnel overhung with thick greenery. At the end was blazing white sand. Anna was thinking about the handgun and American detective books. Maybe one man's fiction was another man's reality. If that was so, she was in the wrong place at the wrong time with the wrong company.

As far as she could tell he was not actually carrying a gun. He wore a light blouson jacket and white slacks, tropical weight, which would not do much to conceal a weapon. But she could not assume anything. What had seemed relaxed and solid about him now appeared to be hard and indifferent.

They emerged from the tunnel onto the beach. There was miles of it – billows of sand dunes with coarse grass and sea oats growing precariously out of them and then the flat sand to the water's edge.

On a day like this any comparable beach in Europe would be packed end to end with frying sun-worshippers. Here, there was hardly anyone about. A few people strolled in ones and twos on the water line. A few lay in the sun, fluorescent swimsuits punctuating the perfect white of the sand. Otherwise it was like the archetype of a honeymoon postcard.

'You don't say much,' Rule said, breaking a long silence.

'Nor do you,' Anna countered. She didn't think she was going to like him.

'I listen.'

'So do I,' Anna said, and they trudged through the dunes.

'Tough,' Rule said eventually. 'It doesn't make for good conversation.'

The dry sand made hard walking: it slid away and gave no purchase. Anna felt the sweat trickling over her ribs.

After a while Rule dropped down in the sand. He switched on his transceiver and muttered: 'Got it.'

'Roger,' someone muttered back. Rule switched off. He removed his sunglasses. Surprisingly, for someone so dark, his eyes were blue. He rolled over and edged, like a marksman, to the top of a sand dune with the binoculars. Anna sat with her back to him keeping an eye out for anyone coming up behind. It was an automatic response, but the familiarity of the action did not comfort her. She had never felt further from home.

'Want a look?' Rule said after a few minutes. He slid down and handed her the glasses. She crawled up and lay in the dent his body had made. It was very hot – as if the sand had absorbed the heat of his body as well as the heat of the sun. She rolled away to a cooler place. He was sitting, where she had sat, chewing on a stem of grass.

The house was a bungalow on eight legs. A porch ran along the whole of the ocean side of it. Casuarinas hid it from its neighbours. The windows were like blind eyes reflecting the light.

While she watched, a window slid open and a woman appeared on the porch. She stood for a moment gripping the rail and staring out to sea. She wore a floppy pink T-shirt which came down to her knees and a large pair of dark glasses. She looked older than Cynthia was supposed to be. Even with the binoculars Anna didn't know for sure.

The woman came down the steps and disappeared behind some dunes. When she re-emerged she was carrying a stack of folded beach chairs. A coloured parasol was lodged awkwardly under one arm. She propped the parasol against the steps and went up with the chairs. She took them inside the house. Then she came back for the parasol. The glass door closed.

'I think they're leaving,' Anna said.

'Shit,' Rule said. 'How do you know?'

'She brought the furniture indoors.'

'Shit,' Rule said again, and switched on the transceiver.

Anna kept her eyes on the house while Rule's voice murmured behind her.

'Anything?' he asked.

'Nothing.'

'Did you get a good look at her?'

'Not good enough.'

'See him?'

'No.'

The midday sun was as heavy as a blanket on her back. No one stirred from the house.

Rule said at last, 'He met with some heavy dudes in Miami. The names won't mean anything to you, but this is a partnership that has money in casinos, connections in Columbia. Scum.'

Anna didn't know what to say. She flicked the sweat off her upper lip and refocused the binoculars.

'Do you hear me?' Rule asked. 'Is this what Ms Crowther wants to know? Or am I telling you stuff you are already familiar with?'

His tone of voice was unmistakably hostile.

Anna couldn't help herself: she started to laugh.

'It is not funny,' Rule said. 'There's people working for Florida-Technics with wives and children.'

'Give me strength,' Anna said. 'I wouldn't bloody be here myself if I'd've known that. You're talking movies.'

'I'm levelling,' he said, still hostile.

Anna slid down the dune and handed him the binoculars. 'Then I'm on the next plane out of here,' she said. 'Did you tell Ms Crowther about Miami? What did she say?'

'Are you serious? She's been stringing us along since the beginning. We kept telling her this was more than a runaway daughter.'

'Not to her it isn't. Bloody hell, she's a respectable business woman. My governor checked her credentials. Didn't yours?'

'Sure he did,' Rule said stiffly. They stared at each other. The hostility was mutual. Anna couldn't see his eyes.

The radio crackled, and Rule turned away to talk. When he turned back he said, 'They're on the road.'

He got up and brushed sand from his slacks. They started the long trek back to the car.

Chapter 51

'SEE, IT'S LIKE this,' Rule said. He was chewing a slice of pizza but he didn't seem hungry. 'Was a guy once – call him Billy. His wife was divorcing him and it was a mess, a real mess. She was asking too much – alimony, you know, and child support. So Billy, well he thought he was tough. He sent someone round to the office where the wife worked, you know, to rough her up a little. Get her to be more reasonable. Only when the guy got there the wife was out of the office. So the guy roughed up the secretary instead. Because, see, she fitted the same description as the wife, and the guy hadn't met either of the two ladies before.' He took another bite of pizza.

Anna waited. There was a chicken sandwich on the dash in front of her, but she wasn't hungry either. The air-conditioner was full on.

'But, the point is this,' Rule went on, 'the office where the wife worked was the development corporation of a big hotel complex. Right here on the Keys. You probably seen it. But the money for the development – the money came from Miami. Some conglomerate on the Gold Coast diversifying, right? The guys we're talking about are not seedy little punks dealing in half ounces. These guys have seedy little punks dealing for them. But they also have attorneys, financial advisers, developers telling them how to invest their money. It's big business. Hotels, condominiums. Respectable stuff. But . . .'

He took a swig from his Coke can, still staring through the windscreen at the ocean. 'But,' he continued, 'it is still dirty money, and the guys we're talking about are still very, very heavy people. Who do not appreciate some little punk roughing up the office staff. What I'm saying is, Billy thought he was in a domestic situation. He thought he was just saving on a little alimony. And the first time he realised his mistake someone was shooting the back of his head off, right next to his own pool. No more Billy, Okay?'

Over the sea, a tern, like a white swallow, wheeled and dived. When it came up, the caught fish was only a glint of silver in the sun.

'Okay?' Rule repeated. 'Am I getting through?'

'Loud and clear,' Anna said.

'Well, thank you, ma'am,' Rule said. 'I thought I was maybe just flapping my gums.'

'So what are we doing here?' Anna asked. 'Why are we sitting here, eating lunch, waiting for your boss to tell us where our so-called "domestic situation" is hiding? Why aren't I packing my suitcase? Why aren't you on your way back to the wife and kids?'

'I don't have a wife and kids.' Rule sighed. 'Because we both work for a couple of assholes,' he said. 'And we both got to make a living.'

'Speak for yourself,' Anna snapped. She was beginning to get a headache. 'What do you do in your spare time? – write film scripts? "Freeze, motherfucker" – that sort of thing?'

Rule sighed again. He said, 'You don't get it, do you?'

'Get bloody what? Hugh Fellows is mixed up with organized crime? But you're sitting on your duff eating pizza because a man's got to do what a man's got to effing do?' She leaned forward and bit a large chunk out of the chicken sandwich. A gob of mayonnaise fell on her thigh.

'I'm off my turf,' she said. 'Mob? For true?'

'That's what it looks like,' Rule said. 'I suspected you already knew. But maybe you don't. I'm just telling you to be careful.'

On the pier a fat family, dressed like easter eggs, walked slowly out towards the restaurant.

Anna said, 'What *do* you do in your spare time?' She had been rude and was trying to make amends.

'I go fishing,' Rule said. 'Every chance I get.' He pointed at the horizon. 'Out there. You don't see land. You don't see anyone. You don't have to talk to anyone. Okay?'

'Okay,' Anna said. She ate the rest of the chicken sandwich in silence.

It was just a story, she thought, as she collected the rubbish from their meal. It didn't have to be worse than it already was. She walked across the sand and threw the rubbish into a bin. Pelicans were snoozing on the water in the shade of the pier.

Looking back at the Buick, she saw Rule talking on the car-phone. He had the car in gear when she got in. He turned south.

'Manatee Key,' he said. 'A motel. It looks like he's stashing her.'

After a while, Anna said, 'That story about Billy – how do you know it was the mob?'

And after an even longer while, Rule said, 'I was the guy working on the divorce. For the wife. I was the guy walked in and found Billy covered in ants. I was the guy warned off. Right?'

He was angry but it only showed in his voice. His big hands seemed quite relaxed on the wheel. Anna hoped they were going close enough to the tennis club for her to pick up her own car.

Chapter 52

THE SAND DOLLAR Motel advertised a heated pool, shuffle-board, colour TVs and Efficiency Apartments. From the road all that could be seen was a two-storey building on two sides of the car park. Anna could not see the Thunderbird.

They drove slowly past and pulled up outside a shop called the Little General. Ethan Callow was drinking coffee from a paper cup. He threw the cup away and came to Rule's door.

He talked across Rule to Anna. 'If you don't mind,' he said, 'we'll go on to your place. I don't like it out here on the main road.'

The tennis club was about a mile and a half further on. Only the two pros were on court. Lew seemed to be conducting a clinic for six middle-aged women. A couple stood on the clubhouse steps. Even numbers, Anna thought, as they drove by. Everyone came in pairs.

Tony and a skinny boy were brushing grit off the white lines on one of the empty courts. He raised his hand in an ironical salute as she let Rule and Ethan into the house.

Upstairs, they sat primly side by side on the sofa. If Rule had been British, Anna thought, he would have looked around at all the designer good taste and said, 'All right for some.' As it was he produced a packet of cigarettes and said, 'Mind if I smoke?'

Ethan looked mildly offended.

There was no ashtray among all the cut glass do-dahs so Anna gave him a saucer. Ethan got up and opened the window onto the screened porch. The phone rang.

Quex said, 'Hello, sweetheart. I've been trying to call you for hours. How's it going?'

'Well, getting busy,' Anna said. Rule lit his cigarette and blew a plume of smoke at one of the Japanese prints.

'When are you coming home?' Quex asked, his voice thin and distant.

'I can't talk at the moment,' Anna said.

'Company?'

'That's right. I'll phone back later.'

'If you can find the time,' Quex said. 'Who knows, you may be lucky.'

'I'll phone later,' Anna said. 'Please.'

Quex rang off.

Ethan said, 'I've put a couple of guys on the beach. If we can get a picture and you identify it positively, we've done our job. I really hope it's the right woman because we've let Hugh Fellows go. Did Rule tell you about Miami?'

Anna nodded.

Ethan continued, 'I mean, there are some things we don't like to mess with without good reason. I told Ms Crowther. We'll do a job for her, of course we will, but she should know that when it comes to defensive rebounding the kind of guys we're talking about play rough.'

'Sorry?' Anna said.

'If it's the right girl,' Rule said, 'you're on your own.'

Anna nodded again.

'I wouldn't put it quite like that,' Ethan said.

'Coffee or tea, anyone?' Anna asked. She wished the two strangers would put on their baby-coloured jackets and get out. Now. She wanted to telephone Quex and have a cosy conversation abut moving house or watering the plants or what Selwyn had been up to.

'Nothing for me,' Ethan said. 'I've got things to do. But I will be in touch.'

He got up and looked at Rule. Rule took a long drag on his cigarette and then stubbed it out in the saucer. He got slowly to his feet.

'Too bad,' he said. 'I never had a British cup of tea before. A nice cuppa tea,' he added in what he probably thought was an English accent.

'Another time,' Anna said, politely holding the door open and stifling a strong urge to plant her foot on his muscular rear as he went downstairs.

She waited until she heard the two cars drive away and then she filled the kettle to make tea for herself. Sod him. But she left the saucer with his cigarette stub in it. It made the place look lived in. At last the perfect living room smelled of something other than flowery air freshener.

She called her own number. The phone rang twenty times. No one answered. She called Selwyn. No one answered. She even punched out Quex's number in Fulham. The kettle boiled.

She made tea in the coffee pot and then called Lara Crowther in New York. Ms Crowther was in a meeting. She dialled Brierly Security's number.

Jenny said, 'Anna Lee! Oh, you are lucky. What's it like over there?'

'Great,' Anna said, glumly. 'Would you put me through to Bernie, please?'

'I bet you're getting a wonderful tan,' Jenny went on. 'Beryl's spitting cinders.'

'Don't tell her I phoned,' Anna said. 'I just want to talk to Bernie.'

'She's in with his lordship,' Jenny said. 'What do you do all the time over there? Are the fellers hunky? – like Miami Vice?'

'I'm on the other side of Florida,' Anna told her.

'Yes but have you met anyone?' Jenny asked, with a special emphasis on the word 'met'.

'There's a dishy tennis pro,' Anna said, wondering why she was playing. 'But he's an Aussie.'

'A tennis pro,' Jenny breathed. 'I'm going to save up for a ticket, starting now. It sounds a t'rific place.'

'It is,' Anna said. 'Can I speak to Bernie now? It costs a fortune phoning transatlantic.'

'Transatlantic,' Jenny said, impressed.

After a few clicks and a whirr Bernie said, 'Hello, love. What can I do for you this drizzly afternoon?'

'Well it's nothing really,' Anna said, 'but just before I left I went to see the accounts manager of the garage William Herridge owes money to. He said he'd go through his files and ring back but . . .'

'Hold hard,' Bernie interrupted. 'William Herridge?'

'You know, that promotion check I was doing before Mr B. gave all my cases to Sean. And he didn't follow up properly.'

'Oh, yes?' Bernie said.

'Can you phone him?' Anna asked. 'The accounts manager, I mean. The details should be in my desk. It's been on my mind because I took off the next day and never followed up myself.'

'Can do,' Bernie said. 'Now, what's up? Feeling lonely?'

'Of course not,' Anna said.

'Just guilty about William Herridge?'

'That's Herridge with a D,' Anna said.

'I know how to spell Herridge,' Bernie said, sounding as if he were in the next room. 'If you want to tell me what's bothering you, ring me at home this evening when there's no chance of Beryl listening in.'

'Give my love to Syl,' Anna said before hanging up.

She took her tea out on to the porch and sat facing the sun and the sea. An hour later she phoned Lara again but she was still in a meeting. Quex still didn't answer.

Anna washed and dried her cup. She washed and dried her tennis clothes. She wrote up her notes. When she phoned again, Lara had gone home and Quex was still out. She rang Lara's private number but all she got was an answering machine.

Anna turned on the TV. She turned it off again. She switched on the radio. It was a programme of oldies – Mick Jagger singing 'Moonlight Mile'. Anna looked in the fridge. There was nothing there she wanted to eat.

'Oh, I am sleeping under strange, strange skies,' sang Mick Jagger.

Anna switched off the radio. She closed the porch door and collected her bag.

Chapter 53

AT THE CLUBHOUSE Elaine was closing the shop. The bar and restaurant were still open.

Elaine said, 'You going to eat here tonight? If you want a change try Eva's down the road. The lasagne is fantastic. You like Italian?'

Anna said she loved Italian.

Elaine switched on an elaborate alarm system and they went through to the bar. It was not busy, and all the ashtrays were clean.

Elaine said, 'That was a cute guy came for you this morning.' She ordered a Coke and Anna asked for a beer.

'Lew figures he's a jock,' Elaine went on. 'But I say he's a cop.'

At the other end of the bar Lew and the blond pro were eating salted nuts. Lew looked over and grinned.

'He's a friend of a friend,' Anna said. 'We had lunch down at the pier on Coquina.'

'Bad Billy's?' Elaine said. 'It's a neat spot, but the food is just terrible. Is he a cop?'

'He didn't say so,' Anna said. 'He knows Ms Crowther so I assume he's in the rag trade. All he talked about was fishing.'

'Lew has a boat. Me, I get sick just looking at a boat. But I get along with cops. Didn't you think he was kind of cute?'

'What made you think he was a cop?'

'Cops have a way of looking at things,' Elaine said. 'Like there was something hidden behind them. See, he just came in and asked where he would find you. So I didn't really talk to him. But I thought, he's kind of cute and then I thought, I bet he's a cop.'

'She thinks he's a cop because she thinks he's cute,' Lew said coming over to stand behind Elaine's stool. 'Or she thinks he's cute because she thinks he's a cop. She's got a thing for cops.'

'I do not!'

'Cute cops,' Lew said. 'I told her tennis pros are a safer bet. Are you eating?'

'Okay,' Elaine said, slipping off the bar stool.

They left by the door which led onto the pool area. Lights were on and the pool glowed turquoise in the dusk. A man and a woman were swimming sedate and patient lengths.

Anna looked into the restaurant. A few couples were eating an early dinner. Even numbers again, she thought, and decided to go somewhere else.

She went back to her house for the car, but by the time she got there her appetite was gone. She walked out onto the beach instead.

The sun had almost disappeared, leaving blood-red stains on the horizon. The sea was black and indigo with a white lacy border where tiny waves licked at the sand.

Anna jumped down from the sea wall and began to walk north. The Sand Dollar Motel was somewhere about a mile and a half away. She wondered if she would know it when she got there.

As it turned out she did not have to know it. A grey figure emerged from among the black of pines and palms, and Rule said, 'Can't keep away, huh?'

He spoke softly, but from behind a screen of sea oats she could hear the sound of hearty voices and smell the smoke and meat of a barbecue.

'Anything happening?' she asked.

'Not a thing.' He led her through dry sand into the cover of some pines. 'Hugh's gone, and she hasn't been out since he left.'

The motel was built like a three-sided courtyard around a swimming pool. In the arc lights the grass looked false, like a snooker table, and the pool shone like coloured glass.

The unit Hugh had taken was on the ground floor closest to the sea. The porch door opened right onto the sand and from there it was only a few steps through the sea oats to the water.

The curtains were drawn but a sliver of flickering blue light showed that the TV was on.

Rule said, 'He left her without a car. She won't be going

anywhere unless he comes back for her. There's a guy out front watching for him.'

Anna sat down in the sand and pine needles. She leaned back against a tree trunk. To her right the sea whispered, and to the left the barbecue party became more raucous.

After a while she said, 'Why do they call you Rule?'

'Raoul,' he said.

'Were you a cop?'

'Yeah. You?'

'Yes.'

By now the moon was up, and it seemed to lie on its back just above the ocean. Rule was just another shadow in the dark. She liked him better that way.

Half an hour later the flickering blue light went out. Rule moved quietly away. When he came back he said, 'I think she's gone to bed.'

They sat and waited in silence. Anna watched the silver road to the moon. Another half hour drifted by, and then Rule said, 'Who is she? If she's the right one.'

'Cynthia Garden,' Anna said. 'Possibly Cynthia Fellows. She ran away with him when she was under age. Her mother's been doing her nut since.'

The tree trunk was digging into her back. She shifted position.

'Apart from you and your mate,' she said, 'is there anyone else keeping an eye on this place?'

'No.'

'What about him ducking and diving?' she asked. 'Has anyone actually seen anyone else following him?'

'No. You think we're interpreting this wrong?' The hostile note was back in his voice.

'No,' Anna said quickly. 'It's just that what you describe is so different from how he behaves in London.'

She remembered Hugh waiting in the queue for a number 31 bus, the women looking at him and nudging each other. She sighed, and was about to say something else when another shadow crackled softly through the pine needles.

Someone said, 'Rule?'

'Yo-o,' Rule said. 'You're late.' He got up. 'We're relieved,' he told Anna. 'C'mon, I'll give you a ride back.'

They walked down the beach and then cut through an empty site to the road.

Anna said, 'Has anyone been back to the house on Coquina?'

Rule looked at her. 'What are you thinking of?' he asked.

'Just curious,' she said. 'Wondering why they left, what they left behind.'

'Yeah,' he said. 'But we aren't finding out. Ethan was happy to let Hugh go. The smart money says leave him be.'

They got into the Buick and Rule dropped her off at the gates of the tennis club.

Tennis players went to bed early, Anna decided. There were only a few cars outside the clubhouse and most of the units were dark and shut up.

She let herself in and went straight to the phone. Lara's answering machine gave out the same message, and when she phoned her own number her own voice told her there was no one there. Quex had obviously come home and remembered to switch on the machine. Or maybe he was there but didn't want to speak to her.

Anna opened a tub of potato salad and made a cup of tea. While she was eating she stared at the phone. Was Lara avoiding her?

She rinsed her plate and cup, took a deep breath and phoned Penny Garden in Oakleigh.

Eventually, Penny answered. She sounded half asleep, and it took her a moment to remember who Anna was. When she did she became quite animated. At any rate she sounded almost normal.

'Larry says you've found Cyn,' she said. 'How is she? What's she doing?'

'Hold on,' Anna interrupted. 'Hugh Fellows is living with a young woman who could be Cynthia. But I haven't seen her properly, so don't get your hopes up yet.'

'Please, please let it be her,' Penny said, as if Anna had the power to force an identity onto a strange girl. 'You can't imagine what it's like – not knowing. You haven't got any children, have you? You can't just let them go – never see them again – not know if they're dead or alive.'

'Tell me about your daughter,' Anna said. 'Tell me what happened.'

'I thought Larry told you.'

'She told me a bit,' Anna said. 'I don't think Lara paid much attention to Cynthia before she left.'

'That's right,' Penny exclaimed. 'She always treated my family as if they were a distraction. She thinks I'm some sort of "artist".' She said artist in an American accent. It sounded almost cruel.

'She's got no idea,' she went on. 'She's never had a child either. She doesn't even *like* Cyn. She hates Chris. She *wants* them gone.'

'She's paying me to find Cyn,' Anna protested.

'Only because I won't work.'

Anna was jolted: won't work and can't work were two very different conditions.

'You don't think she actually wants Cyn to come back?' Penny continued. 'God, I remember one time when Larry was here in the afternoon and she gave Cyn money to stay away. I didn't know about it till she came back at suppertime. Larry had met her when she came home from school and sent her off again. She went to the local coffee bar and arcade, where all the rough kids go, and she had a whale of a time. But she was only twelve, and I was furious with Larry'.

'Tell me about when Cyn first met Hugh,' Anna asked.

'That was a couple of years later – we were all up in my workroom,' Penny said. 'Larry had brought Hughie to meet Chris and me. We were looking through some drawings for the spring collection. Cyn had just been shopping with a friend from school and she'd bought a skirt and top – which she was wearing. And she burst into my workroom saying, "Look! What d'you think?" Anyway, she was a bit punky at that stage, you know, a bit anti-style, and she looked – well – funny. Larry thought she looked terrible. But Larry's taste is awfully mainstream.'

'Do you remember how Hugh reacted?'

'He just laughed, I think. It never occurred to me then that he was a paedophile.' Penny sounded vicious. 'If I'd known what he was up to I'd've cut his heart out.'

'You don't know when it started?'

'I didn't know anything. She was just a normal teenager. I worked it out afterwards from what her friends said, but I don't know how or when it happened. I thought Hughie came here to see Chris and me. I've never been able to talk about it to Chris because he left too. He just walked out. He said he wanted more out of life and he has never been back. Not a letter, not a phone call. Nothing.'

'Nothing at all?' Anna asked, wondering how much to say. 'What has Lara told you?'

'Nothing. Nothing about Chris. Have you found him too?'

'Well, no,' Anna said. 'But I've heard he was operating from Italy.'

'Italy?'

'Yes. As far as I can tell he does the buying while Hugh does the selling.'

'Doesn't he care at all?' Penny cried. 'How could Chris still be working with Hughie. Cyn is his daughter too.'

'I don't know,' Anna said. 'What do you think?'

'Me?' Penny said, sounding surprised to be asked. 'Sometimes I think my relationship with Larry has poisoned my family against me.'

It was Anna's turn to be surprised. 'What do you mean,' she asked.

'Nothing,' Penny said. 'Nothing specific.' She rang off, leaving Anna feeling uneasy.

Chapter 54

LARA HAD SAID they all met on the lawn. Penny said it was in her workroom. Perhaps no one had noticed when Cyn first met Hugh.

Anna went to sleep thinking about how little adults know about their children's lives. And vice versa. She dreamed about a large house where the people who lived upstairs had no notion that a family of dwarfs inhabited the cellar.

She woke up at three o'clock sharp, heart pounding and ready for anything. Jetlag had to be good for something, she reasoned, when half an hour of tossing and turning had done no good at all. In the end she got up, dressed, and took the Tempo out of the garage. It was as good a time as any for a drive to Coquina. The road was empty. She felt as if she were the only person in the world awake. A light mist had rolled in from the sea and the air was clammy.

On Pier Drive she stopped the car short of the stilted house, and walked towards it through the dark. She could just make out the shape of the house and the tilt of the stairs up to the porch. She circled once, and then again. Nothing stirred. Even the sea seemed to be holding its breath.

She switched on her torch, and, covering most of the light with her hand, crept up the stairs.

She was not the first. A quick sweep of torchlight showed her that the screen on the door to the porch had been slit. The door swung back at the touch of her hand. She switched the torch off. The lock had been forced and the glass door into the house slid open. She moved slowly forwards and came face to face with drawn curtains.

Advance or withdraw? The smart money, as Rule put it, said withdraw.

Anna advanced, very slowly, very carefully, pushing aside the curtain. The air was quite still and smelled fetid. When she was quite certain she was alone she turned the torch on again and was met by a scene of complete chaos.

The room had been turned upside down. Armchairs, sofas, were on their backs with the bottoms ripped out. The carpet was torn back and floorboards jemmied up.

The two bedrooms were in a similar condition. Plasterboard had been levered from the walls, the ceilings and light fixtures similarly attacked.

In the bathroom the lid was off the lavatory cistern and the ceiling had been utterly destroyed. No doubt someone had gone up to look in the water tank.

She did not need a torch in the kitchen because the refrigerator door was open. The light from the fridge reflected in puddles of water from the defrosting freezer mixed with cereal from emptied packets.

It was not senseless vandalism. It was the result of a systematic search which included the fabric of the house itself.

Something had been found.

There were two empty cartons on the floor. Both had Cara Cosmetics stencilled on them. Close to the boxes were three empty jars. Anna picked one up. The label on it read Cara Defoliant Cream. But the jar was absolutely clean – not a trace of cream, defoliant or otherwise. Three clean jars. But the boxes had been torn open. They had obviously contained something. And that something was now missing.

Anna wiped the jar she was holding on the hem of her T-shirt.

She left the ruined house and drove back to the tennis club, shivering.

So much for jetlag. It was a pulse-racing business, out at the dead of night in a foreign country.

Chapter 55

'SHE DOESN'T PLAY tennis,' Betsy Hicks said, talking about her daughter. 'But she's on her college track team. Eight hundred metres. Ver-ee competitive. It's hard to get selected.'

The others murmured congratulations. They were gathered around the water fountain at the end of the game. Anna sat in the shade feeling about as competitive as a used tea bag.

'My son,' Marcia said, 'Monty, the one at medical school, you know? He played a lot of basketball in high school. Was on the school team. But it is so-o different in college. Bigger kids, kids on sports scholarships. He gave it up. I guess track is still relatively relaxed, some places. They don't have the same pressure, like with inducements and sponsorship and all the other stuff.'

Over on the pro courts Anna could hear Lew yelling, 'Hustle, Dave! Move those feet. Punch it away.' Another giant teenager was being put through the wringer under the eyes of his admiring grandparents.

Anna's foursome left the court to an ancient mixed doubles match, and Anna went back to shower and change. The word was that tomorrow Carol Biermann would be back. Anna hoped she would get a day to recover. Her muscles felt empty – there was no coil left in her spring. A 3 am start to the day had not improved her stamina.

The doorbell rang just as she got out of the shower. Looking down from the window she saw Rule, arms folded, leaning against the Buick watching the action on the nearest court. He looked nonchalant to the point of boredom. Anna ran down, wrapped in a towel, to let him in.

'You play tennis?' he said, following her up to the living room.

Anna hitched the towel firmly round her. It was not the way she preferred to open the door. The phone rang.

Lara said, 'You called Oakleigh last night.' She sounded furious. 'I will not put up with you bothering Penny. She's under enough pressure. I employed you to sort out her problems, not add to them.'

'Did you?' Anna asked. Rule sat down. She turned her back on him. 'I called you four or five times yesterday, and left four or five messages. I do not have enough information. I've never had enough information. I should have talked to Penny long before now.'

'What did she say?' Lara squawked. 'She's in the middle of an emotional breakdown – she doesn't make any sense half the time.'

'She makes sense,' Anna said, keeping her voice level against a rising tide of temper. 'What's senseless is you ignoring warnings about what's been going on here.'

'You've been talking to Ethan Callow. The man is a paranoid. It's an occupational disease. I thought you, at least, would have enough nous to recognize that.'

'Did he tell you that Hugh moved house yesterday?'

'No.'

'Well he did, and the house he moved out of was turned over last night – broken into and torn apart. Professionally. I think the people at Florida-Technics know what they're talking about.'

Lara said nothing. Anna heard Rule get out of his chair. She swung around to face him. She said, 'Any comment, Ms Crowther?'

Lara was silent.

'Because you've got me sitting out here like a bleeding lemon with no information and . . .'

Lara hung up.

Anna put the receiver gently into its cradle. She said, 'I'm having what you might call a breakdown in communications. In other words the woman was bloody gob-struck'. She stamped upstairs to dress feeling angry and undignified. She was never at her best in a bath towel.

When she came down again Rule was on the porch watching a lone Chris-Craft motor across the horizon. She put the kettle on and made tea.

From the porch, Rule said, 'I guess she's been giving you the run-around too. Ethan told me he couldn't get a hold of her last night either.'

Anna took the tea out and put it on a little glass table. Rule stood with his hands in his pockets watching her pour.

'I brought you some pictures,' he said. 'See if you can identify them.' He looked suspiciously into his teacup.

Anna looked at the pictures. They were of Cynthia Garden. Without the big sunglasses she could see her mother's wide grey eyes, broad cheekbones and brow. She seemed to be collecting sea shells. The shadows were long. There were twenty shots in all. Cynthia walked towards the camera carrying a plastic bag. She wore shorts and a rugby shirt. In a couple of shots she was rinsing something in the sea. And in the last two she was looking almost directly into the lens.

'It's her,' Anna said. 'I suppose that means I'm on my own.'

'We got lucky,' Rule said. 'There was a flock of ibis out on the beach early, and our guy just had to look like he was taking pictures of birds.'

'If I stay, that is,' Anna said. 'I've half a mind to pack it in anyway.'

'Is that straight goods about the house on Pier Drive?' Rule asked.

'More than half a mind,' Anna said. 'I've worked for some lulus in my time but that woman takes the cake.'

The phone rang again. Rule said, 'The house on Pier Drive – did you really go back there last night?'

'Yes,' Anna said and went to answer the phone.

Lara said, 'Anna, I'm sorry. I really want to apologise. I don't know what you must think of me.' She sounded quite different. Her voice was low and under control.

'That's all right,' Anna mumbled awkwardly. She was not frequently apologised to and she felt disarmed by it.

'I didn't get back to you last night because I was with my mother,' Lara went on. 'She's eighty-three and not in the best health. It's no excuse, but if I over-reacted it's partly because I'm worried sick about her.'

'It doesn't matter,' Anna said.

'Well, it does. You're right – I have just one aim in mind, contacting Cyn, and I've ignored the other issues. But don't you see, if Hugh has gotten himself mixed up with something bad it's vital we get her out of there. She's only, what, seventeen, eighteen? Do you know where she is? Have you identified her positively yet?'

'One of Mr Callow's men is here right now,' Anna told her. 'He brought some pictures. It's Cyn all right.'

Lara sighed. 'Good,' she said. 'So what happened yesterday? You found her and then they moved out?'

'They found where Hugh was living, but I couldn't be sure about who he was living with. And he only stayed long enough to pack a bag and move out.'

'So where are they now?'

'I don't know where Hugh is. But Cynthia's at a motel not far from here. He left her and went off again. I don't know if he's been back. Mr Callow doesn't want anything to do with Hugh any more, and after last night, I can see his point.'

'You went back to the house he moved out of?'

'Yes.'

'And you found it had been searched?'

'Yes. Thoroughly.'

'You mustn't take that kind of risk,' Lara said. 'It is all very well in London where you know your way around. But not here. You've got to keep a low profile. Concentrate on Cyn. We have got to get her out of there.'

'She might not want to go,' Anna said. 'From what you told me she could be married. This is what I mean about not having enough information. You didn't tell me that till a day or so ago. Both you and Mrs Garden talk about Cyn as if she's a little girl who was abducted by a dirty old man. That's emotional, not factual.'

'Well, then you must establish the facts,' Lara said. 'I don't know them. But not knowing is no excuse for not trying. And it *is* a fact that Cyn is in her teens whereas Hugh is in his forties. I think that is some indication that undue pressure was brought to bear. And if Hugh is in trouble that means she needs protection. We've got to try. Don't you think we have to try?'

'I suppose so,' Anna said. 'But it's her decision in the end.'

'Right,' Lara said, sounding satisfied. 'I'll go with that. And I'll talk to Ethan Callow – make sure you have some back-up in case you need it. I mean,' she added hurriedly, 'if he doesn't want to mess with Hugh that's fine by me, but if they move again you might need some help finding them. Is there anything else I can do?'

'Money,' Anna said. 'I thought I might move into the motel myself.'

'Use your credit card. I'll reimburse you.' Lara paused. 'You have got a credit card, haven't you?' She rang off suddenly as usual.

Anna's tea had gone cold and she poured herself another cup.

Rule said, 'I'm not wild about your tea. It's not bad, but I'm not crazy about it.'

The sun was streaming onto the porch. Anna sat down and closed her eyes.

Rule said, 'I guess you are not going home.'

'Not today,' Anna said. 'Where do you live? Tampa?'

'Talked you out of it, did she?'

'She appealed to my sense of responsibility for damsels in distress.'

'Damsels, huh?' Rule said. He had his feet up and his hands behind his head. 'I'll try another cup of that tea. Could be it grows on you.'

Anna poured him another cup. If it were just the tennis and the sun, life would be perfect. Even the sense of lassitude would be enjoyable.

'What did you find at Pier Drive?' Rule asked.

'A shambles. Why? I thought you didn't want to know.'

'I don't like unanswered questions. Was it big or small?'

'I'd say they were looking for something big or a lot of something small. They had the plaster off the walls, they'd been through the ceiling, had the floorboards up, that sort of thing.'

'Any ideas?'

'Something he air-freighted over in cases of Cara Defoliant Cream. They found some of that.'

Rule sat up and sipped his tea. It had not, apparently, grown on him, and he put the cup down unfinished.

'Where's his warehouse?' Anna asked. 'Has anyone had a look at it?'

'You know what I'm thinking?'

'What? Drugs?'

'The guy he met in Miami is known in that connection.'

'But,' Anna said, 'This stuff comes from Italy. It's repackaged in London. Drugs from Milan to Miami – it's a bit arse forwards, isn't it?'

'Yeah.'

'Does Hugh have a record over here?'

'No. We checked that out.' Rule got to his feet. 'I gotta go,' he said abruptly.

Anna blinked at him.

'Mind if I give you some advice?' he said. 'Stay away from Hugh Fellows. I'm not going to give you his warehouse address because you might take it into your head to toss it yourself. You already took an awful chance going back to Pier Drive. If you got to involve yourself with the girl, be careful, you hear?'

He turned back at the door. 'I live in St Pete,' he said. 'You can always find me through the office.' He went.

Chapter 56

ANNA REGISTERED AT the Sand Dollar motel under the name of Ann Johnson. Hugh might never have seen her, but he knew her name because Sonia Casey would have told him.

The woman in the office had beige hair and sat behind a sign which read, Mrs Katheryn Katz, Reception. She wore her glasses on a chain round her neck and seemed worried that Ann Johnson had no husband.

'I would just hate to go on a trip solo,' she said, critically. And then, when she showed Anna the unit, she added, 'Of course, this is really a family motel.'

Anna's unit was on the ground floor of the main building behind the pool. There was a small bedroom and shower, a living room with a kitchenette, and a screened porch. In comparison to the house at Manatee Key Tennis Club it seemed distinctly cramped and a little shabby. Anna felt comfortable in it.

She slid open the glass doors onto the porch. Outside, sun-chairs and loungers were grouped around the pool. People lay like beached whales in the sun. In the pool a couple of children kicked and screamed in the shallow end and a large woman floated on her back in the middle.

Cynthia was not among the sunbathers.

Anna changed into shorts and a T-shirt and went outside. She skirted the pool and walked down to the Gulf.

Cynthia was on the beach lying face down on a sunbed. She was very brown. Close by, a muscular young man in shorts was raking pine needles and dried seaweed from the high water line. Shirtless, he flexed his pectorals, trying vainly to be noticed. Cynthia turned her head away from him and looked directly at Anna. Anna raised her hand in a casual greeting to a fellow guest and continued to walk down the beach.

Tiny coloured seashells speckled the sand. Anna picked up a few. It became like a treasure hunt, a mesmeric occupation: the slow walk, eyes down, hands pecking here and there for pretty colours and strange shapes.

Returning, she washed her trophies in the sea. Cynthia lay propped on one elbow reading a paperback.

'Do you know what these are?' Anna asked, displaying some shells on the palm of one hand.

Cynthia raised her dark glasses and said, 'Coquinas, kitten paws and scallops.' She sounded bored.

'I thought Coquina was a place,' Anna said.

'It's named after the shellfish,' Cyn told her. 'See those bubbles coming up when the waves pull back. Those are coquinas breathing. That's what the birds peck at in the sand. Where are you from?'

'London,' Anna said. 'You?'

'Oh, I've been everywhere,' Cyn said. 'I'm not from anywhere in particular. My parents were in the forces – we lived everywhere. Are you staying here long?'

'A few days,' Anna said. 'It's a great place for a holiday.'

'My husband's on business here,' Cyn said. 'So it's not really a holiday. Have you got a car?'

'Yes.' Anna was beginning to feel there was something odd about Cynthia. She had an 'I've seen it all' tone to her voice, but the look in her eye was of a child with a stolen treasure behind its back – a mixture of fear, guilt and triumph.

'Only my husband's taken our car,' Cyn went on, 'and I can't get out to the shops.'

'I'm going to Bay Plaza,' Anna said. 'You're welcome to come with me if you want.'

'San Isabel Circle's better.' Cynthia got to her feet. She moved stiffly. 'Come on, I'll show you.'

Anna wondered if Cyn had a stomach ache; she walked a couple of steps slightly bent over before straightening up. She was wearing a silver, pink and blue swimsuit, cut high at the bottom and low at the top – not the sort one would ever get wet. She did not, Anna thought, have her mother's subtlety with colour.

'What's your name, by the way,' Cyn asked.

'Ann,' said Anna.

'Serena,' said Cynthia.

'I'll put something on and see you in the parking lot,' she added.

The muscleman with the rake came over and said, 'You want to go out, I'll take you when I get through here.'

'No thank you very much,' Cyn said, in an accent which was pure Knightsbridge. She swept past him and entered her own unit via the porch, locking the screen door behind her. Anna went back to her room to change.

She waited in the car with the engine running and the air-conditioner turned full on. When Cynthia showed up she was wearing a bright yellow sundress which was split up to the thigh, showing a lot of tanned leg. She had done a full make-up job and looked about ten years older.

'Who's the feller with the muscles?' Anna asked as she joined the traffic on the road to San Isabel.

'We could have lunch at Cool Katie's,' Cynthia said. 'I'm starving.' She sounded like a kid on a treat. 'I haven't had any decent food for ages. I hate cooking, and Hugo never wants to go out. Then he goes off on a business trip and leaves me miles from any good shopping centres.'

'How long have you been married?' Anna asked, slowing down for an aged gent in a Cadillac.

'Nearly two years,' Cynthia said. 'But Hugo still wants to keep me all to himself.' She fluttered her fingers and made a modest little pout.

There was something so false in her delivery that Anna's hackles started to rise.

She drove past Manatee Key Tennis Club in silence.

Cynthia glanced at the little gold watch on her wrist. 'They drive so slowly here,' she complained. 'Don't you just long to put your foot down?'

Anna could not decide what she was up to. It almost sounded as if she were pretending to be English – the archetypal English woman in a Thirties play.

They crossed over from Manatee to San Isabel and Cynthia

gazed languidly out of the window as the bright green golf courses sailed by.

'Burt Reynolds lives here,' she said brightly. 'A lot of big stars have condos on these islands. My husband, you know, is a producer – a sort of impresario. He's putting a movie together right now. We met when I was at RADA.'

'You're an actress?' Anna murmured hopelessly.

'There's plenty of time,' Cynthia said. 'I'm recovering from a serious operation. I almost died, you know.'

'What was the matter?'

'Hole in the heart,' Cynthia said. 'It's the sort of thing that should have been diagnosed in childhood but I led such a gypsy life, you know, we never had a proper family doctor. And my mother was so neglectful, she never noticed anything was wrong.'

'That's a shame,' Anna said, nonplussed.

'The doctors in Mexico were wonderful,' Cynthia continued. 'Some of the best doctors in the world practise in Mexico City. I got married in Mexico City. My husband was making a movie out there. All the stars came to our wedding.'

Chapter 57

'GREAT VALUE PARTY Platters,' the sign read, 'Big Shrimp Spectacular!'

Cynthia had changed her mind about where to meet for lunch, and her second choice was Mario's Marina where the tables were outside under an awning, and the chowder smelled of diesel from the adjacent refuelling dock. The sign there said, 'Fuel Only. No Parking. No Smoking.'

While Anna waited, a boat as tall as a house, bristling with rods and aerials, manoeuvred backwards into the fuelling bay. The boat was named M.T. Pockets.

Anna waited a long time for Cynthia. When she turned up she was almost invisible behind a load of shopping bags, several of which came from Phoebe's Fashion and Sweet Petites.

'I just love shopping for clothes,' she said. 'Don't you? It's wonderful to be able to buy whatever you like. My parents were very well-off, but they were awfully mean. I never had a proper allowance.'

She ordered Baked Stuffed Shrimp, french fries and a mixed salad. Anna was amazed at how much she put away, the piled plates emptied in no time at all. But at least eating stopped her talking. She finished with a hot fudge sundae while Anna, rather flattened by the heat, was still spooning up her chowder.

'I can eat anything I like,' Cynthia said, 'and I never put an ounce on.'

She went to the ladies, and when, after nearly a quarter of an hour, she had not come out Anna followed. She found Cynthia, pale and shaky, leaning against the basins.

'I was sick,' she said, almost proudly. Her upper lip was damp with sweat.

'What's the matter?' Anna asked. She ran cold water over a paper towel and gave it to Cynthia to dab on her face.

'I haven't recovered from my operation yet,' she said. 'I almost died. Did I tell you that? It's a good thing I'm seeing my doctor.'

'When?'

Cynthia looked at her watch. 'I'll be late if I don't hurry,' she said.

'You didn't tell me you had an appointment.'

'Why should I tell you?' Cyn said rudely. 'You're not my mother.'

'I'm not your sodding chauffeur either,' Anna snapped. 'I was just giving you a lift to the shops. Remember?'

'I'm sorry,' Cyn said calmly. She gave Anna a long assessing look. 'I've been in a lot of pain lately.' She smiled bravely. 'You've been very kind. But if you want to go I can manage perfectly well on my own. I'm used to it.'

Anna stared at her. She had almost certainly been sick. That was no lie. Surely. Cynthia lowered her tawny eyelashes. Sweat stood out on her smooth brow.

'Well?' she asked without looking up.

In yet another copper-coloured mirror Anna saw herself, taller, straighter, stronger than wan Cynthia. Everyone's older sister, she thought, mournfully.

She said, 'Let's get you to the quack, then. Only less of the bullshit. All right?'

The doctor existed, and Cynthia did have an appointment. Anna sat in the waiting room under the eyes of a starlet in nurse's uniform and read *Smithsonian* for twenty minutes. Across the corridor a Cosmetic Dental Surgeon had his office, and through the glass doors people with already perfect smiles came and went.

The doctor seemed to be an ordinary general practitioner, not, as Anna might have expected, a psychiatrist. She couldn't make up her mind whether Cynthia was disturbed or simply reinventing herself in a silly pretentious way. It was something teenagers sometimes did – inventing a personality that went with their feelings rather than the facts, if the facts were unacceptable.

And reinventing yourself was a freedom offered by a foreign country as well. When there was no one around to remind you of who you were, you could be who you liked.

But whatever Cynthia was doing, it made things tricky for Anna.

Anna dealt in hard currency, not in Monopoly money. She could not assess what Cynthia would do when faced with the truth.

Your husband's in serious bother, Anna wanted to say. Your mum sent me to fetch you home. Do you want to come? Yes or no.

Did Cynthia know anything about Hugh? It was impossible to say.

Anna thought about Hugh. King Groper, he had been called. He was Sonia Casey's lover. He made the girls who worked for him on the King's Road blush. Lara said he was an animal. Cynthia's mother said he was 'public school smarmy'. He was not an honest man. He had dangerous connections in Miami. His house had been turned over by experts.

He was married to Cynthia. Or was he? How would he react if someone tried to take his woman away? At least he knew he was courting danger – Cynthia, perhaps, did not.

And then, as if she had conjured him, Hugh Fellows walked into the waiting room.

Anna took a brief and startled glance before burying her nose in *Smithsonian* again. He spoke to the receptionist and then came over to Anna's chair. He cleared his throat. Anna looked up politely.

He said, 'I gather you were kind enough to bring my wife here.' Very courteous, very urbane.

'Hello,' Anna said. 'It was no trouble. I had some shopping to do anyway.'

'I knew she had an appointment.' He sat down beside her. 'I came back specially but found she had already left. She must have thought I would forget.' He gave her a winning smile which almost concealed hard curious eyes. 'Are you staying at the Sand Dollar?' he asked.

'I came this morning,' Anna said. 'It's a lovely part of the beach, isn't it?'

'Lovely,' he said. 'Not many people know about it, fortunately. How did you?'

'Well, some friends in Sarasota told me how beautiful the Keys were. And I was driving past and it looked like one of the few places I could afford to stay in.'

'A happy accident.' He smiled his actor's smile.

'Oh yes,' Anna said enthusiastically. Her mouth grinned while her hands perspired. Nice tourist talk – nothing to worry a worried man. She looked into cold eyes and couldn't help remembering Coral's phrase, 'Gangrene of the heart.'

'You sound like a Londoner,' he observed smoothly.

'Shepherd's Bush. And you?' She had to ask. No curiosity would be just as suspicious as too much.

'Dorset, originally. But I've lived all over the world since then.'

'This is the first time I've been to the USA.' Out of the corner of her eye she saw the doctor's door open. She turned her head just in time to catch a look of complete dismay flash across Cynthia's face when she saw Hugh.

Anna kept talking. 'In a way, this was my last chance to come,' she said.

'Darling!' cried Cynthia. 'I wasn't expecting you. How nice!'

'Apparently not,' Hugh said. He got up and planted a kiss on her cheek. 'We must have got our wires crossed.' His arm went around her shoulder, hers around his waist – a picture of affection.

Anna said, 'I'll be on my way then.' She stood.

But they left the office together.

Hugh said, 'Darling, your friend was just telling me this was her last chance to come to the States.'

'Really?'

'You haven't introduced us,' he said, chidingly. Sweet, forgetful little wife.

'How silly of me,' she said. She looked as if she were trying to still chattering teeth. 'Hugh, this is . . . Ann.' She had to search her memory for the name.

'How do you do?' His handclasp was warm and lingering.

Anna said, 'Well, nice to have met you.' The afternoon sun was low and glaring. She walked away towards her car, but after only a few steps, Cynthia caught up with her.

She said, 'I left my shopping in your car. I just want to take two bags. Please. Hugh mustn't know how much I spent.' She spoke hurriedly, in a whisper.

Hugh came up behind them. 'Secrets?' he said in a jolly tone.

'Darling, don't be mad with me. We went shopping. Ann wanted to go shopping. And I bought a couple of dresses, just to keep her company.'

'Why should I be mad with you?' he asked, smiling at Anna.

'He thinks I'm extravagant.'

'Of course I do,' he said, fondly. 'That's my job.'

Anna said, 'Why don't we sort it out back at the motel?' She didn't want to open the boot in front of Hugh. Cynthia's 'couple of dresses' filled the whole space. 'I'll have to open all the bags to find yours,' she went on. 'And I'd rather not do it here.'

'Okay,' Cynthia said. She took Hugh's arm. Anna couldn't tell if she was relieved or not.

She drove away leaving them arm in arm — Cyn in her yellow sundress, Hugh elegant in a lightweight suit — a lovely couple.

As she drove she swung her head to loosen the tension in her neck. She went twice round San Isabel Circle to make sure Hugh was not following her, and then went back to the motel.

Just how extravagant Cynthia had been only struck her when she carried all the purchases into her room, and stowed them in the bottom of the fitted wardrobe. There were dozens of bags and boxes, everything from underwear to make-up, shoes to earrings — hundreds, perhaps thousands of dollars worth.

Frenzy feeding, she thought, and recalled the speed at which Cyn had guzzled her lunch.

Anna put away the groceries, and thought that it was much more reasonable to suppose that Cyn was replacing things lost at Pier Drive. She had, after all, left the house with only two suitcases. But if so, why was she afraid to admit it to Hugh? There could be no mistake about that. Cyn was afraid of Hugh.

Anna made a cup of tea in the tiny kitchenette. She now had

two kitchens, whereas at home in London, soon, she might not have even one.

The palms and pines cast long shadows over the pool. All the swimmers and sunbathers had gone in, leaving only the muscleman who was rearranging the chairs into tidy lines. Anna watched him, and wondered about Hugh's sudden appearance at the doctor's office. Suppose, she thought, Muscleman did not simply fancy Cynthia; suppose he was her minder.

If Cyn were not quite stable wouldn't Hugh employ someone to keep an eye on her, take her to the doctor? Then when Cyn unexpectedly went off with a stranger wouldn't her minder contact Hugh straightaway?

Chapter 58

IT WAS GROWING cold and the air was damp. For the first time since Anna had arrived she found herself in need of a sweater. She closed the glass doors and continued to watch Muscleman from behind the glass.

He had a T-shirt on now and was skimming the pool with a big net. The long muscles in his back stood out as he worked.

While he worked, Anna worried. What if Hugh and Cyn did not come back? Suppose Hugh had made the connection between nosey Anna Lee of the Official Receiver's Office in London and nice helpful tourist Ann Johnson? He was cautious enough to suspect her of anything. Perhaps she should have called herself Jane. Ann only brought Anna to mind.

What if Lara forgot to pay her back for the motel bill? Anna needed every penny she had to move house when she got home. Suddenly Anna couldn't imagine what she was doing in a motel on Manatee Key, USA, when she had so many pressing problems at home in London. Quex was quite right – she would go anywhere rather than face her own difficulties. Quex might be phoning her at the tennis club right now.

Mr Muscles finished with the net. He stacked it beside a hut which looked as if it hid a generator, and turned on the outside lights. A bank of cloud had built up on the horizon, hiding the sunset, and dusk that night was grey and gloomy. The pool lights seemed to extinguish what was left of the day.

A blue heron stalked up from the beach and stood on one leg staring at nothing. Lights went on in apartments all over the motel. Anna couldn't see Cynthia's window because it faced out to sea. She went through the apartment to the bedroom which looked onto the car park. There were a lot of cars but no

Thunderbird – which did not mean much. Hugh drove more than one car.

While she watched, Muscleman emerged from the walkway between pool and car park. He too seemed to be counting cars. After a moment he unlocked a grey pick-up truck, swung himself into the cab and drove away.

Anna let herself out of her apartment and walked down to the beach. It was becoming misty and the tide was out. There were no lights on in Cynthia's window. Shivering, she went back.

She stayed in the bedroom with the lights off, watching the car park. One by one, couples, dressed for an evening out, got into their cars and left. The receptionist locked up the office. She left too.

It was obvious, Anna thought. She had alerted Hugh. He had another bolthole. She would have to start again from the beginning.

Headlights swung into the car park. A tan Toyota Camray manoeuvred into a space. Hugh and Cynthia got out.

Anna let the curtain fall. She went through to the living room, and a moment later saw Hugh on the walkway. Cynthia was trailing disconsolately behind. They disappeared round the corner.

About ten minutes later Hugh came back alone. Again, Anna went through to the bedroom and watched while he got into the Toyota and drove away.

No sooner had his tail-lights vanished than she heard someone tapping at the glass doors. Cynthia had let herself into Anna's porch. Anna opened the doors for her.

'I can't stay long,' Cynthia said, breathlessly. 'He's coming back.' The yellow dress looked limp and grubby, and Cynthia herself had lost a lot of her starch.

'Can I take some of my things?' she asked. 'I don't know what I'm going to do with the rest. I can't even return them without him knowing. I don't know what I'm going to do.'

Anna took her into the bedroom and watched while she rummaged through the bags and boxes.

'Oh, God,' Cynthia moaned. 'What am I going to do?'

Anna said, 'You shouldn't be scared of your husband, love.'

'You don't know him,' Cynthia said. She stood up with a scarlet cocktail dress. 'What about this one? Isn't it great? Why, oh why did I buy all this?'

'You shouldn't be here,' Anna said. 'It's all wrong.'

'You won't tell him, will you?'

'I mean you shouldn't be married to someone you're afraid of.'

Cynthia picked out something pink and shimmering. 'You don't understand,' she said. 'It was a love match. It was Abelard and Eloise. Dante and Beatrice. We had the whole world against us. We still have.'

'What do you mean?' Anna asked. 'You've still got your family haven't you?'

'Help me,' Cynthia wailed. 'I don't know what to do. Just pick out two dresses for me. I can't choose. I told him it was only two, didn't I? And listen, you can keep whatever you like if you'll just take the rest back for me. I haven't got a car and he has me watched. He won't let me have anything. He's worse than . . .' She broke off and sat down heavily on the bed.

'Uh-oh,' she said. 'Those bloody pills are kicking in. I shouldn't have come out.'

'What pills?'

'Tranquillizers. He gives me tranquillizers.'

'When?'

'About ten minutes ago. I think. I should be in bed. He's coming back, didn't I say?'

'You did say,' Anna said. She picked up two dresses – a striped one and a blue one. She stuffed them in a carrier bag. 'You'd better hop it while you can still walk.'

'I should,' Cynthia agreed, still sitting. 'But I feel quite good really. It's the only time I ever feel good – before I go to sleep. I haven't done anything bad. No one can blame me. You know what my friend in Mexico said? She said, "It's never too late to have a happy childhood." Isn't that lovely? And she was old – thirty-five at least.'

'It's a nice thought,' Anna said. 'But when is Hugh coming back?'

'Don't know.' Cynthia lay back supporting her head on her hand. 'I never know. He never says. He does what he wants. And I do what he wants. I always do what people want. Except that then they don't want it anymore. But that's not my fault, is it? If people say they want something and I do it, and then they change their minds, I'm not to blame, am I?'

'Perhaps you should do what you want for a change,' Anna suggested. She stood there, holding the carrier bag, listening for cars in the car park.

'I don't know what I want,' Cynthia said dreamily. 'All I ever wanted was someone to love me. Something of my own.'

'Love,' she added, in a singsong, little girl whisper. 'It all turns out so dirty. He said I was all he ever wanted. He said I was young and pure. And I said, if what you want is young and pure why did you sleep with my mother? And he said it was because he wanted to get closer to me. But he didn't tell me till afterwards, when I wanted to go home. It's all so complicated – dirty and complicated.'

'Oh, shit!' Anna said, because it did seem dirty and complicated. 'Did you believe him? I mean, maybe he said that to stop you going home.'

Cynthia closed her eyes. 'I believe him. My mother never let me have anything of my own. I was always in the way. That's the story of my life – always in the way.' Her elbow gave way and she rolled onto her side. Her eyes opened a crack and she smiled sloppily.

'Never too late to have hap-pee chil-ood,' she mumbled and stuck her thumb in her mouth.

'Come on, ducky,' Anna said urgently. 'Time to go.'

Cynthia's eyes closed tight.

'Come on!' Anna shook her. 'This is the worst place to go bye-byes.'

Cynthia was fast asleep.

Headlights strafed Anna's curtains. She lifted the corner and through the crack saw Hugh get out of his car. He was carrying a pizza box. She dropped the curtain. There was not enough time to get Cynthia back to her own room.

Chapter 59

S HE COUNTED TO ten slowly. Then she grabbed her bag and keys. She hauled Cynthia up to a sitting position. She was as floppy as a rag doll but a hundred times heavier.

Anna let her go again. She ran out to the car and opened the back door. Came back, grabbed Cynthia, jostled her into an untidy fireman's lift. Bowed over under the weight she staggered out of the motel room. Cynthia slid inexorably down her back.

It was all for nothing: Hugh, out of breath, appeared from the side of the building.

He said, 'What the hell do you think you're doing?'

Caught.

'Where the hell were you?' Anna said furiously. 'Your wife's ill.'

When caught, lie your head off.

Hugh ran at her. He pinned her against the car and dragged Cynthia off her back. Cynthia slid to the ground and lay at their feet.

'Hello,' she said groggily.

'What're you doing?' Anna shouted, sandwiched between Hugh and the car. 'Your wife collapsed. I'm trying to get her to hospital.'

'Oh, yes?' he asked calmly. 'What hospital? Where? How would you know where to find a hospital? Aren't you supposed to be just a simple tourist?'

He jerked his arm up catching her a hard blow on the back of the head. She lashed back with her elbow. But he was too close, leaning on her back, and the blow didn't count.

He hooked her feet out from under her, forcing her over the boot of the car, face down.

'I didn't think they'd send a woman,' he said. One hand was

in her hair pressing her face into the cold metal. The other started to search her.

'Keep your fucking hands to yourself,' Anna yelled. Where was everyone?

'This is the fun part,' he said, taking his time. 'Nice of them to send me a girl.' His hand crawled. 'I like girls,' he said, in a voice distorted by loathing.

'Not even armed,' he said.

'You're wrong!' Anna screeched, her teeth scraping against paint. 'Nobody sent me.'

The hand seemed stuck between her legs. Anna twisted her hips, drew her legs up, and kicked. Everything was wrong. She had no balance, no purchase, no steel caps to her shoes. All she achieved was to get rid of the hand. The other yanked her hair even tighter and twisted her neck.

'Bitch!' he hissed. 'Keep still!' He raised her head by the hair and banged it down on the metal.

'You're making a mistake,' she yelled.

'I don't make mistakes,' he whispered and banged her face again.

Anna stopped struggling.

'That's better,' he said. 'I like my women to lie still.'

Cynthia said, 'It was better in Mexico City.' Her dopey voice seemed to come from under the car.

'Really,' Anna said, 'this is a mistake.' Her face felt hot and swollen. Her teeth ached.

'Where are your friends?' he asked.

'What friends?'

She felt him move behind her. An icy point cut into her neck.

'Knife,' he informed her. 'Next to your carotid artery. Stand up. Very slowly.'

Anna stood up. Very, very slowly.

As she did so she saw the black shape of a car, without lights, slide into the entrance of the car park. She thought: 'A witness.'

Hugh said, 'Do you really think you can get to me through *her*.'

Cynthia was asleep on the asphalt. He kicked her head. The black car crept slowly closer. Why were there no lights?

Hugh said, 'Tell them I'm done with her anyway. They can have her. Tell them I work for myself.'

He did not see the black car until it was half way across the car park. He wheeled around. Anna felt the burn of the blade. She flung herself away from him, falling over Cynthia's legs.

The rear door of the car swung back before it came to a stop. A man got out. He was pointing. Pointing.

Anna rolled.

A gun went off.

Anna leaped up, grabbed Cynthia's leg and dragged with all her might. She tumbled back towards the motel room. Cynthia's body came with her.

The gun roared a second time. Something black and wet hit her in the chest. She fell backwards through the door.

One more pull. Cynthia slid across the threshold. Anna slammed the door.

She heaved Cynthia up and slapped her hard on both cheeks.

'Hugh? What?' Cynthia said. 'Is it a thunderstorm?'

'Come on!' Anna screamed. She got her arm around Cynthia's waist, lifting her, dragging her out of the bedroom.

There was a deafening crash — half the door splintered and vanished. A jagged hole opened in the wall opposite.

Anna staggered through the living room, through the porch, to the screen door. She was hauling Cynthia through tar, through wet cement.

The pool lights were blazing. There was nowhere to hide.

She gripped Cynthia and ran, stumbling, so slowly, between the chairs, beside the pool. Towards the dark. Towards the Gulf.

Cynthia, trying to help, infected by panic, not awake. Cynthia, heavy, helpless, lurching across the sand.

Weeping, Anna pushed Cynthia into the sea. To wake her up. To wash the viscera and urine from her own clothes.

Chapter 60

CYNTHIA SAT IN the shallow water. 'My back hurts,' she said.

'Shut up,' Anna hissed. 'Not a sound.'

She waded further out. The slime and splinters that had once been Hugh clung to her shirt. Some of the splinters had torn the fabric and pierced her skin. She vomited into the waves. That came back and hit her too.

She leaped away. The sea flamed round her neck.

'I'm cold,' Cynthia said from out of the dark.

Anna struggled towards the voice. She had not been shot. She thought she had been. Anyone could have been. But she wasn't. Anna had not been hit. Cynthia had not been hit. It was Hugh. Hugh had been hit.

That was what happened, she thought. The water tugged at her legs. That's what happened. They shot Hugh.

Lights. The lights were on in the motel. Had no one called the police?

'Somebody was shooting at us,' Cynthia said from close by. It was blessedly dark in the water. Anna reached out and found Cynthia's living hand.

'Are you okay?' she whispered.

'My back is all scraped,' Cynthia complained. 'And I'm cold.'

'Hush,' Anna said. Cynthia's voice was shrill in the silence.

Why was it silent? Where were the sirens, the voices?

'Come on,' Anna said. 'Quick.'

She led Cynthia out of the water and along the beach.

'Don't run,' Cynthia gasped. 'I feel awful. Where are we going?'

'Away,' Anna said.

A shot had blasted away half the motel door – a shot meant for Anna or Cynthia, Anna and Cynthia. Hugh was already dead.

Cynthia tripped in the sand. Her hand was freezing. The night was black and Anna could feel mist like clingfilm over her face.

'What happened? Where's Hugh?'

'Someone shot at us,' Anna said, feverishly urging Cynthia on. She felt herself burning, moving at lightning speed. Why was Cynthia walking so slowly?

'Oh, my God.' Cynthia panted. 'Why?'

'I don't know.' Something, driftwood perhaps, caught at Anna's leg and she fell, bringing Cynthia down beside her.

She scrambled up.

Cynthia said. 'The police will come. If Hugh sees the police he'll never come back.'

'No,' Anna agreed, and burst out laughing.

'What's funny?'

'Nothing.' Anna felt the vomit rise in her throat again.

'Come on!' she said, helping Cynthia up. She looked back. Mist pressed against her eyeballs. She could hear nothing but the slap and sluice of the ocean. If the sea would only shut up for a moment maybe she would hear the sound of footsteps behind them.

'Listen,' Cynthia said. 'Sirens.'

In the distance they heard the whoop and wail approaching like a troop of gibbons.

'Come on,' Cynthia urged.

They stumbled on like a pair of demented joggers, breath hissing in jagged gasps.

Keys, Anna thought. House keys. They were in her pocket. The car keys . . . As she went along she tried to order the chaos. The car keys were in the car. She had put them there before going back for Cynthia, before Hugh came back. The car was in the motel car park. Other keys. Keys to her flat in London. They were in her bag. Her bag was in the car. The car was in the car park.

What was in her bag? What had she been carrying which might connect Ann Johnson with Anna Lee and the house at Manatee Key Tennis Club? She could not remember.

Cynthia was tired, trying to hurry, dragging her feet.

'How much further?' she said.

'Not far now. There's a house near here. We can rest there.'

But not for long – not if someone had found her bag and there was something in her bag. Not if someone traced the Hertz car to the tennis club. Who were the rental papers made out to?

The police would be along sooner or later. That was all right.

'I think it's all right,' Anna said aloud.

'What?'

'Nothing.' It wasn't the police Anna was afraid of.

Cynthia was afraid of the police. Anna was afraid of whoever had blasted Hugh's blood and bone all over her shirt.

She felt the scrape of the seawall on her left hand.

'Here,' she said. 'Up here.'

Chapter 61

'LOOK AT MY dress! It's ruined,' Cynthia said.
       'Have a hot bath,' Anna suggested.

Cynthia was shaking like a faulty engine and she was blue around the mouth.

'It's nice here,' she said. 'Where are we?'

'Have a shower. I'll make some tea and find you something to wear.'

Anna thrust a pile of clean towels into Cynthia's arms and left her in the spare bedroom.

In her own bathroom she ripped her shirt off. Hugh's blood was no more than a sea-washed stain, but her collar and shoulders were scarlet with her own blood. There was a clean slice round her neck close to the carotid artery. Her chest and stomach looked raw and grazed. Her face was bony and her eyes enormous.

She stood under a hot shower for a couple of minutes and then got hurriedly out. The cut on her neck began to bleed freely again.

She wound a towel round it and dressed rapidly in jeans and a sweatshirt. The sound of running water came from the other bathroom.

She ran downstairs and dialled Lara's home number. Lara's voice said, 'Lara Crowther is unavailable just now. But if you have a message . . .'

Anna swore. After the tone, she said, 'This is an emergency. Phone me as soon as you hear this.' Her voice sounded like breaking glass.

She phoned Florida-Technics. The woman, who introduced herself as 'Night desk', would not give her Rule's number. She took Anna's number and promised that Mr Suarez would 'Get right back'.

Anna put the kettle on. She could not keep still. She ran upstairs. In a drawer beside the bed she found her passport and the wallet containing driving licence and insurance. They were there because she had not wanted to take anything to the Sand Dollar motel which might make Hugh suspicious of her.

She ran down again, stuffing passport and wallet into her pockets as she went. Half way down, she stopped. Ticket and money. She went back to gather up traveller's cheques and the airline folder.

The kettle had not yet boiled. The phone was mute, Cynthia was still in the bath. The world was taking a very long time to respond to Anna's emergency.

She rang Brierly Security. There would be no one there but she could leave a message on the machine. She wanted to warn Mr Brierly that trouble was on its way. She might need a lawyer, she would need somewhere else to stay. Cynthia needed . . .

Even as she spoke her mind wandered. She shouldn't be using the phone, Lara or Rule could be trying to get through.

She put the phone down hurriedly.

It rang again straightaway.

'Rule?' Anna asked.

'Elaine,' said Elaine. 'I tried to call you earlier but I guess you were out. I haven't got a game for you tomorrow, but I'm looking for a woman to fill in – mixed doubles – the day after.'

'I'm sorry,' Anna said, wondering which one of them was batty. 'I don't think I can manage that.'

'Too bad,' Elaine said. 'Say, someone came round to see you this afternoon. Young guy. Looked like a body builder. You sure have some cute visitors.'

'Who was he?' Anna asked, hair stirring on the back of her neck.

'Didn't say his name,' Elaine said. 'I think I've seen him on the keys sometime, so I guess he's local. I could ask Tony – he's into weights and stuff.'

Anna thanked her and rang off. Her hands were shaking so badly she could scarcely set the receiver onto its cradle.

She made tea, pouring most of the boiling water into the coffee pot. Some of it splashed on the counter. Sugar for Cynthia: Cynthia was probably in shock, she would need sugar.

Upstairs, she found slacks, a sweater and some underwear. She dumped them on the spare bed and then took the tea into the bathroom.

Cynthia was stretched out as far as she could in the small bath, up to her neck in steaming water. She looked as if she had dozed off.

'Tea,' Anna said. 'Wake up. We'll have to move on soon.'

'I thought I'd never get warm again.' Cynthia opened her eyes and saw the tea cup. 'Haven't you got any Coke?' she asked.

'Sweet tea,' Anna said firmly, leaving the cup where Cynthia could reach it.

Hole in the heart, my Aunt Gertie, she thought on the way downstairs. But if there was no sign of heart surgery, there had been two small, recent scars on Cynthia's belly. She almost went back up to ask about them but the phone rang.

Rule said, 'You want to talk to me.'

'Hugh Fellows was shot at the motel tonight,' Anna told him.

'Dead?'

'Very.'

'Okay,' Rule said. 'What do you want me to do about it? You in a jam?'

'Yes,' Anna said. 'I was there. So was Cynthia. Someone shot at us too. I took Cynthia down the beach. We're all right. But someone's been asking about me at the club. We shouldn't stay here. But my car's at the motel.'

'You're speeding,' Rule said flatly. 'Slow down — it's that British accent.'

'Got wax in your ears?' Anna asked angrily.

'You are a witness, right?' Rule said, ignoring her. 'When did this happen?'

'About . . .' She looked at her watch. Was that all? 'About forty minutes ago.' It felt like four hours. Or seconds.

'Sorry,' she said. 'I *am* speeding.'

'Yup,' said Rule. 'You talk to the cops?'

'We left before they arrived. Also, Cynthia is scared of them, and – oh shit!' She had forgotten. 'And Cynthia doesn't know Hugh is dead.' Anna would have to tell her.

'How come?'

'She was asleep,' Anna said. 'Look, all that can wait. The police can find me here because I left the car and my bag at the scene. But the point is – so can whoever shot at me. You said they were professionals.'

'I think maybe you better move,' Rule said. 'I'm on my way now.'

'I'll call a taxi,' Anna said, stiffly.

'Oh, right,' Rule said. 'I guess that's why you got me out of the shower – to tell me you were going to call a cab. I told you, I'm on the road right now and you won't lose much time waiting. Call a cab if you want, but that'll be one more place your name and face will be logged.'

Anna bit her lip.

Rule said, 'So just shut up, right? Make yourself one of your cups of tea and sit tight.' He rang off.

'Sod you too,' Anna said to the dead line. Why had she called him? He wasn't a mate. He wasn't on her side – like Bernie, Johnny, Phil or Tim. Even that tosser Sean.

Rule was just another bastard with a gun.

She couldn't rely on him. But he was the only one she knew.

She stared at the Japanese irises.

There was someone on the stairs. Footsteps.

She leaped to her feet, lunged into the kitchen and grabbed for a knife. Waited, teeth rattling, for the door to open.

Nothing.

She opened the door herself. No one.

She tiptoed down to the front door. It was locked.

The door from the garage was locked too.

Upstairs she checked every room. They were all empty. The windows were securely fastened.

In slow motion, the motel door splintered again. Her nose filled with the smell of blood.

She rapped on the bathroom door. 'Get a move on!' she shouted. 'Get dressed and come down.'

'Coming,' Cynthia called back sleepily.

In her bedroom, Anna threw random armfuls of stuff into her case. She dragged it down to the front door. Checked the lock again. Went up to the kitchen.

Her tea was cold on the counter. She made some more.

Chapter 62

ANNA FORCED HERSELF to sit still. She held the cup in both hands to stop the hot tea sloshing. She unclenched her teeth so that she could drink. Will power was all it took.

Will power worked with teeth and teacups. It wasn't much use for the big things like blood and bone, like holes in doors.

Cynthia appeared at the doorway. Wearing Anna's clothes she looked smaller and more normal. In her hand she carried the tattered and soiled yellow sundress. She looked around the kitchen till she located the washing machine and then dropped the dress into it. She measured out some washing powder and switched on the machine.

Anna watched, incredulous.

'It'll be all right,' Cynthia said. 'They do some amazing washable fabrics over here.'

The washing machine hummed and whirred.

'Are you all right?' Anna asked. 'Are you feeling better?'

There was an angry red patch on Cynthia's cheekbone. Maybe that was where Hugh had kicked her. Or had Anna caused it?

Cynthia said, 'I've got these weird grazes on my back. Can I go to bed soon? I'm really tired.'

'We're waiting for a friend,' Anna said. 'We can't stay here. Do you want some more tea?'

'I only drink tea in England,' Cynthia said contemptuously. 'They can't make it here. You look awful.' She stared at Anna. 'Did someone try to cut your throat?'

Anna touched the towel. She had forgotten about it.

'I think I'll go and lie down,' Cynthia said. But she wandered into the living room and switched on the TV. The sound of gunfire cracked out.

Anna jumped.

'Bonnie and Clyde,' Cynthia called. 'I love it. It always makes me cry. Come and watch.'

'Watch something else,' Anna said. 'And turn the volume down.'

'I can't not watch Bonnie and Clyde.'

'Try!' She ran upstairs to change the stained towel round her neck. No wonder she could smell blood.

In the living room Cynthia was stretched out on the sofa still watching the film.

'For Christ's sake!' Anna said, and snapped the TV off. 'Someone just shot at us.'

'So what?' Cynthia yelled. 'It happens all the time over here. Everyone's got a gun. Don't you know *anything*?'

'Don't talk stupid!' Anna shouted back.

'And don't tell me what to watch on telly! You're not my mother.' It was the second time she'd said that.

Anna said, 'Why was someone shooting at us? What has Hugh been doing?'

'Was Hugh there?'

'Yes.'

'Where is he now?'

Break it to her gently, Anna thought. She sat down next to her. The only thing she could think of was a modification of a sick joke: All right, you women! Everyone with a live husband take one step forward – *not* so fast, Cynthia Fellows!

Anna shook her head trying to clear it. She was becoming as potty as Cynthia.

Cynthia said, 'Hugo's dead, isn't he? That's who got blown away. I think I saw it but I thought I was dreaming.'

'I'm sorry,' Anna said uselessly.

'An eye for an eye.' Cynthia got up and turned the TV on again. 'Actually, I dreamt I shot him. Do you know, that if you don't show your emotions, you'll never get lines on your face?'

By now, Anna was so off balance she felt that if she were to stand up she would fall over.

'It wasn't me who axed him, was it?' Cynthia said, in a tone of polite inquiry. 'No, I didn't think so. But you know, you have to be careful what you wish for, especially over here. You can get what you want in this country – if you've got the money.'

'I think you should go home,' Anna said. 'I think you've been through something terrible. You should go home and sort it out.'

'Did I tell you Hugo killed my baby?' Cynthia asked. 'It's a terrible thing to get what you want when you're in two minds about it. I mean, you can want quite opposite things at the same time, can't you? I wanted my baby, but it would have ruined my life. I was much too young. I was a child bride, you know. Did I tell you that?'

'I know that,' Anna said, thinking, would the real Cynthia Garden please stand up. Talking to Cynthia was like continually dialling a series of wrong numbers. She could have coped with grief, anger or hysteria, but this string of inappropriate reactions was beyond her. All of Anna's responses were geared to something far more conventional. She was prepared to comfort Cynthia, or protect her. She wanted information from her. But Cynthia was like an automatic bank teller which played 'Moon River' instead of dispensing cash.

Her skin was muddy beneath the tan and there were black circles under the wide grey eyes, but she stared at Anna quite steadily and burbled in a perfectly reasonable tone of voice. It was impossible to tell the difference between fact and fantasy.

A job was just a job, Anna thought, trying not to twitch. Everything was relatively simple until you got involved with the people. Find these sweaters. All right, she'd found them. Find out who's peddling them. Fine. Follow that man. Done. There were techniques for that. You could watch and wait and answer your own questions.

And then along came Cynthia – a one-woman Bermuda Triangle where professionals foundered, where solid information disappeared without trace.

'Cynthia,' Anna said firmly. 'Who was out to get Hugh? Why were you hiding?'

'It was a paramilitary burn,' Cynthia said without taking her eyes from the TV screen. 'I told you my father was in the army, didn't I? One of those spook special regiments. My guess is that he and some of his friends wanted to teach Hugo a lesson. In the old days, my father was Colonel in Chief, and Hugo was his right-hand man. They went all over the world together, until Hugo fell in love with me. We've been on the run ever since.'

'Mmm,' said Anna. In spite of the TV she heard a car approaching slowly.

'It was a deadly secret,' Cynthia said. 'But now that Hugo's been so tragically wasted, I suppose I'm free to tell my story.'

'Just a minute.' Anna ran upstairs. With the lights off in the spare room she looked down onto Rule's Buick. He got out and lifted his head so that she could see his face.

'Take it easy,' he said, when she let him in. 'There's no one around. I checked. All the action is out at the motel. That's crawling with cops.'

'It's not the cops I'm worried about,' she said as they went up to the living-room.

'Where's the subject?'

'Watching telly.'

'She know?'

'Well,' Anna said, 'I told her, but she doesn't seem to mind.'

Rule stared at her and then pushed open the living-room door. Cynthia glanced at him and then got up. She switched the TV off and came over, hand extended.

'Hi,' she said, giving him an up and under look. 'I'm Cynthia. Can't I get you something – tea, coffee, a drink?'

To Anna's astounded ear, she sounded genuinely American: in fact she sounded like a Pan Am stewardess.

Rule said, 'We should be leaving. You okay?'

'Sure,' said Cynthia. 'Why not?' She paused. 'I'm a widow now, you know.' She smiled sadly.

'No kidding,' said Rule, looking at Anna.

Anna said, 'Let's be off.'

'It's very kind of you to help us like this,' Cynthia murmured, switching to English. 'I don't know what we'd have done if you hadn't.' She touched the back of Rule's hand, a tiny gesture of gratitude and helplessness.

'Flaming Nora!' Anna said.

On the way down to the car Cynthia whispered, 'You've got to make them think they're wonderful or they won't help. You'll never get anywhere with a mouth like yours.'

'What's she saying?' Rule asked.

'Nothing,' Anna said, through clenched teeth.

'I should be wearing black,' Cynthia mused. 'You can't go wrong with basic black.'

She made as if to get into the front seat with Rule, but Anna shepherded her into the back and told her to lie down. She felt as if her head were mounted on a ball bearing – swivelling this way and that as they drove out of the club – peering into shadows, fearing dark cars and ambush.

'Relax,' said Rule.

The mist gathered like rain on the windscreen. He set the wipers going.

'I cruised before I came to your house,' he said. 'It's clean, I'm telling you.'

Cynthia popped up from the back seat and leaned forward almost touching Rule's collar. She said, 'Where are you taking me?'

'Friends in Bradenton,' Rule said.

'Lie down,' Anna said.

'I'll get car sick,' Cynthia warned brightly.

'Want some music?' Rule asked. He selected a Billy Joel tape and slipped it into the cassette deck. He turned the volume up loud and tuned out the front seat speakers.

'I was listening in to the cop's frequency on the way over,' he told Anna. 'Your name did not come up yet. I called Ethan because he has some connections in the Department – to warn him as much as anything – so we could get news from him.'

'I saw Billy Joel live in Concert,' Cynthia said, popping up again from the back seat and practically hanging on Rule's neck. 'I went backstage afterwards. He literally crackles with energy – wow! You remind me of him a bit. Not to look at, but . . .'

'Down,' said Anna.

'I mean, you're much better looking,' Cynthia went on, ignoring Anna.

Anna turned in her seat. 'Get down,' she said, 'and shut up!'

'She's jealous,' Cynthia told Rule. 'Older women always are. They try to keep us down because we've got the one thing they want.'

'The one thing I want out of you,' Anna snarled, 'is a piece of bleeding hush!'

Rule said, 'Lie down, honey.' And Cynthia subsided gracefully, smiling at him in the mirror as she did so.

'Jee-zus!' Rule muttered out of the corner of his mouth.

'I'll have to talk to the police,' Anna said. 'But I wasn't going to wait for them back there.'

'She's a witness too,' Rule said, gesturing with his thumb.

'Wonderful,' Anna said. 'In the first place she was zonked out on tranqs. Then she said she thought she did it. And just before you arrived she said it was her father.'

'No shit,' said Rule. He kept the car at a steady forty-five in the direction of San Isabel.

'What really happened?' he asked after a while.

Anna took a deep breath. 'The three of us were in the car park,' she said. 'Hugh, her and me. I was blown. He knew I wasn't just another tourist.'

'How?'

'I don't know. But I can guess. There was a feller working at the Sand Dollar who seemed to be acting as Cyn's minder, and I think he's the same one asking about me at the Club.'

'Name?'

'She'll know,' Anna said, thumbing towards the back seat. 'But what she'll tell you is anybody's guess.'

'Go on,' Rule said.

'I think Hugh thought I was one of your Miami heavies. He said things like, "Tell them I work for myself." And, "They can't get at me through her."'

'And then?'

'And then a big black vehicle, no lights, no motor, crawls into the car park . . .'

'What make?'

'You'll be lucky,' Anna said. 'I don't know American cars.

Bigger than this Buick. More bonnet and boot. Sharp angles. Dark glass. It didn't have a local number plate.' Where had that detail come from? Anna closed her eyes. At the time she hadn't noticed anything. 'Connecticut,' she said.

'Okay,' Rule said. 'Then what?'

'Passenger side rear door opens, man gets out. Single shot. Which I think must've missed.' She looked at her hands and noticed she was gripping her own knees as if they were safety rails. She went on, 'The second shot took his head off. The third went through the door to my motel room. I don't know what happened after that because I was legging it with her in tow. I don't think we were pursued. I didn't hear any other shots.'

'Slow down,' said Rule. They were passing over the bridge between Manatee and San Isabel. Wheels rattled hollowly on the metal.

'Was that your first time?' Rule asked.

'What?' Anna twisted round to look at Cynthia. She seemed to be asleep.

'First time under fire.'

'Yes. It was a bit of a shock.'

'A bit of a shock,' Rule repeated. He laughed.

'Well, sorry,' Anna said defensively. 'I didn't notice a lot of detail.'

'Take it easy,' Rule said. 'You're doing fine.'

He sounded like Lew teaching a new stroke.

Chapter 63

NANCY'S HOUSE WAS in a brand-new development on the edge of Bradenton. From the road all that could be seen was a wall. But once inside it was like a small town with matching grey roofed houses winding round in a complicated network of streets.

Nancy was over six feet tall, big-boned but slim. She wore her hair in a sleek bob, and even in a lumpy towelling bathrobe she looked as if she should be modelling sports equipment.

'We used to work together,' Rule said enigmatically. 'She says you can stay here tonight.'

'Thank you very much,' Anna said.

'Sure,' said Nancy, looking from Anna to Cynthia and back again. 'No problem.'

'Did Rule explain?' Anna asked.

'Rule? Explain?' Nancy chuckled. Rule shrugged.

'I'm tired,' Cynthia said, looking at Rule.

'Go to bed,' he suggested. But she just stood there, waiting.

Nancy said, 'You'd better let me take a look at your neck, Anna. You might have to soak that towel off.'

'How'd it happen?' Rule asked.

'My back hurts,' Cynthia said, hopefully.

The blood had dried, and Anna knew the cut would open again as soon as she took the towel off. She said, 'Maybe we should call the police first, and let Lara Crowther know what's . . .'

'No, no, no!' screamed Cynthia.

Everyone stared at her.

'No!' Cynthia went to Rule, hugging his arm. 'Don't let them,' she cried. 'They're trying to kill me.'

'Who?' said Rule, trying to disengage his arm.

'Them.' Cynthia pointed at Anna. 'She abducted me! I understand it all now. That woman sent her. She's a lesbian!'

'Who?' Rule asked again.

'Lara Crowther. She seduced my mother. She tried to seduce me too.' Cynthia hung on to Rule's arm as if it were a tree in a hurricane. 'I'm frightened,' she said. 'Ann's a lesbian too. They're all in it together. She made me have a bath. Hugo warned me about her. He should know. He was married to her.'

'Who?' Anna asked.

Cynthia hid her face in Rule's shoulder.

'Who, honey?' Rule asked, staring at Anna.

'Lara Crowther.' Cynthia looked up at him, eyelashes working double time. 'It was a marriage of convenience. He didn't really love her. He wanted to stay in America.'

'True?' Rule asked Anna.

'God knows,' said Anna, shrugging helplessly. 'She never told me anything like that. She only said Hugh worked for her a few years ago.'

'She's a lesbian and a ball-breaker,'Cynthia told Rule. 'She's a witch, and her mission is to castrate men and seduce young girls and make it so that they can never have any babies. She did it to me, you know.'

'Isn't this getting a little out of hand?' Nancy asked quietly. 'Why don't you go to bed . . . Cynthia, isn't it? There's a room upstairs and the bed's all made up.'

'You see what they're doing?' Cyn cried. 'They're trying to convince you I'm in the way. They'll send me to bed and then they'll call that witch in – and the police, and they'll take me away, and then we'll never see each other again.'

There was a moment's silence while Rule, Nancy and Anna looked at each other. Cynthia was still nestled against Rule and he looked extremely uncomfortable.

Nancy grinned suddenly and said, 'Well, come on Anna. I've got a medicine chest in my bathroom. You want to get that neck fixed?'

'Yes, thanks,' Anna said gratefully. She hadn't a clue as to what to do about Cynthia. The scene she had created left her feeling paralysed.

Nancy started upstairs and Anna followed.

'Hey, you guys,' Rule said, 'what am I supposed to do?'

'The magic word is "honey",' Anna said tiredly. 'Do what you can with it.'

'Thanks a whole bunch,' said Rule.

'We could run away,' suggested Cynthia.

There was a moment, half way up the stairs, when Anna, looking down at Cynthia, felt she had seen the sum total of Cynthia's life: her fears, her fantasies and her manoeuvres. She shook her head and went on up. Maybe they were a lot of women's fears, fantasies and manoeuvres, but Cynthia's had raced out of control.

Anna was very, very tired.

Chapter 64

'THIS LOOKS LIKE a knife wound,' Nancy said. Her bathroom was big and bright and full of mirrors.

'Maybe you should get it stitched.' She was sure-fingered and competent.

'It'll be all right,' Anna said. 'It's clean. If we sort of press the edges together with strips of adhesive . . .'

'Okay,' Nancy said. 'You had a rough night, huh? Hold still.'

In the mirror, Anna watched Nancy's hands. She seemed to know what she was doing.

'That kid's disturbed,' Nancy said. 'You feel everyone else has a bit part in her personal movie. Only she's kind of wacky about the casting.'

'That's a good way of putting it,' Anna said, impressed.

Rule came in without knocking. Anna grabbed a towel.

Nancy said, 'Hold still.'

'Got anything to make her sleep?' Rule asked. 'She's in bed but she won't stop talking.'

'That's what Hugh Fellows did,' Anna remarked. 'He stuffed her full of tranqs.'

'Shit,' Rule said. 'Well, maybe he had a point.'

'There's some sleepers in the cabinet,' Nancy said.

Rule found the pills and left scowling.

Anna said, 'I think he thinks we stitched him up rotten.'

'Don't talk,' Nancy said. 'Every time you say something you move and this thing opens up.'

After a while she said, 'Anyway it'll do him good. They always think the women and kids are our job. If someone needs care, leave it to us.'

She was doing a good job of caring for Anna and Anna wondered if she had been a cop too.

Anna said, 'It's very kind of you to put us up like this.'

'That's what I'm talking about,' Nancy said, snipping off small pieces from a roll of plaster. 'He'd never think of calling up one of his men friends. I said, "Rule," I said, "my name is Nancy, not Nanny." Don't get me wrong, it's okay, and if it was me in a jam I wouldn't hesitate to call him. Hold still, I'm nearly done.'

Anna held still. The cut should have been hurting, but it wasn't. Altogether, Anna felt curiously numb. For a while she worried about not feeling anything but in the end decided it didn't matter. Nothing mattered very much. She looked at her own blood on the swabs and towels, and it didn't mean anything. It was simply red.

She went downstairs with a neat white bandage like a dog collar round her throat. Nancy had lent her a sweatshirt which was far too big.

Nancy poured scotch for herself and Rule. Anna didn't want anything.

Rule said, 'Cynthia says we can't call the cops because if we do she'll never get Hugh's money. She just offered me twenty-five thousand bucks to take her to Mexico.'

'I know a great travel agent,' Nancy said, perching on the arm of his chair.

'A rich widow,' Anna said. 'How lucky can you get?' She felt a lot more comfortable with Rule knowing he had a friend like Nancy.

'Okay,' Rule said patiently. 'But how much of what she says do we take seriously?'

'I don't know,' Anna said. 'Some of what she says is absolute bollocks, some of it seems truish, and some of it looks like embroidery.'

'How do you mean?' Nancy asked.

'It's hard to explain,' Anna said slowly. 'When I first met her of course I was expecting her to lie about herself and Hugh. And she did. That's natural. But it wasn't just lying it was more like sort of demented fantasies. For instance, she said she had just had major surgery – hole in the heart – she said she was ill. Well, at the time I thought she had just made herself throw up – after bingeing at lunch, but it turned out she really did have a doctor's appointment. And then when she was in the bath . . .'

'You mean you *did* force her to have a bath?' Rule asked.

'Don't be daft, she wanted a bath. We were both freezing from having been in the sea.' Anna stopped. After all she had pushed Cynthia into the water.

'In the bath?' Nancy prompted.

'I took her a cup of tea, and clearly she hadn't had any heart surgery . . . but there were two recent scars on . . . oh shit a brick!'

'What?' said Nancy.

'I've seen scars like that before. I think she's been sterilised. She's only eighteen and someone's sterilised her.'

'That is just awful,' Nancy said, appalled.

'And she said Hugh had killed her baby . . .' Anna stopped again. 'Rule,' she said. 'I think it might be a good idea if we checked whether Lara Crowther and Hugh Fellows were ever married.'

'You think she might be on the money there?'

'I mean, we should check before I tell Lara where we are.'

'I *knew* there was something,' Rule said, looking oddly satisfied.

'Ethan reported back to her, didn't he? – when he found the house on Pier Drive. And it was tossed. I didn't tell her the name of the motel, but . . .'

'Ethan did,' Rule said. 'Remember, we couldn't get hold of her after Hugh Fellows left Pier Drive? So we couldn't let her know he had moved until the next day. And we can't get a hold of her now. You think she might have fingered the guy?'

'This is speculation,' Anna said.

'But worth a try.'

Nancy said, 'I shouldn't really be hearing this. I'm going to bed.'

'Night,' Rule said without looking up. 'We could use some background on Ms Crowther. Any ideas?'

'Property,' Anna said. 'Elaine told me Lara was a friend of the developer who built the tennis club. You said there was dodgy Gold Coast money in development on the Keys.'

'Right,' Rule said. 'And we should find out for sure what Hugh Fellows was into.'

Nancy, half way up the stairs, said, 'What're you going to do about the kid? You forgotten about her?'

'Nancy, honey,' Rule began.

'No,' said Nancy. 'Unh-unh, N-O No. Honey ain't no magic word on me. The kid needs professional help and a safe place to stay, and it ain't me, babe.'

'We'll figure something out in the morning,' Rule said, turning back to Anna.

'It's nearly morning now,' Nancy said inexorably.

'I should really take her home,' Anna said. 'But I can't.'

'Why?'

'No passport,' Anna said. 'And that's another point, Rule, if Hugh and Cynthia were at the Sand Dollar under aliases, maybe their passports were somewhere else. Like the Style File office.'

'I was wondering when you'd get round to that,' Rule said. 'I'd better talk to Ethan. Anything else?'

'The feller working at the Sand Dollar. Elaine said she might be able to find a name for him. If not there's the motel itself.'

'Investigators!' Nancy exclaimed disgustedly, and disappeared upstairs.

Anna did not want to think about Cynthia. Cynthia was a victim. She was an abused and manipulated child. Terrible things had been done to her. But she was also a monumental pain in the neck. And if Anna were to keep her safe for the next few days and somehow manage to get her home she would probably end up abusing and manipulating her too. The process had already begun.

Cynthia was simply an object to everyone involved: to Penny she was the daughter used to manipulate Lara: to Lara she was an impediment. To Hugh . . . well, Anna didn't even like to speculate what she had been to Hugh. To Anna she was a giant problem.

She said, 'Can we keep Cynthia away from the cops?'

Rule didn't answer. With his head thrown back against Nancy's raspberry-coloured furnishings, his legs crossed at the ankles, he looked nearly asleep.

'The cops are a bit iffy for me too,' Anna went on. 'I wouldn't know how to explain myself. I'm supposed to be on holiday. I'm not supposed to work over here, and you people have to be licensed.'

She thought about it for a while, but her brain did not seem to be doing anything constructive.

She said, 'Perhaps the easiest thing would be if Cynthia and I got ourselves deported . . .'

Rule finally stirred. He yawned and said, 'If that's what you call your British sense of humour I guess I'll be running along. You should get some sleep.'

He got up. 'I put your bags in the den.' He led her into a smaller room off the living room and showed her how the sofa there turned into a bed.

'You going to be all right?' he asked. 'I could stay if you like.'

The bed suddenly looked enormous.

Anna said, 'Thanks, but we'll manage.' She was feeling very uneasy again: uneasy because, inexplicably, she did not want to be alone, and uneasy because all she had to do was ask him to stay. She did not want to ask.

Awkwardly she said, 'Listen, I want to thank . . .'

'You bet,' he said quickly and left the room.

A couple of minutes later she heard the front door close.

Chapter 65

WHEN ANNA WOKE up she was in exactly the same position she had lain down in. The sun was nearly overhead and she had not moved for six hours. Nancy placed a glass of fresh orange juice on the floor next to her.

'Ethan Callow rang,' she said. 'They're sending the ambulance round in an hour.'

'The what?' Anna sat up, heart hammering. 'Has something happened to Cyn?'

'She's still asleep. She's okay, but there's this private clinic or nursing home Ethan knows about. She'll be safer there.'

'I don't know,' Anna said doubtfully. 'Do you think she'll agree?'

Outside, the bright yellow-green grass led down to a canal where three boys were fishing.

'I don't think she gets the choice,' Nancy said quietly. She shrugged and looked out of the window too. On the far bank of the canal a pair of egrets watched the fishing lines expectantly.

'I suppose it's for the best,' Anna said, drinking her orange.

'I suppose so,' Nancy said. Their eyes did not meet.

Anna showered and dressed quickly. She felt stiff and heavy. She did not look at herself in the mirror. She fumbled with buttons, hands still shaky from last night, and forced herself to perform small tasks methodically. She had a strong urge to rush: as if she were being chased. She breathed deeply to steady herself.

In the kitchen, Nancy was scrambling some eggs, muttering and swearing to herself.

'I can't cook, I don't like cooking,' she said. 'Maybe I should convert this kitchen into a gym. If it wasn't here I wouldn't feel I had to use it.' The eggs were sticking. 'Damn things,' Nancy groused. 'Put some bread in the toaster, will you. I guess you could do this better.'

'I could,' Anna said, grinning. 'And I'm pretty bad at it too.' She felt better talking to Nancy.

'If you can't be the best, be the worst,' Nancy said. '"Don't go for Mr In Between." You gonna take something up to the kid?'

'I suppose so,' Anna said. 'Hope she doesn't throw it at me.'

'She'll be okay: Rule isn't around. You were always going to be the enemy with him around.'

'Think so?'

'Sure,' Nancy said. 'She's man-oriented, poor kid. I don't know where she learned it, but that's the way she is.'

'She doesn't seem to be too fond of her mother.'

'There you go,' Nancy said. 'Her first success was playing the mother off against the father so she's stuck with it.'

Anna laughed.

'What?' Nancy asked.

'Acute observation,' Anna said. 'Reasoning – a bit previous.'

'That's me,' Nancy said. 'Kitchen psychology a specialty. It's a winner with burned eggs. *Damn!*'

Anna carried burnt eggs, toast and orange juice upstairs to the spare room. She put the tray on the night table and half opened the curtains. Cynthia was sleeping on her side, hair glossy and tumbled across her face.

'Breakfast,' Anna said. 'Wake up.'

Cynthia stirred and stretched before opening her eyes.

'I was dreaming,' she said, smiling and rosy with sleep. 'I was a dolphin and I could take off in any direction – up, down, side to side, anywhere. I could breathe under water – the water was just like air.' She stopped to think. 'Actually,' she went on, 'the water *was* air. Isn't that funny?'

'Nice,' Anna said, sitting on the end of the bed.

Cynthia reached for the tray and began to eat. She wrinkled her nose at the burnt eggs, but ate them.

Anna said, 'There's someone coming for you shortly. We had to find a safe place for you, somewhere you could have proper medical attention.'

'Okay,' said Cynthia, continuing to eat. She watched Anna carefully from behind her hair.

'Not the police,' she said after a couple of minutes.

'Not them,' Anna said. 'They won't know where you are. Nor will Lara Crowther, or the people who shot at us last night.'

'Okay,' Cynthia said again.

She was amazingly passive, Anna thought, wondering about it. However peculiar the things she said were she always seemed to do as she was told.

Anna said, 'Where's your passport, Cyn?'

Cynthia shrugged.

'Because if you're in bother here, you know, you should leave.'

'There isn't anyone to go with,' Cynthia said.

'I can take you back home,' Anna suggested.

'I always wanted to go to France.'

'What about your parents?'

'I'm an orphan,' Cynthia said. 'Hugo was my father.'

Anna sighed. 'You've got a mother in Oakleigh,' she said tiredly. 'And your father's somewhere in Italy, last I heard.'

'"Last I heard,"' Cynthia mimicked. 'You're not very classy, are you? "In bother." Sometimes you talk like a pleb, actually.'

'Not to worry,' Anna said, standing up. 'You talk like a raving dip-brain all the time. Don't you really know where your passport is?'

'I have no country,' Cynthia proclaimed. 'So I need no passport.' She looked as though she'd said something extremely clever.

'Well, bully for you,' Anna said and took the tray downstairs. Fault, double fault, she thought: she simply could not get her serve in when playing Cynthia.

The trouble was that Cynthia was Anna's responsibility, although quite how much Anna didn't know. A job depended on the client, and now that she could not trust the client the job seemed to fall apart.

'I'm only as good as my client,' she told Nancy, moodily in the kitchen. 'If my client has rotten intentions, my actions turn out rotten too. But I've no way of knowing in advance.'

'Trust yourself,' Nancy said, carelessly. 'It'll turn out okay, you'll see.'

'How can you say that?' Anna asked. 'You don't know me from Adam. You think I'm okay because Rule brought me here and you trust *him*'.

'It's more than that,' Nancy said. 'I get instincts about people.'

'So do I,' Anna said gloomily. 'And half the time I'm wrong.'

'So, half the time you're right.' Now that she was no longer cooking Nancy's mood had improved considerably.

All the same, Anna was anxious. Cynthia was to be carted off to some unknown sanitorium because Anna did not know what else to do with her. She was making decisions by default, decisions she was not qualified to make. Her client was dodgy and her boss was on the other side of the Atlantic. Somewhere, perhaps close by, was someone who pointed a gun at her and pulled the trigger. She couldn't think properly. Instead she sat down and ate burnt eggs.

The ambulance, when it came, was in fact a limousine. Shiny, cream-coloured, with darkened glass, it looked more like a liner than a car, and Cynthia treated the two attendants as if they were her personal chauffeurs. But her eyes, when she looked back at Anna, were glazed and perplexed. The front she put up was one thing, Anna thought, but she had never seen anyone so lost and bewildered. Now that she was someone else's responsibility, even if only temporarily, Anna could afford to feel very sorry for her.

As the limousine rolled slowly away, Anna noticed Rule's Buick parked in front of another house a few doors down.

Coward, she thought, with understanding.

He came in a few minutes later, hands in pockets, dark glasses hiding any expression.

'Sleep okay?' he asked, neutrally. 'Everything smooth? So, let's go.'

'Where?' Anna asked.

'You want to take a look at the Style File,' he said. 'So we'll take a look.' He did not mention Cynthia at all.

In daylight Anna could see that the development Nancy lived in was only half complete. The finished houses were neat. There were sprinklers on the lawns and swimming pools in back gardens. But outside an inner residential ring the rest of the estate looked like a building site.

Rule drove out of it onto the main Bradenton to Sarasota road.

He said. 'Ms Crowther *was* married to Hugh Fellows. She filed for divorce about three years ago, and he stiffed her for some heavy bucks.'

'She was paying him alimony?' Anna asked.

'That's what I said.'

Anna looked at him, but he kept his eyes on the road.

'He had a resident's permit,' Rule went on. 'And a green card. Permission to work – in case you don't know. That's as much as we could get out of New York and Washington so far.'

'But if he was married to Cynthia,' Anna said. 'Wouldn't that stop the alimony?'

'If Ms Crowther knew about it,' he replied. 'If they really were married.'

'She knew they went off together.'

'And I'll bet,' Rule said, 'I'll bet she's had someone looking for him before. Some place, there's another agency.'

'But, first off, I was never employed to look for Hugh,' Anna said.

'No. You were employed to look for Cynthia.'

'Not even that. When I first met her we were putting in an estimate for alarms and stuff in her brother's house. Then she wanted me to find out what'd happened to a bankrupt stock of sweaters – Cynthia's mother's work. I only came across Hugh by accident.'

'Some accident,' Rule said. 'I'd say you'd been had.'

'But her reasons always looked good. Penny Garden can't or won't work because she's been ripped off for everything. Lara Crowther depends on her designs for her own reputation. She thinks she can get Penny back to work by solving some of her problems.'

'How about what the kid said about her mother and Ms Crowther?' Rule asked. 'Any truth there?'

'Dunno,' Anna said. 'They're friends. They are closely involved with each other. But anyway, so what?'

'Just interested,' Rule said, keeping his eyes on the road. His profile was a bronze mask.

There was such an explosion of new building along the highway that it was hard to see where Bradenton ended and Sarasota began.

'Property,' Rule began. 'We started with the tennis club, like you said. She owned three of the units there – including the one you had. But two of them she sold on.'

'I wonder why Elaine never told me that,' Anna said. 'Elaine didn't seem to know her at all.'

'She has a property company – Shiras Holding. She inherited it from an ex-husband. Her name wouldn't have to appear on the deeds. The developer himself, chairman of the board, is a guy called Amos Farr. He's, so far as we know, on the up and up. We don't know anything about the rest of the board – we haven't had time.'

While he was talking, Rule pulled off the main road, and a few blocks later made a left turn.

'Are you married?' he asked suddenly.

'No,' Anna said surprised. 'Why?'

He turned off the road into the forecourt of a small industrial group of buildings and parked in the shade of a warehouse.

'Over the road there,' he said. 'That white building. You can't see the sign from here.'

Anna leaned forward. There was a bathroom centre, a laundry and a furniture storehouse, as well as the low, white building. Several cars were parked outside.

Rule took his binoculars out of the glove compartment and scanned buildings and the car parks.

'We're meeting the locksmith here,' he said. He sat back in his seat. The motor was still running and the air-conditioner raised goosebumps on Anna's arms.

I'm in the USA, Anna thought. You don't just break into a

place here – you call a locksmith to do it for you. It made breaking in almost respectable.

All the same, as the minutes passed she felt her breath become short and the palms of her hands grow damp.

Chapter 66

IN SPITE OF the noon sun, the locksmith wore a knitted cap on his head. He was an old man with skin the colour of overdone toast. He walked slowly on his heels, wearing his potbelly like a pregnancy. This was not one of the superannuated boys Anna saw in such numbers on the Keys. His teeth were black and worn down, and Rule carried his tool kit for him as he huffed and puffed up to the Style File doors.

His hands were knotted and speckled with age, but he opened the door in no time at all.

Inside was a lobby with a few chairs grouped around a coffee table. The locksmith opened another door into a small office and then another one which led from the office into a dark, cold storage room.

'You better wait in the lobby,' Rule told him.

The locksmith shrugged. 'It's your nickel,' he said, and shambled away.

'Okay,' Rule said, when he had gone. 'What are we looking for?'

'The light switch,' Anna said. She felt along the walls by the door. Her fingers slithered on the paintwork. She wanted to get this finished as soon as possible.

The locksmith poked his head round the office door and said, 'You got company. I guess I won't wait after all.'

'Shit!' said Rule under his breath. He went towards the lobby, unbuttoning his jacket as he walked.

Unbuttoning his jacket! Anna spun round. Was the stupid bastard armed?

'Thanks for you help, Mr Smith,' Rule said in a hearty voice. 'We'll call if we need you again.'

Almost unable to stand, Anna slipped into a chair behind the desk. She found herself looking at an electric typewriter. She switched it on.

In the lobby a bass voice said, 'Where's Dredge? This is too much.'

Rule backed through the door followed by a giant in a jump suit. Anna's eyes were fixed on Rule's hands. What was he going to do? The giant was saying, 'Yesterday pm, the guy said. He didn't show. Either I get what I paid for or . . .'

Giving Rule no chance to do anything, Anna said, 'I'm so sorry. Mr Dredge was unavoidably detained. His wife was taken ill.'

The giant stopped in mid-stride. Rule whipped his head round to look at Anna. She sat on the edge of her chair, fingers poised over the typewriter keys There was no paper in the machine, but the giant didn't seem to notice.

She said, 'How may we help you, Mr, er?'

'Ah . . . Smith,' the giant said at random. He was in his early forties, massively built, with hands like sledge hammers. He turned towards Rule and said, 'Ain't I seen you someplace before?'

'I think I would have remembered you.' Rule's hands were hanging loose at his sides.

Anna said, 'How may I be of assistance, Mr Smith? During the regrettable but uncircumventable absence of Mr Dredge I am temporarily responsible for the continuation of normal working procedure. However, I will have to ask your forebearance due to my relative lack of experience in such matters.'

'You British or something?' the giant asked. He looked at Rule. Rule raised his eyebrows and gave him a long suffering wink.

'I gotta see Dredge,' the giant said uneasily. 'But I guess it can wait.'

'Mr Dredge has asked me to say that he will return tomorrow at three pee em precisely,' Anna said. 'At which time normal service will be resumed. May I pencil you in for three, Mr Smith?'

'Yeah, do that,' said the giant, frowning savagely. 'And tell him he better be here.' He swung round, brushing Rule against the wall as he made for the door. They heard him tramp across the lobby and wrench open the outer door.

'Just tell him to be here,' he bellowed. The door slammed.

'Any more Mr Smiths?' Anna asked. She sat back in the chair. Her hands were dripping onto the typewriter.

'Jee-zus!' Rule said. 'That accent just about kills me.'

'It's a bleedin' marvel, innit? From someone who can't even find a light switch.'

'I'll get the lights,' Rule said. 'You shut up and wind down.'

'Mr Smith didn't exactly look like someone interested in European fashion,' Anna remarked. She rubbed her hands up and down on her thighs to dry them.

Rule switched the light on in the storage room. A Nissan Pathfinder was parked by the double doors.

'Well, well,' said Rule.

'I wonder where the Thunderbird is,' Anna said. 'He was driving a Toyota last night.' To herself, she sounded as if she were still babbling.

'Yeah,' said Rule, looking around. Crates and boxes were stacked against the walls, but what had caught his eye was a steel locker bolted to the wall. 'Maybe we better get the locksmith back in.'

They returned to the office, and Rule dialled a number on the desk telephone. While he waited, he said, 'Mr Smith is definitely not interested in European fashion.'

He spoke briefly into the phone and then hung up. 'You want the passports?' he asked, and gave up his place at the desk. Anna sat down and started to go through the drawers.

'Does he know you from somewhere?' she asked.

'Who?'

'Mr Smith.'

'He would if he had a better memory,' Rule said. 'I played football for him in high school.' He began to open drawers and cupboards too. 'Coach Cairns,' he said. 'A grade A bastard.'

Anna stopped searching the desk and watched him. He was methodical. His big brown hands moved and replaced papers, opened boxes.

'Yeah,' he said. 'When I left the cops I coached for a while too. And I heard he was canned for some ticket scam. It didn't make me too unhappy. A lotta kids got hurt playing for him.'

He lifted a box file from a top shelf and brought it to the desk. Anna bent her head and opened another drawer.

'You gotta be tough to play football,' Rule went on. 'Even in high school.' He began to sort through the file contents. 'But the big kids aren't necessarily the tough ones. Maybe they just grow fast. You gotta know that – coaching kids. Some guys you gotta be patient with.'

There was nothing in the desk to interest Anna, but she went through the motions.

'Some schools,' Rule said, 'you know, rundown area, it's all they got – the team. And some kids, it's all they got too. It's their ticket to better places.'

He replaced the file on the shelf and picked out another one.

'A coach has a lotta power,' he said, with his back to Anna. 'He talks, you listen. He says, "do this," you damn well better do it.'

'What is it?' Anna said, at last.

'What?'

'What are you getting at?'

Rule turned and looked at her. 'You figure it out,' he said. 'Stuff coming in from Italy. Drug connection. Goddamn Coach Cairns.'

He was angry. In spite of his methodical hands and even voice he was boiling.

'Performance enhancing drugs,' he said patiently. 'Steroids, speed, diuretics. Stuff that puts on bulk, stuff that lets you play on an injury. Masking agents. Crap that can hurt you real bad. What I want to know – Is fucking Coach Cairns still coaching kids?'

Chapter 67

An hour later they had everything. What Rule wanted was in the steel locker. What Anna wanted was in the Nissan.

'Well,' Anna said. She was sitting on a crate swinging her legs, impatient. 'Now we know.' The search had taken too long.

'Now we know,' Rule echoed. He shook a cigarette out of its packet and lit it. He was not going to be rushed.

'Look at it,' he said neutrally. Anna looked. It was like a chemist's store cupboard. There were boxes of mega-vitamins, syringes, eye-droppers. There were small bottles, some still in cosmetic packaging. The jars might be labelled 'Skin Toner', but inside were vials with stickers on them identifying primobolin, decoderobolin, stanozolol, dianabol, human growth hormone.

'Yeah,' he said. 'That's all these guys are to a bum like Cairns. Big meat, fast meat, aggressive meat. Get an edge. Get a jump on the opposition. Lotta these guys have wrecked livers by the time they're twenty. Was a guy I heard about, died – he injected some gear direct into his thyroid. Thought it would act faster that way. Into his thyroid!' Unconsciously, Rule touched his own throat. 'Big,' he said. 'You got to get big real quick or you're nothing.'

The yellow fluorescent light picked up the mess they had made – the opened boxes and packages, the fabrics, cosmetics, polystyrene chips, paper. It was Hugh Fellows' whole enterprise, legitimate or otherwise. Whatever he could buy cheap and sell for a profit. Plus a line in what Anna described to herself as hooky pharmaceuticals.

'Doesn't seem enough to get him topped, does it?' Anna said, feeling queasy.

'Depends,' Rule said. He sucked in smoke and blew it in a long stream at the ceiling. 'Could be he was on some other guy's territory.'

'Maybe.' Anna didn't know what it took to get a man killed here. '"Tell them I work for myself,"' she quoted.

They were almost the last words Hugh had ever spoken. He had held a knife to her throat and given her a message for people she didn't know and hoped never to meet. A mistake. While he was sending them a message they were creeping up behind him in a big, black car. A bad mistake. He had been so careful – watching his back, thinking he was one step ahead of the opposition.

She looked at the Nissan Pathfinder. It was packed, like a camper, with clothes for Hugh and Cynthia, papers, passports. And money – a lot of money. A strongbox contained thousands of dollars in cash and traveller's cheques. There were bank books and credit cards. It was a mobile safety net, a holdall for everything Hugh needed if he had to move suddenly.

It could be, Anna thought, a safety net for herself and Cynthia. Take away everything which needed Hugh's signature and there was still enough cash to stuff a duvet.

She eyed Rule speculatively. Rule eyed her back. He did not seem to be in any hurry. Tension strung Anna's backbone tighter than a guywire.

She said, 'Why aren't the cops here?' She wanted to remind him they were on enemy turf.

Rule grunted. 'Yeah, well,' he said, 'They're investigating a British tourist, name of Joseph King, and not getting very far.'

'Joseph King?' Anna laughed suddenly.

'What?'

'Joseph King,' she explained, 'Joe King – joking. A bit wittier than your average heavy.'

'That's witty?' Rule asked.

Anna swung her legs some more and kept her mouth shut.

After a while Rule said, 'Your car was hired by Shiras Holdings – one of several. So they don't know who you are either. They're looking for Ann Johnson.' He stared at her suspiciously. 'Nothing "witty" about Ann Johnson, is there?'

'No.'

'And they're trying to find Joseph King's young wife, Serena. No theories. They are kind of worried because it looks like a professional hit, but the target is not known to them. Usually with a hit like that the reasons are clear. Not this time.'

He ground out his cigarette on the concrete floor, and went on, 'There's a pretty good description out on "Serena King", but I guess no one took much notice of you. What they have on you is vague. Could be anyone.'

'So there's no panic at the tennis club?'

'No.'

'Have you been out there?'

'Not me,' Rule said, 'But Ethan has a coupla guys keeping an eye on the place. Here too. Ethan is not a happy man.'

'Why?'

'Could be because Ms Crowther owes him a few grand.' Rule grinned briefly. 'And now he's wondering if she's playing hardball in the Miami major league, you know, using him to finger Hugh Fellows, making him look bad with the Department. Reason we're still on this – Ethan wants to keep everything quiet.'

'There's more than a few grand here,' Anna said, jerking her head at the Nissan. This was what she wanted to talk about. She tried to read Rule's eyes through his dark glasses. Didn't he ever take them off?

'What's he going to do?' she asked. 'Turn all this over as evidence?'

'Got me,' Rule said. 'His number one priority is keeping his nose clean.'

'Good,' Anna said. 'Then let's hoist this bleeding Nissan, and get the fuck out of here.'

Rule took off his dark glasses and gave her a cool blue stare. 'You nervous?' he asked.

'Of course not,' Anna snapped.

Chapter 68

'Y OU GREW UP in London?' Rule asked. They were sitting in the shade of some pine trees and looking out at the Gulf. Behind them, the Buick and the Nissan sat side by side too. There were plenty of cars parked under the trees. It was a public beach. All Anna wanted was to be in the shade and let the tension drain away. But Rule wanted to talk.

'I don't know anything about you,' he went on. 'If you were from here I'd know right away.' He leaned back on his elbows, not looking at her.

'Yes, London,' Anna said. 'Dulwich. South of the river.' As if that would mean anything to him.

'Dull itch,' Rule said. 'That a classy neighbourhood?'

'No.'

'See, I can't tell from the way you talk.'

'I can't tell anything from the way you talk either.'

'But you were a cop?'

'Yes.'

'I guess that'll have to do,' Rule said. 'Now what?'

Anna watched the lazy ocean, and the couples walking to and fro in their garish beach wear. She stretched her legs into the sun. Now what, indeed. She wanted to sleep. She wanted to go home. She wanted to turn the clock back to when the sun and sea and fresh orange juice were all she knew about Florida – before part of a mans head had exploded against her chest.

Her neck burned where the scab was forming. She touched the bandage and shivered.

'That hurt?' Rule asked. He didn't seem to be looking.

'No,' Anna said. 'But I think about it all the time and I can't believe how it happened.' She wanted to ask him if he had ever been shot at and if so how he'd felt about it. But somehow the question seemed impertinent, or naive, or both.

After a while she said, 'Rule, why did you leave the cops?'

He grunted. 'It was a traffic accident. One night – there had been a lotta rain – on Interstate 75, and this Plymouth hit a truck, see, and there were three young kids in the back. The couple driving the Plymouth, they were mashed up real bad, but alive. But the three kids . . . well, one of them, the baby, we couldn't even find her. And when we did – it was morning by then – she was hanging upside down off this bush. She'd gone through the windscreen and just kept on going till she hit this bush. No arms though. She left her arms on the windshield.'

He stopped talking and looked at his hands. Then he looked at the Gulf.

'When you're a cop,' he said at length, 'you never know what you will have to deal with, what you are going to have to see. I never wanted to see anything like that again.'

'Yes,' Anna said again. Maybe it *was* enough just to know someone had been a cop too.

After a long pause when nothing was said, she began, 'If I went back to the tennis club would you watch my back for me?'

'What do you want to go back there for?' he asked.

'I left my new racket behind,' Anna said. 'I don't want to go home without it.'

He laughed and got to his feet. 'Okay, don't tell me,' he said holding out a hand to help her up. The hand was dry and very warm. Anna did not hold it long.

They went in Rule's car, leaving the Nissan on the beach. As they crossed Manatee Bridge onto the Keys, Anna said, 'You see, I think she'll come looking for me. Lara Crowther. I think she'll want to know what happened, and she'll come and see for herself. I haven't been in touch, except for a message on her machine last night. She'll have rung me back when *she* was ready. Then when she couldn't find me . . .'

'She called Ethan early this morning,' Rule said. 'Ethan said he hadn't seen you, didn't know diddly.'

'You didn't tell me.'

'Didn't ask.'

'Did Ethan tell her anything about last night?'

'Not a thing.'

'She'll come,' Anna said, suddenly convinced.

Nothing had changed on the Keys. They drove slowly past the joggers, the cyclists, the motels and golf courses.

'I wouldn't,' Rule said, at last.

'Wouldn't what?'

'I'd stay in New York, let you make the next move.'

'Me too,' Anna said. She thought about Lara, trying to explain it to herself: the competence, the directness, the control. Was that it? Lara's need to control things? She thought about Lara's reluctance to give any information. It was only when Anna became annoyed, backed off, or acted independently that Lara would come to her with information. Lara used information as currency to keep Anna tied to the job — tied, in fact, to Lara.

Most of all she thought about the tennis game in Battersea Park: Lara winning easily until Anna stiffened, and then, when Anna was catching up, the limp, the fatigue, the shoelaces. Anything to keep the upper hand, anything to keep Anna on the hook.

Had she acted the same way with Penny Garden — making Penny dependent on her? She did not like to lose control of people.

'She'll want to reassert control,' Anna said. 'She wants me to respond to her. If I don't, she'll come.'

'You want to see her?' Rule asked curiously.

'Yes,' Anna said. 'I want to know.'

'Hah!' Rule grunted. 'She won't tell you. If she set Hugh up she will not tell you.'

Anna sighed. 'Probably not,' she agreed. 'But I'm not after evidence. I just want to know . . . for myself.'

'Cop's disease,' Rule said, and drove on in silence.

A little later Anna said, 'I can't understand why a lady like Lara Crowther has, what you call them, major league associations. She's so respectable. I don't understand it at all.'

Rule didn't seem very interested. 'Investors,' he said, 'Big investors, little investors. Clean money, dirty money. It's all money.

You want in on some project you don't ask where the other investors got their money.'

Manatee Key Tennis Club was quiet in the afternoon sun. The sprinklers played over the outside courts. Only Lew was working.

'Eight hours a day on court,' Anna muttered. 'And not a hair out of place.'

'What?' said Rule.

'Lew. He must have legs like steel.'

'Great strokes,' Rule said, winding his window down to watch.

'Bend those knees!' Lew called to an overweight teenage girl as she came puffing to the net. 'You gotta bend those knees for the half court volley – get down to it. Right?'

The girl said nothing and plodded back to the baseline as if she were looking for the nearest bed. Around the Coke machine, in the shade, parents and grandparents smiled indulgently.

Rule parked the car and they walked to the clubhouse. Elaine was unpacking boxes of rackets and at the same time selling a hot-pink tennis outfit to an elderly woman.

'Cool wash, cool dry,' she was saying. 'Hi, Anna, where yah been? Great colour isn't it? Never fades, never loses it's shape. I was looking for you. Ms Crowther called, wanted to know where you were. Shall I charge that Mrs Adler?'

Anna waited while she filled out the sales docket and bagged the goods.

'I called you,' Elaine said, 'because I had a game for you this morning, and then Ms Crowther said she couldn't find you either.'

'I was staying with a friend in Bradenton,' Anna told her.

'That's nice,' Elaine said, looking at Rule. 'And I found out who that guy is, you know, came looking for you yesterday.'

She was still looking at Rule, her dark eyes very bright.

Anna grinned and said, 'This is Rule Suarez. Rule – Elaine.'

'Hi,' said Rule.

'You a cop?' Elaine asked, straight out.

'Was a cop,' Rule said.

'See?' Elaine said, triumphant. 'I always know. I said you were a cop, didn't I, Anna?'

'You did,' Anna said.

'Lew, now, he said you were a jock.'

'Was a jock too,' Rule said.

'No kidding!' Elaine said. 'Lew, he's from Australia so he doesn't always figure out people the way I do. I just knew you were a cop.'

'Elaine knows everyone,' Anna said. 'So who was the chap who came yesterday?'

'I *knew* I'd seen him,' Elaine said. 'Works on the Key at the Sand Dollar Motel. You see what happened there last night?' She reached under the counter and slapped a newspaper down for them to see. The headline read, TOURIST SLAIN.

Elaine was sparkling and excited. She turned to Rule and went on, 'They say it was a mob killing. But on the news they said the guy was just a British tourist. But I told Lew, I said, "If it's a mob killing the guy musta had mob connections." Am I right?'

'Seems logical,' Rule said.

'What about the chap asking for me?' Anna put in quickly.

'Dave Douglas, didn't I say?' Elaine turned back to Anna. 'See, he and Tony work out at the same gym. Competitive body building. I thought Tony would know, see, because there's this sorta fashion where all the guys bleach their hair, looks kinda cute with a tan, like in California. You musta noticed Tony dyes his hair, right?

'Well, this Dave Douglas used to do the snacks at the Cabana at the Holiday Inn, which is where I guess I knew him from. But something happened and they let him go. So now he does pool and yard work out at the Sand Dollar.'

'Why was he looking for me?' Anna asked.

'Well that was kinda funny,' Elaine said. 'He didn't know your name except he thought you were called Ann, but he described you and your car. Said he'd seen you on the beach and you'd left your camera, which I thought was weird because you don't have a camera I've ever seen. I asked Lew and he said he'd never seen you with a camera either. So I thought maybe the guy wanted a date or something. But I acted cagey and said you came in sometimes and if he left his name and number you'd maybe give him a call. Or, I said, why didn't he leave the camera and I'd give it to you. But he wouldn't. So anyway I didn't tell him your real name or the number of your unit because, see, he's cute, but he's not the kinda guy our members usually associate with.'

'Thanks,' Anna said, relieved.

'No problem,' Elaine said. 'I was right, wasn't I, not giving out your personal details?'

'Absolutely right,' Anna said.

'What time was this?' Rule asked.

'Let's see,' Elaine said, 'had to be sometime before lunch yesterday, because Bucky had just come in for his lesson at twelve-thirty.'

Rule looked at Anna, and she nodded.

'I took Cynthia shopping about an hour earlier,' she said.

Elaine looked from one to the other as if she were following a ball. The phone rang.

Anna said quietly, 'I think he was just working for Hugh. When I went off with Cyn he would've rung Hugh, and he might've seen my car or something, turning in here.'

Elaine said, 'Someone wants to talk to Rule Suarez.' She handed the phone over the counter.

After listening and muttering for a few minutes, Rule put the phone down and said, 'That was Ethan. The lady wants us to trace you. She thinks you might be here, not answering the phone. She wants to know immediately we locate you.'

Chapter 69

'Y OU'RE STILL A cop,' Elaine said.
    Rule leaned big brown arms on the counter and said, 'Elaine, I'm gonna tell you something confidential, okay? I was a cop. Now I'm a private investigator. So is Anna here.'

'I knew it!' Elaine said, eyes brilliant. 'I knew it. Jeez, that must be interesting work.'

Anna closed her eyes briefly and wondered what on earth Rule thought he was doing.

He went on, 'I can't tell you what we're working on, Elaine, you know that, but you could be a big help to us. We're going over to Anna's place now, and . . .'

'I know,' Elaine said. 'I call if I see anyone I can't account for or anyone asking for you.'

'That's it,' Rule said. 'You know everyone, what deliveries you're expecting. It'd be a big help.'

'I can do that,' Elaine said, 'no problems.'

'Thanks a lot,' Anna said. 'There's one thing . . .'

'You don't have to say it,' Elaine said. 'I know how to keep my mouth shut.'

'Even Ms Crowther,' Rule said. 'If she comes, Elaine, we want to know. It's just you, me and Anna here, right?'

In the Buick, Rule took the gun out of the glove compartment and stuck it in his jacket pocket. Anna turned away as if he were doing something indecent.

He said, 'You pissed off or something?'

'Of course not,' Anna said. 'But do you go round telling *everyone* your business?'

'Sometimes it's a real good move,' he said thoughtfully. 'Believe me – I know Elaine. I only just met her and I know her better than I'd know you if you'd been around a whole year. No offence

— some people you take one look you know which way they jump.'

'She thinks you're cute too,' Anna said sourly. Rule grinned.

They put the car out of sight in the garage under the house, and Rule went upstairs first. He's probably got that bleeding gun out, Anna thought, and he's jumping across doorways as if that'd do any good. Depression descended on her like a black felt hat. This was a bad idea: she couldn't afford to have ideas in a country she didn't know.

'You coming?' Rule called. 'There's no one up here but me.'

'Then I think I'll stop in the garage,' Anna muttered.

'What?'

'I think I'll lock the garage,' Anna said, having already done it and checked the locks twice.

Rule was in the kitchen. He said, 'You got ham and eggs in the refrigerator. I'll fix us something. I bet you haven't eaten since yesterday.'

'I had breakfast at Nancy's,' Anna said, stiffly.

'Nancy made breakfast?' Rule asked. 'And you are still walking? What did she give you?'

'Scrambled eggs,' Anna said, feeling more comfortable all of a sudden. 'Flambé,' she added with a sheepish smile. The gun was out of sight and Rule looked altogether more attractive with a frying pan. The phone rang, and Anna went to answer it. Rule stopped rattling the pan.

Martin Brierly said, 'Have you any idea what it costs to telephone the United States? No? Well let me tell you . . .'

'Don't tell me,' Anna interrupted. 'It's too expensive.' And life was too short, she realised, much too short.

'I *beg* your pardon,' he exclaimed, the phone straining his normally fruity voice so that it came out thin and weak.

'May I remind you,' he said, 'that it is in response to a garbled message from you we are speaking now.'

On the off-peak rate, Anna thought, the habit of silence reasserting itself.

'Not only that,' Martin Brierly went on, 'but I have had to respond to frantic calls from your client who, it appears, does not know where you are. She was under the erroneous impression that, as you are employed by this agency, you would be in constant touch with this office. I have to confess to a similar error of judgement.'

'There is a very good reason for that,' Anna said. 'As a client, Ms Crowther is unreliable. I think she has been using me, us, to do a job other than the one stated. Someone was shot last night . . .'

'Shot, Miss Lee?' Brierly said. 'What in the world have you been up to?'

'Trying to find Ms Crowther's friend's daughter,' Anna said. 'Only the daughter . . . look, Mr Brierly, the point is that Lara Crowther isn't to be trusted.'

'I think I told *you* that, Miss Lee,' he said, smugly. 'From the beginning she was obviously more than parsimonious with the necessary details.'

'So I might need your help,' Anna said doggedly. Something very like despair was boiling up inside her. He could have asked how she was, or had she been hurt, instead of 'I told you so,' and complaining about the phone bill. He hadn't even got in touch until he could do so on the cheap rate.

'I hardly see how I can help at this distance,' he said. 'Your predicament is largely of your own making.'

'You haven't even asked what my "predicament" is!' Anna shouted.

'I should be very careful, if I were you,' Martin Brierly said. 'It's fortunate for you, with your tendency towards pigheadedness, that I had the foresight to demand a healthy retainer for your services.'

Anna hung up. 'Fucking toe-rag,' she said, looking at the bright blue Gulf. She wished she had said it to him before cutting him off – made it official. A snatch of an old song came into her mind: 'The tide is high and I'm movin' on . . .'

She went into the kitchen, her mind practically empty. Rule was just turning the eggs.

'Coffee or beer?' she asked.

'Coffee,' he said.

She filled the coffee maker while he served up the ham and eggs.

'Good,' she said with her mouth full. He nodded.

'Who was that?' he asked.

'My boss.'

'What is a toe-rag?'

Anna put down her fork. 'An insult,' she said. 'An expression of extreme contempt. It's probably from a time when beggers and tinkers had to wear rags round their feet instead of socks and shoes.'

'No kidding,' Rule said. 'Eat.'

She ate.

He said, 'You should tell him to take a hike.'

'Yes,' she agreed. 'Except I think that was him telling me to take a hike.'

'You don't know?'

'He isn't all that straightforward,' Anna said. They finished the meal in silence. Anna poured the coffee and they took it into the living room to drink. The silence was comfortable.

After a while Rule said, 'There's something I want to ask you.'

'Yes?' Anna said.

The phone rang.

Elaine said, 'I just seen Dave Douglas. He parked his truck where he thought I won't see it and he went round back of the clubhouse.'

'Can you see him now?' Anna asked.

'He's round back,' Elaine said. 'You want me to check him out?'

'No,' Anna said. 'We need you to watch the entrance.'

'It's kinda good there's only one entrance,' Elaine said. 'I'm glad now the developer didn't clear all the mangrove even if we do lose a lot of balls in there.'

'Right,' Anna said. 'I'm going to hang up now and go to somewhere I can see from.'

'Bedroom,' Elaine said. 'There's a real good view of the club from the small bedroom. Is that Rule still with you?'

'Yes, do you want to talk to him?'

Elaine laughed and rang off.

'Dave Douglas,' Anna told Rule. She ran up to the small bedroom, and stood a pace or so away from the window where she could see without being seen.

It struck her again how oddly like a village Manatee Key Tennis Club was – with its houses grouped around the courts and clubhouse as if around village green and church. It was isolated in a billowing green sea of mangrove, and its western border was the Gulf. A sleepy village. Both Lew and the other pro were on court, but Anna was too far away to see or hear.

Rule came up and handed her his binoculars. She swept the scene slowly. Lew's lesson was a dark, intense woman with a tendency to overrun the ball.

She paid special attention to the path that led from behind the clubhouse, behind the central courts towards the beach. The screens were in the way, but after a few minutes she thought she saw the movement of figures behind the screen. She followed the movement, and sure enough, caught a glimpse of two blond and muscled men as they walked casually from the shelter of the screen to the house closest to the courts. They disappeared behind it.

'Yes,' she said. 'He's here with Tony. They're coming this way.'

She left Rule with the binoculars and went into the big bedroom to dial Elaine's number.

'Does Tony know we're here?' she asked when Elaine answered.

'He only just got in,' Elaine said. 'He was out picking up some hoses from Harry's Hardware which is where we have an account.'

'Right,' Anna said. 'Does he have keys to the houses?'

'Sure he does,' Elaine said, 'so's he can let the agency people in to clean.'

'Thanks,' Anna said. 'As long as we know.'

She passed this information on to Rule.

'Okay,' Rule said, and went downstairs. Anna remained by the window, watching.

Soon enough Tony appeared, on his own, carrying a long-handled broom. He looked up at the house and then started to sweep, looking this way and that. Finally he nodded, but continued to sweep.

Anna grinned tightly. She took off her shoes and padded downstairs. At the bottom, by the front door she noticed that the door through from the garage was open slightly.

'One,' she said, in a low voice. 'Any minute.' Then she went up. In the living room she slid behind the curtains, not exactly hidden, but not immediately obvious either.

Two minutes later she heard the front door open, and then footsteps on the stairs. He went into the kitchen first.

If he had any sense, Anna thought, he'd know someone had cooked there recently. In fact he'd have known as soon as he set foot in the house. But he did not seem to know. He moved quietly but not cautiously.

He came into the living room, and went straight to the only cupboard – a lacquered bow-fronted cabinet. He squatted and opened the doors.

Anna did not hear Rule follow him up, but she assumed he had. While the blond man was still squatting she moved away from the window and said, 'Hello, mate. I didn't hear you knock.'

He turned his head quickly enough to give himself whiplash. Anna pushed the sofa abruptly at him and knocked him over onto his back.

Rule appeared from the doorway with his hands in his pockets.

'Shee-it!' said Mr Muscles.

'Stay where you are,' Rule said.

Anna threw him a cushion, and said, 'Get comfy but keep lying flat on your back.'

Mr Muscles clutched the cushion and looked furious.

'You stick the cushion behind your head,' Rule said, sleepily. 'And you clasp your hands on your chest, see, and you cross your ankles. Right?'

'Fuck you,' said Dave Douglas. 'I came to check the water tank.'

'Be still,' Rule said. 'This is not a banana I have here in my pocket.' He turned to Anna. 'Defence of property, y'know. A citizen has a right.'

Dave Douglas stared at Rule's pocket.

'Hey, look man,' he said. 'I haven't touched anything, right? The maintenance guy is a good friend of mine. He let me in. I help him out sometimes.'

'Behave,' Anna said. 'We know who you are.'

'Screw you,' he said. 'I knew you were trouble.'

'Never mind her,' Rule said. 'You're talking to me now, so watch your mouth.'

There was a silence, Dave staring at Rule, thinking about it. He looked about as tense as a recumbent man could. His white T-shirt rose and fell with his hurried breathing. Just above his canvas shoes a pulse beat visibly in his ankle. His fingers twitched.

Rule sighed. 'Turn over,' he said. 'I don't want to see your face when I do it.'

'I was looking for some stuff,' Dave said, in a rush. Sweat leaked from his forehead and ran down into his ears. 'Mr Dredge owes me. It's mine. You took it, see. I seen you at Style File. We had a deal, Mr Dredge and me. He owes me. I watched out for that crazy chick, I did loading, unloading for him. He gave me stuff. I was a sorta distributor and I got a percentage, right? Now you took him out, it's mine, way I see it. But hey, I'm not greedy, I can work for you same's I work for him, right? But I gotta have some stuff. I got my reputation to consider. Guys on programmes gotta have a regular supplier, they'll go elsewhere.'

Once started he was unwilling to stop. His eyes jerked between Rule and Anna, and the words tumbled out.

'See, he told me you guys was after him,' he went on. 'Gonna take away his business, move him into a higher risk area. Right? This is a profitable market. I mean it's a really profitable market, man. I got all the connections, know all the guys. And it's an expanding market — really young guys gettin' interested. I mean, hey, you let me take care of business for you we could clean up. And if you got other stuff you want pushing, hey, no problem.'

'Tell me,' Rule said mildly, 'is Coach Cairns still teaching kids?'

Chapter 70

'WHAT I COULD do is sleep in the Nissan,' Anna said. It was getting dark and she had had a couple of beers. 'Elaine will be going home soon and I don't want to hang about here after dark.'

'It should be safe,' Rule said. 'Probably.' He had drunk a couple of beers too, but it didn't seem to be affecting him. Anna was quite shocked at the speed with which two weak beers had worked. Or she would have been shocked if she hadn't felt so relaxed. She couldn't understand it at all.

'What's safe?' she asked. 'Anyway, "probably" safe isn't safe enough.'

'That little creep thought *we* blew Hugh away,' Rule said. 'So he isn't in touch with the guys who did blow Hugh away.'

'But what about Lara?' Anna said.

'I'll take you back to Nancy's house,' Rule said. 'We can start again in the morning.'

'We left the Nissan on Bay Beach,' Anna said.

'But I have all the stuff in my vehicle.'

'You sound like Dave Douglas,' Anna remarked. 'Stuff!'

'Fucking toe-rag,' Rule said. Anna began to giggle. He watched her for a moment, smiling patiently.

Anna said, 'You were going to ask me something.'

'What?'

'I don't know. You said you wanted to ask me something before Dave Douglas came.'

The phone rang. Rule got to it first.

'Yes?' he said. Then, 'Okay Elaine. Good work.' He put the receiver down.

'White Mercedes,' he told Anna. 'Ms Crowther, she thinks. No passengers, she thinks. How d'you want to play it?'

'Buggered if I know,' Anna said. 'I want to play it hard and low over the net, make her work to get the ball back and stop her lobbing into the sun.'

'You okay?'

'Of course,' Anna said. 'I mean I just want to keep her honest.'

'I know what you mean,' Rule said. 'It's just you had a coupla beers and every time you say, "Of course" you seem to mean the opposite.'

Anna stared at him. He said, 'I'll get lost. Right? She probably won't talk to you unless she thinks you're alone.'

He stood up and they heard a car door slam below.

'Not too far,' Anna said.

'I'll be there,' Rule said. 'Don't worry.'

'Of course not,' Anna said. And then to cover up, she added, 'Don't forget your cigarettes.'

The front doorbell chimed. Rule took his cigarettes and left. She waited. She thought he had probably gone upstairs but she couldn't hear him. For a big man he moved very well.

The bell chimed again, and then she heard a key in the lock. She listened. There was only one pair of feet on the stairs.

When Lara saw her she only paused for half a second. She put her handbag on the coffee table and dropped her keys beside it.

'Hi, Anna,' she said. 'Why didn't you come down and let me in?'

'This is your house,' Anna said. 'You've got your own keys. You can come in whenever you like.'

'That's right,' Lara said. She sat down and crossed her legs. She was wearing a pink and lime green dress, made of silk with fine pleats in the skirt. She arranged the pleats precisely over her knees. 'Well?' she said.

Anna waited, watching her.

She had on pale green eye shadow which went well with the gold hair and tan. A colourful woman, Anna thought.

'Look,' Lara said, 'we're a little out of sync here. You left an urgent message on my machine last night. I didn't get home till the early hours so I couldn't respond. When I called you back there was no reply. I called Florida-Technics. I called Elaine at the club. I even called your office in England. Nobody had seen you or heard from you.'

'So you came,' Anna said. 'Why?'

'Why?' Lara said. 'Because I thought you might be in trouble. It sounded as if you were in trouble.'

'How kind,' Anna said. 'But as you see I'm not in trouble. There was a spot of bother last night but that was last night.'

'So?' Lara said.

'So what?'

'So, have you anything to report?' Lara asked, like a very patient woman. 'I don't want to waste my trip entirely.'

'Have some coffee,' Anna suggested. 'It won't take a minute.'

'Look, I'm sorry I didn't call you right back,' Lara said. 'If that's what's bugging you.'

'I'm not bugged,' Anna said. 'Where were you last night?'

'I'm sorry?' Lara said in offended tones.

'With your mum again?' Anna asked politely. 'Is she any better?'

'As it happens, yes, I was visiting with my mother.' Lara frowned.

'I could verify that?' Anna asked. 'I mean, are there three independent witnesses to this visit?'

'I don't get it,' Lara said. 'I feel this terrific hostility from you.'

'Hostility?' Anna asked. 'Of course not.'

'Quit fencing,' Lara snapped. 'If you have something to say to me, say it.'

Anna looked puzzled. 'I haven't got anything to say to you,' she said. 'You came to me. I didn't come to you.'

'I'm paying you to report to me,' Lara said. She was getting angry.

'No, you're not,' Anna said, thinking – fifteen, love. It had taken a while, but sometimes even a single small point took patience.

'What do you mean?' Lara said. 'I am your employer.'

'No, you're not,' Anna repeated. 'It's all over.'

'It's all over when I say it is, not before,' Lara said angrily. 'Now where is Cynthia?'

'I don't know,' Anna said.

'What do you mean you don't know?'

'I just don't know,' Anna said pleasantly. 'They didn't tell me where they took her.'

'Who took her?' Lara asked. She looked shaken.

'They didn't tell me their names.'

'You took her,' Lara exclaimed. 'They didn't take her.'

'Now we're getting somewhere,' Anna said, relieved. 'Thirty, love.'

'Are you crazy?' Lara shouted. 'What has come over you?'

'It's something you told me once,' Anna said.

'What?'

'You told me not to ignore the mental game. I always pay attention to what you say. I'm a big admirer.'

'That was tennis,' Lara said.

'No. You said it was my whole attitude to life. The game was a draw. Remember? You said I should have won and that therefore I had let you beat me. Because I ignored the mental game.'

'Jesus!' Lara said. 'It was only a game.'

'Isn't that what I'm supposed to say?' Anna asked. 'That's what the loser says, right?'

'What are you talking about?' Lara said, exasperated. 'All I did was ask where Cynthia is. Is that too much for you? What am I going to tell Penny? That poor woman. Hasn't she been through enough?'

'Ah, the old shoelace trick,' Anna said approvingly. 'Why not wheel in your sick mother while you're at it? Come on, Lara, Cynthia is just a point in your game with Penny. You don't give a wet fart what happened to her.'

'I told you I never cared for Cyn,' Lara said. 'But I do care for Penny. I never saw you as a hard woman, Anna, but how in hell can you use that child against Penny? You really must tell me where she is.'

'You don't believe me, do you?' Anna said calmly. 'I told you, they took her away.'

'They did not take her away!' Lara raged.

'I was there, you weren't.'

Lara fell silent. Anna waited. Lara rearranged the pleats, and then leant forward to pick up her handbag.

'I could make you tell me,' she said quietly. She put the handbag on her knee and undid the clasp.

'How?' Anna asked, watching carefully.

'Your Mr Brierly may not look like much, but one word from me . . .'

'That wouldn't work.'

Lara sighed. She fiddled with the clasp of her handbag. In the end she said. 'This is ridiculous. What do you want?'

'Nothing,' Anna said. 'I've got everything I want.'

'More money?' Lara suggested. 'A bonus? Cash.'

'I've got loads of money,' Anna said. 'Enough to stuff a duvet.'

Lara's eyes narrowed. 'I see,' she said slowly. 'You switched sides. They paid you. Now I understand. This is a hostage situation.'

'No, it isn't,' Anna said.

'I thought you were straight,' Lara said. 'I got to hand it to you – I didn't see this coming at all.'

'I thought you were straight too,' Anna replied.

'Why?' Lara asked. 'I thought we got along.'

'You made a convenience of me,' Anna said.

'Pride,' Lara said. 'I should have known.'

'One of the first strategies of the game,' Anna told her cheerfully. 'Know your opponent. I slipped up there myself. I should've checked the details – like who you were married to . . .'

'You know about that?'

'And how much you were paying him in the settlement.'

Lara sighed again. She seemed much more sure of herself now that she was convinced of Anna's dishonesty. But she seemed tired too.

'You understand then,' she said. 'You and I both know what it is to be made a convenience of. I thought I knew all the tricks. God, he made a sucker of me! It was that smooth British charm. If it hadn't been for that I'd have seen him coming a mile off.'

'You divorced him.'

'It wasn't enough. I had to pay him off and even then I couldn't

266

get rid of him. Every way I turned I tripped over him. He used my contacts, my outlets. He used my name. So then he runs away with my designer's daughter, and my label goes up in smoke too.'

'He wasn't a nice man,' Anna agreed.

'Nice!' Lara made an explosive sound in her throat. 'He . . . I can't tell you . . .' She began to count on her fingers. 'He was a cheat, a thief, a liar. He was sexually promiscuous. He used drugs. He smoked. He sold drugs.'

'You knew about that?' Anna asked.

'Sure I did. It was the final straw. He was importing steroids and God knows what else in consignments of *my* garments. If anyone had got to know about that my whole operation would have gone to hell. As it was he sold the goddamned things at my racket club. I mean he was only a member because he was my husband.

'People knew!' Lara said emphatically. 'He was talked about. And it was *my* goddamned reputation.'

'You should have told Penny,' Anna said. 'You could've saved her a lot of grief.'

'I'm talking about my reputation!' Lara snapped.

'I'm talking about your friend!'

'I guess you're right,' Lara said tiredly. 'But I felt such a fool. I didn't even tell her I was married. He was a few years younger than I, and I thought she'd lose respect for me.'

'So poor Cynthia was sacrificed to your reputation.'

'I don't think you have the right to talk to me like that,' Lara said. 'You've been bought. It cost me a lot of money to find Hugh and Cyn. You were paid. Now you want me to pay again.'

'No I don't,' Anna said.

'Well, you tell Mr Fantini or Fantoni or whatever he chooses to call himself he won't get a single cent out of me. I gave him information but I will not buy Cynthia. I'm through. He can't get at me through her.'

'That's exactly what Hugh said.' Anna sighed. 'Poor Cynthia. She isn't worth very much to anyone. Except her mother, perhaps.'

'She can't pay you,' Lara said quickly. 'She's had no income for over a year. Why, I'm practically keeping her.'

'More fool you,' Anna said.

'What do you mean?'

'I don't really know,' Anna said. 'It's just an instinct. I could be wrong.'

'Penny loves me,' Lara said. 'We've been friends for years.'

'Friends are equals. You made a dependant out of her.'

'Penny loves me,' Lara insisted.

'But do you love Penny?' Anna asked. 'You didn't give her the information she required to keep her family together. Maybe you even encouraged Hugh. Maybe you thought things would be better for you with them out of the way. You only tried to get Cynthia back when Penny stopped working. And then you used the excuse of finding Cynthia to get Hugh killed. Don't you understand? You nearly got Penny's daughter *shot*!'

'You have nothing to be self-righteous about,' Lara said. 'If any harm comes to that kid now it will be your fault. If anyone sold her this time it was you.'

'Wrong,' Anna said. 'You haven't been listening. I don't know Mr Fantoni. He hasn't paid me anything. I have not switched sides. This is not a hostage situation. I don't work for you anymore but I don't work for anyone else either.'

'I don't believe you,' Lara said. 'What do you want?'

'Take a hike,' Anna said. 'If I wanted anything, it was simply to hear everything you just told me.'

Chapter 71

'YOU HAVE BEEN stringing me along,' Lara said, sitting very still, handbag on her lap. For a second she seemed to pull herself up and became very alert. But as Anna watched something seemed to drain out of her and when it was over she looked like any other ageing woman.

'I don't feel too good,' she said. 'You manipulated me.'

Anna looked away. A clean, pure moon hung over the Gulf. Game, she thought. Had she won? It didn't feel like winning. Or if it did winning wasn't very pleasant.

'I could kill you for that,' Lara said wearily.

'Mind if I look in that purse, ma'am?' Rule said from the door. Lara did not even look surprised. She raised shaky hands to massage her temples. Anna ignored her.

Rule took the bag, flipped through the contents and handed it back to her.

'Police?' she said.

'No,' Anna told her. Rule went to stand by the window. He looked at the moon too.

'Boy,' he said, 'you sure took your time.'

'What do you want?' Lara asked again, making an effort to sit up straight. 'I don't know what you think you understand by this conversation. I haven't admitted anything.'

'Not really,' Anna agreed. 'But if I wanted to make a case I could. All the elements are there – your marriage, your business, Hugh's naff little operation, your connection with Fantini-Fantoni through Amos Farr and the development corporation. It'd take a lot of work. It might even be worth it. You very nearly killed me.'

'I did not,' Lara said. 'I had nothing to do with it.'

Rule said, 'What do you think a professional hit is? Do you

think any witnesses stand much chance? You let guys like that loose on a target, they're gonna let a witness walk away?'

'Two witnesses,' Anna said. 'Maybe you meant to get Cynthia killed. Tell you the truth, I think you did. After all I would never have put you in the frame if Cynthia hadn't told me you and Hugh were married. Not in a million years.'

'What has she been saying about me?' Lara asked. 'You cannot believe one word she says. I've known her since she was a child.'

'And she's known you,' Anna said flatly.

'You said you didn't know where she was,' Lara said.

'I don't. But I'm going to take her home.'

Lara seemed to crumple. 'She'll tell Penny.' All the colour drained from her face leaving a mask of cosmetics. 'She'll tell Penny everything,' she said, and tipped forward.

She fell out of her chair, struck her head on the edge of the glass coffee table and lay in a heap on the carpet. A tiny worm of blood crawled out of the golden hair.

'Shit a brick!' Anna said. She knelt by Lara feeling for a pulse.

Rule pulled the coffee table aside. They straightened Lara and turned her. Her eyes were open, baby blue.

'Stroke!' Rule said sharply. He stared at the panic-stricken eyes. 'I've seen it before.' He got up and went to the phone.

The scalp wound seemed superficial. Anna put a cushion under her head. She pulled Lara's skirt down over her legs.

'It's all right, ducky,' she said, and took Lara's helpless hand. Lara's mouth was open but she did not speak.

'Don't worry,' Anna whispered. 'There's help coming.'

Chapter 72

Anna took Cynthia home. She left her with Penny one dark chilly morning four days later. She hoped Penny was prepared. Bernie had been looking after that side of things — arranging for Penny's doctor to be present and informing the social services.

'How did it go?' Bernie asked curiously. 'She's a funny one, that Mrs Garden. A bit do-lally, if you ask me.'

'I didn't stop,' Anna said. 'The house was full of do-gooders. There wasn't anything else for me to do.'

They were sitting in Bernie's kitchen and Anna was warming her hands on a cup of tea.

'You look knackered,' Bernie said. 'You should take a break, go somewhere nice.'

'Florida?' Anna asked, and laughed.

'That's better,' Bernie said. 'I thought you were going to keel over from a state of terminal depression. Have another slice of cake. Syl will never let me hear the end of it if there's any left when she gets back.'

It was chocolate fudge cake, dark and reassuring — the kind of cake grown-up children dream about. Anna took another slice. Bernie poured more tea, and Anna told him everything she hadn't already told him on the phone. Almost everything.

'Don't take it so hard,' Bernie said, when she finished. 'Strokes just happen. You didn't make it happen.'

Which was roughly what Rule had said too. 'You weren't too tough on her,' he said. 'Jeez-us, waiting out there, I thought you were *never* going to hit her with it. All that crap about the mental game. What you did was more like fishing than tennis.'

'Fishing takes time,' Anna said. 'And patience and subtlety.'

'Subtlety!' Rule snorted. 'I'll take you out on my boat tomorrow. You'll see how "subtle" a swordfish is.'

But Anna had not seen, because there weren't any swordfish biting.

She smiled, remembering.

'That's the spirit!' Bernie said. 'Life's not so bad.'

'It sure beats the hell out of death,' Anna said, trying out her new American accent. Bernie looked mildly surprised.

'Actually,' Anna said, 'I could go back. I mean, what have I got to stay for? Old fart-face has given me the push. Jobless, homeless . . .'

'Brainless,' Bernie supplied. 'You can get your job back if you want it. I know for a fact he'll be shorthanded come New Year. Young Sean's moving on. Some brewery interviewed for a security manager, and I happen to know he was the successful candidate. If that young puppy can swing a cushy number like that, think what you could do for yourself.'

'I dunno,' Anna said.

'Security's still an expanding market.'

'Maybe that's what's wrong with it.' Anna sighed. 'Everyone's at it. I might as well be a sewing-machine demonstrator.'

'Except you can't sew.' Bernie grinned at her. 'Aren't you a bit young for a midlife crisis? Or is this our old friend jetlag?'

'It's all so narrow here,' she complained. 'Cold, pinched and narrow.'

'Definitely jetlag,' Bernie said, nodding to himself.

'Can I stay here tonight?' Anna asked suddenly.

'If you stop complaining about poor old London,' Bernie said. 'It really gets on my wick the way people talk when they've just come back from the States. I must go there sometime myself.'

'I've got to sort things out at home,' Anna said, not listening. 'I've got to talk to Quex, but I really can't face him today.'

'Poor chap,' Bernie said.

'What do you mean?'

'Well,' Bernie said, 'you'll marry him or you'll give him the chop. Either way, poor chap.'

'Thanks a bundle!'

'Admit it,' Bernie said. 'You're no gift in your present mood.'

'I'll give him a bell,' Anna decided, starting to get up.

'Not now, you won't,' Bernie said. 'Whatever it is you'll mess it up proper if you do it today. Sit down and I'll make another pot of tea. Don't you want to hear about your pal, William Herridge.'

'Who?'

'William Herridge-with-a-D. You rang me all the way from Fantasy Island about him, didn't you, Miss Memory? Couldn't wait to get the poor bugger sorted.'

'Of course I remember,' Anna said.

'Well then, what're you grinning about? Got wind?'

'Nothing,' Anna said. 'What happened about William Herridge?'

'He ordered four racing tyres from F.J.P. Garages,' Bernie began. 'Not radial tyres, *racing* ones. F.J.P. got radials in for him. He stopped the cheque – wouldn't pay. F.J.P. put him down as a bad debt. It appears Herridge's hobby is rally driving. He wanted those particular tyres for a race. He paid by cheque in advance. When F.J.P. got him the wrong ones he stopped payment and told them to get stuffed. But the accounts department had already done the paper work. They kept dunning him for the money. He kept writing to say he didn't have the tyres. Meanwhile the accounts department had informed the credit company.'

'I thought it was something like that,' Anna said. 'He just wasn't the bad debt type.'

'Right,' Bernie said. 'Well spotted. F.J.P. accounts man has promised to do what he can to get the credit block lifted.'

'What about his promotion?' Anna asked.

'Another story,' Bernie said. 'All this took some time. Sean, as you no doubt remember, had written the report without doing the work. Well, just after you left Beryl discovered the report was missing. Big fracas.'

'Dear, dear,' Anna said piously.

Bernie's lips twitched. 'Sean swore he'd handed it in. Beryl swore it had been approved and was on the pile to be sent to the client. They both decided you had nicked it.'

'But I'd never nick a file,' Anna said crossly.

'Then you rang from the States and asked me to follow up. Which I did. While I was pursuing my enquiries, Beryl found the file behind the word processor.'

'Actually,' Anna confessed, 'it was behind her floppy disc box.'

'Well anyway, she sent the bloody thing to the client.'

'Shit!' Anna said. 'Couldn't you stop her?'

'I tried, but she was so annoyed with you I think she did it out of spite. I went to Old Nobble Nut and he said, I quote: "I think, Mr Schiller, we will have to let the report stand. Public relations are not benefited by an appearance of wavering." Silly old sod. So I finished my enquiry double quick and rang the client direct. Too late. He told me he was satisfied with Sean's report. He had already made his decision and he wasn't going to change it. William Herridge did not get his promotion. Not only that, the client put his cousin in as manager and William Herridge was so browned off he's looking for another job.'

'Typical,' Anna said, depressed. 'That is so effing typical. Everyone standing foursquare behind their mistakes. That is so bleeding small-minded. *Everyone*, all the way from the garage to the client with Brierly sodding Security in between.'

'Yes,' Bernie said soberly. For once he did not try to cheer her up or tell her to be philosophical.

'That settles it,' Anna said. 'Martin Brierly can stuff his job. I wouldn't take it if he handed it to me in a Fabergé egg.'

'Don't go off half-cocked,' Bernie said. 'Get some sleep, shake off that jetlag, then decide. Everyone you work for is the same when you come down to it.'

'Maybe I don't have to work for anyone,' Anna said slowly. 'There's this guy I met in the States. He was fed up working for his boss, and he's thinking of starting on his own.'

'Wouldn't work here,' Bernie said. 'You need too much capital.'

'I wasn't thinking of here. This guy's looking for a partner.'

'This guy?' Bernie said. 'You couldn't work abroad.'

'That's what I told him,' Anna said. 'But I could always change my mind.'

Bernie stared at her. 'Maybe we should have a word or two about "this guy",' he said, shaking his head. 'Jetlag's a terrible condition, you know.'

Chapter 73

Anna stood in the driving rain fumbling with the front door keys. She let herself in and went upstairs. The house already seemed abandoned.

Quex was not in her flat. It was cold and the air smelled stale. Automatically, she filled the kettle for tea and lit the gas fire. There was half a pint of nearly fresh milk in the fridge but nothing else.

Anna looked in the bedroom and bathroom. Quex's clothes were gone from her cupboards, his toothbrush missing from her mug.

Selwyn tapped on the door and came in.

'The return of the native,' he said. 'Did you have a good time? You look amazing – I don't think I've ever seen you so brown before. In fact you look quite different.'

'I don't think I've ever heard you comment on my appearance before,' Anna replied. 'What's up? Why are you using your eyes after so many years blind drunk?'

'Don't forget the "inward eye",' Selwyn retorted. 'Actually, my analyst has observed that my eye is a little too inward for complete mental health.'

'Get along!' Anna said. 'You're never seeing a shrink?'

'Group therapy, actually,' Selwyn said. 'I can't afford anything else. But, you see, a brush with death puts things in perspective. I decided I needed to talk to someone . . .'

'Brush with death!' Anna snorted. 'Seven flaming aspirins if I remember right.'

'It isn't the quantity,' Selwyn told her. 'It's the intention.'

'I'd judge the strength of the intention by the quantity,' Anna said, and went to pour the tea.

'Where's Quex?' she called from the kitchen.

'Ireland.' Selwyn came to lean against the door jamb. 'He left a couple of days ago. He'll be back at the weekend but he's moved into the Fulham flat.'

Anna gave him a mug of tea and they went to sit by the fire.

'I've got a letter for you,' he went on, and began to search pockets already stuffed with crumpled bits of paper. When he found it she saw he had written, 'Bread, spuds, bog roll, library', on it. Selwyn was doing his own shopping.

'How's Bea?' she asked. She did not want to open the envelope until she was alone.

'Happy as Larry,' Selwyn said grimly. 'Queen of all the soft furnishing departments from Wapping to Watford. You know, Leo, I'm beginning to see Bea in her true colours at long last. She is irretrievably suburban whereas I am . . .'

'An irretrievable flannel merchant.'

'Don't sneer,' Selwyn said. 'I know you like Bea. And you're right – she's a good woman. But, honestly, a good woman is not what I need these days.'

'Selwyn,' Anna interrupted, 'you don't need a bad woman either. A bad woman would cut off your goolies and lose them on the lawn. What you need is a sodding minder.'

'It's my last chance,' Selwyn said. 'I'm a dreamer. I've never really lived. It's all right for you – you go out and do things. I just sit and think about them. I've got to make a change.'

'What things are you going to do?' Anna asked, reluctantly sympathetic. 'Staying here and defying the developers isn't exactly constructive either.'

'Oh that!' Selwyn waved his hand airily. 'No, I've given that up.'

'Why?'

'Well, actually,' Selwyn said, looking a little shamefaced, 'West London Properties is, um, sort of, paying me to drop the fight.'

'How much?'

'Well, enough to go to Greece for a few months,' Selwyn said. 'You don't think I'm selling out, do you, Leo?'

'That's just what you're doing,' Anna said, laughing. 'More power to you! You always wanted to go to Greece.'

'So I'm sending some of my stuff to Fulham for you and Quex to look after, and next week I'm off. Christmas in Crete, I thought. What d'you think?'

'I think it's terrific,' Anna said. 'You're putting West London Properties' money where your mouth is. Good on you.'

Even if he came back broke, and ended up in Potters Bar, she thought, at least he would have had a stab at something different – something he had never done more than dream about. It was a big improvement on getting drunk every night and bitching about the triviality of life with Bea.

When he had gone, Anna opened her mail. Most of it was from estate agents, and most of it went straight into the bin. There was a letter from her sister inviting her to spend Christmas in Orpington. She put that aside.

Finally she opened the letter from Quex.

'Dearest Leo,' he wrote. 'When you come home I will either be in Ireland or Fulham. I thought it best to give you time and space to think. I have been crowding you.

'You don't like to talk about the big things, I understand that. So I have decided to put everything in a letter. Then you can decide on your own, without any influence from me. This way, too, I will have to be honest about what I want.

'I want to settle down. I want to marry you. Failing that, I want to live with you.

'The thing is that I just like to be with you. Life is more fun and more interesting when I'm with you. I would like to make it permanent.

'On the other hand, life with you would be neither fun nor interesting unless you could write your own terms – about work, for instance, or privacy.

'That's it, really. I'm sorry I was so snotty on the phone the other day. Sometimes I feel pushed out and rejected and I do not react very well.

'Think, Leo, and talk to me when you've decided – all my love . . .'

He was a good man, Anna thought. He had the sense to know that she was only able to think clearly about him when he was not in the same room. When he was in the same room it always became too small.

Anna thought about this. It was not a good sign. Other big men did not shrink rooms.

She sat in the empty house thinking about big men and small rooms.

About the Author

Liza Cody's first Anna Lee mystery, *Dupe,* won the John Creasy Award for best first novel and was nominated for an Edgar. Her most recent, *Under Contract,* was shortlisted for the Golden Dagger Award. Liza Cody, who grew up in London and studied painting at the Royal Academy School of Art, has worked as a painter, furniture-maker, photographer, and graphic designer. She is active in mystery writers' organizations on both sides of the Atlantic.